DESOLATE PLACES

KATE CHARLES

This book is licensed to you for your personal enjoyment only.

This is a work of fiction. Names, characters, places, and incidents are either products of the writer's imagination or are used fictitiously and are not to be construed as real. Any resemblance to actual events, locales, organizations, or persons, living or dead, is entirely coincidental.

Desolate Places
Copyright © 2021 by Kate Charles
Ebook ISBN: 978-1-64197-170-6
Print ISBN: 978-1-64197-172-0

ALL RIGHTS RESERVED.

No part of this work may be used, reproduced, or transmitted in any form or by any means, electronic or mechanical, without prior permission in writing from the publisher, except in the case of brief quotations embodied in critical articles or reviews.

NYLA Publishing
121 W 27th St., Suite 1201, NY 10001, New York.
http://www.nyliterary.com

This book is dedicated to all of my faithful readers –

thank you for your support through the years

ACKNOWLEDGMENTS

This book was supported by two generous donations to charitable causes, with the donors bidding for a character bearing their name. Sir Leslie Fielding's donation to the Conservation Trust for St Laurence, Ludlow has resulted in a character who is perhaps not quite what he was expecting, but I have faith that his legendary sense of humour will enable him to take it in the spirit in which it was intended. Dr Sein Lwin of Myanmar is more likely to recognise himself in his namesake character, whose role in the book is small but important. His generosity was in support of Project Burma. Many thanks to Sir Leslie and Dr Lwin.

Thanks, as always, to my good friends and first readers: Marcia Talley, Deborah Crombie, Suzanne Clackson, and Sue Mansell.

And thanks to my splendid agent Nancy Yost, for everything.

DRAMATIS PERSONAE

In London

The Church

Callie Anson – Curate
Brian Stanford – Vicar, Callie's boss
Jane Stanford – Brian's wife
Frances Cherry – Hospital chaplain
Graham Cherry – Vicar, Frances' husband
Fr Michael Fairfax – Vicar
Willow Tree – Sacristan
Barbara Grant – Vicar's wife
Pippa Masters – Curate's wife
Mildred Channing – parishioner

The Law

Sgt Mark (Marco) Lombardi – Family liaison officer, Callie's fiancé
DI Neville Stewart – Homicide Detective
DS Sid Cowley – Neville's sergeant
DCS Idris Evans – Neville's boss
Colin Tompkins – police pathologist
Danny Duffy – computer expert

Yolanda Fish – Family liaison officer

The Regent Hotel
Ronald Wicker – hotel manager
Zuzanna Dabrowska – cleaner
Angel Reyes – cleaner
Les Fielding – in the kitchen
Tariq Sadek – in the kitchen
Dr Sein Lwin – hotel guest

Londoners
Peter Anson – Callie's brother
Laura Anson – Callie's mother
Serena di Stefano – Marco's sister
Angelina & Chiara di Stefano – Serena's daughters
Grazia Lombardi – Marco's mother
Andrew Linton – an estate agent
Triona Stewart – Neville's wife
Lilith Noone – Representative of the Press
Rob Gardiner-Smith – Lilith's boss
Kamala Gupta – Neonatal unit manager
Julian St Clair – a man of mystery
Olivia St Clair – Julian's wife
Ben Chapman – a man of importance
Danielle Fisher – Ben's partner

In Devizes
Felicity Chapman – Ben's mother
Alan Chapman – Felicity's husband
PC Grace Long – Wiltshire Constabulary
DS Tom Burton – Grace's boss
Maggie Ruddle – taxi driver
Paige Mason – Alan's secretary

In Oxford

Charlie Stanford – Brian and Jane's son
Simon Stanford – Charlie's twin brother
Ellie Dickinson – Simon's fiancée
Hugh Dickinson – Ellie's father
Georgina Dickinson – Ellie's mother

I

It was every clergyperson's worst nightmare.

'Therefore if any man can show any just cause, why they may not lawfully be joined together, let him now speak, or else hereafter for ever hold his peace.'

A mere formality, legally required as part of the marriage service. A hold-over from days long gone by, when betrothals were binding. No one expected anyone to speak, yet the fear was always there at the back of one's mind. What if ...

Callie Anson, as a mere and lowly deacon, wasn't able to perform weddings herself, but she'd been asked by Brian, her training vicar, to help out with this one. Brian, who'd planned to do the wedding himself, had a schedule conflict pretty much at the last minute and had found a retired priest from a nearby parish to fill in, with Callie's assistance. 'Father Benedict is a bit past it, so you'll just need to keep an eye on him,' Brian had said. 'It should be very straightforward. A nice couple. Not church-goers, of course, but they live in the parish. It will be fine,' he'd added.

And up to that point it had been. No drama – the bride on time, the organist on good form. Lovely spring weather, and a good-sized congregation with everyone smiling.

Until Father Benedict pronounced the line about the just cause. It wasn't a man who responded to the invitation to speak, but a woman.

One of the pink-clad bridesmaids, in fact. 'He's a lying toe-rag,' she announced loudly during the two-second pause which was customary to allow for theoretical objections.

Callie, standing just behind and to the side of the elderly priest, could see their faces – the bride and the groom, in the split second before they swivelled to face the objector. The bride, eyes wide, her mouth a sudden O, frozen in horror. And the groom: guilty as hell, obviously.

The bridesmaid hadn't finished. 'He said he loved me,' she stated. 'He doesn't love her. He never has.'

Things happened quickly after that. The bride fled back up the aisle she'd so recently come down, followed by her father and then her mother. The wronged bridesmaid threw her flowers in the direction of the groom, burst into noisy sobs, and flung herself face-down on the floor. The groom turned to his best man, shrugged, then sloped off towards the side door, closely followed by the best man, presumably heading for the nearest pub rather than seeking out his intended bride.

THAT NIGHT, not surprisingly, Callie dreamed about a wedding. This time, though, it was Brian who was officiating, standing in front of the familiar altar at All Saints'.

And Callie, facing him, was the bride.

She couldn't really see her dress, but the expression of approval on Marco's face, as she turned to smile at him, was confirmation enough that she looked the proper part.

The bridesmaids were arrayed on her left, dressed in pink – just like the real, aborted wedding. Her friend Tamsin, Marco's two nieces – Angelina and Chiara. And Marco's sister Serena. Surely Serena was a bit old to be a bridesmaid? And pink didn't really suit her, with her red-gold Venetian colouring.

Brian smiled benignly and said the Prayer Book words, just as Father Benedict had said them. 'Therefore if any man can show any just cause, why they may not lawfully be joined together, let him now speak, or else hereafter for ever hold his peace.'

Serena was the one who opened her mouth, her beautiful face contorted with hatred. 'No!' she shouted. 'He can't marry her. It's all wrong! She doesn't belong. She'll never be part of *la famiglia*. Never in a million years!'

Callie woke up with a gasp, tears on her cheeks, her heart thudding. And it was a long time before she was able to get back to sleep.

FATHER MICHAEL FAIRFAX was surely the best-looking priest in the Church of England.

At least that was what Peter Anson thought, the moment he'd met him.

In spite of the fact that his sister Callie's life was bound up in the C of E, Peter had no particular interest in that institution.

Until he laid eyes on the beautiful Michael Fairfax.

Coup de foudre – that's what the French called it. A lightening strike to the heart. Love at first sight, to use the more prosaic English phrase.

Peter had been in love before – plenty of times. Far too many times for his own good; he didn't need Callie to tell him that. He fell in love too easily, and more often than not with the most unsuitable men. Jason, and before that a long line of others. From the time he was a young boy, he'd been falling in love on a regular basis with one handsome face after another.

But Father Michael was different. Or at least that's what he told himself.

He'd met Father Michael while Callie was away in Cambridge and he was staying at her flat, looking after her dog Bella. The priest had called at the flat, looking for Callie. He was new in the area, he said, and wanted to introduce himself to his fellow clergy.

Tall, of course. Well-built. You could tell that, even under his black clerical shirt – not a garment that Peter had ever before considered to be remotely sexy, but Father Michael took it to a whole new level.

And he was drop-dead gorgeous: there was no other way to put it.

Bradley Cooper, Peter thought instantly, with those laser-blue eyes and mobile, sensuous mouth. Hair you just wanted to run your fingers through.

When he smiled, Peter knew that he was lost.

'She's not here,' he stammered.

'You're her husband?'

Peter corrected him swiftly. 'Her brother.' Was it possible, he asked himself, that this gorgeous man was eyeing him up? Or was that just wishful thinking? 'She's away this week. I'm ... looking after things. Taking care of her dog.'

Father Michael's smile broadened. 'Oh, what sort of dog?'

'A cocker spaniel.'

As if on cue, Bella appeared at the door, swishing her tail.

'I'm a lab man, myself,' the priest said, leaning down to stroke Bella. 'I have a black lab. Colin. Silly name for a dog, I suppose.' He added, 'We're lucky, being so close to Hyde Park. Great place for dog walking.'

And that was that. Father Michael had said he'd come back another time, and had cheerfully taken his leave.

But Peter couldn't get him out of his head. For the rest of the week, he'd taken Bella for long walks in Hyde Park several times a day, hoping for a glimpse of the delicious priest. A few times he'd thought he spotted either a black shirt or a black dog, only to be disappointed.

And once Callie had returned, he didn't even have the excuse of a dog to be in Hyde Park.

Some lateral thinking was called for, Peter decided.

He remembered every word of his brief exchange with Father Michael; he'd replayed it over and over again in his mind. And he recalled that the priest had said he was the new vicar of St John's, Lancaster Gate.

That would be his next port of call.

MONDAY WAS the customary day for Callie's weekly meeting with Brian, when they talked about plans for the coming week and dealt with any issues which had arisen in the previous one. So she was a bit surprised when, at the end of the Sunday Eucharist, he stopped her at the vestry door. 'I'd like to see you for a little chat. Tonight,' he said. 'After Evensong. In my study.'

She nodded her agreement as he hurried on.

Had he heard about the wedding fiasco, then, and couldn't wait until tomorrow to call her on the carpet? She *had* been planning to tell him about it, of course, but she supposed that someone had beat her to it. Inevitable, really – she should have expected that.

Callie sighed.

Just her luck that it had happened on her watch, when he'd left her in charge. It hadn't been her fault; she couldn't have done anything to stop it. Brian was the one who had done their marriage preparation sessions. If anything, he should have picked up on any potential issues involving bridesmaids.

Well, she thought philosophically, if he blamed her, she'd just have to suck it up. That was what curates did. She'd learned that much from the recent Deacons' Week at her old theological college.

And this would give her a chance to talk to him about another wedding: her own.

She'd been waiting for the perfect opportunity to discuss it with Brian. Things with Marco had been up in the air for a while after his proposal; he'd wanted them to tell his family before they told anyone else. Before they started making plans.

Now Marco had told his family, though not in the way they'd intended. Not together. Instead he'd told Serena in the midst of what must have been a horrendous row, and at the end of it he'd announced to Serena that if he had to make a choice between *la famiglia* and Callie, he would choose Callie.

As far as Callie knew, Serena hadn't spoken to him since.

Shortly after the row, he'd told his parents. According to Marco, they were very happy for them both. Callie wasn't so sure that was the case, but she was willing to go along with his version of the conversation for the time being.

Angelina and Chiara, at least, were unambiguously and predictably delighted. They were going to be bridesmaids – that was established immediately. Regardless of their mother's feelings on the matter.

And now it was time for Callie to start dealing with her side of things. She'd told her brother Peter, and her friends from theological college. But she was going to have to talk to Brian, and she hadn't yet summoned up the courage to tell her mother.

In fact, Callie hadn't even yet introduced the two of them, so it would be a double shock for Laura Anson: her daughter had a new man in her life, and she was going to marry him. Callie didn't expect her mother, who had never liked surprises, to be very pleased.

But first, Brian.

SUNDAY LUNCH WAS OVER, the washing-up done and everything put away.

It was early in the year for doing much in the way of gardening, but the day was fine and warm and Felicity Chapman's green fingers were itching for the feel of soil.

Alan was on the sofa in the drawing room, surrounded by the Sunday papers. 'I'm going out to the garden,' Felicity announced at the door.

He looked up with a vague smile. 'Okay.'

In the utility room she pulled on her welly boots, shrugged on her Barbour jacket and tucked her phone into a pocket; her son Ben customarily rang on a Sunday afternoon and she didn't want to miss his call. Her first stop was the greenhouse, where she collected her flowered gardening gloves and a few tools for weeding, then she went to the nearest bed, knelt down and got stuck into the task at hand.

When her phone pinged, she dropped her spade and reached into her pocket, rocking back on her heels.

Not Ben's phone call, though: it was a Facebook notification. A friend request.

Felicity was puzzled; she didn't really use Facebook much, except to keep up with Ben's postings. She had only a handful of Facebook friends.

She thumbed the button and a window popped up. 'You have a friend request from Julian St Clair,' it said.

For just a split second, Felicity stopped breathing.

CALLIE FELT she'd adequately psyched herself up for her meeting with Brian, and rang the bell with her shoulders squared and her courage screwed to the sticking place.

Brian, however, evidently had an agenda of his own.

He, rather than his wife Jane, met Callie at the front door and ushered her into his study.

'Sit down,' he said, gesturing to the chair where Callie usually sat for their weekly meetings. He seemed nervous – embarrassed, almost. That surprised her; she was prepared for confrontation, for some sort of rebuke, not for his apologetic demeanour. Thrown off, she sat down and immediately blurted it out. 'Marco and I are going to get married.'

It was as if he hadn't really heard her. 'That's nice,' Brian said, then sat down behind his desk. 'You are meant to be priested in the autumn,' he went on.

'Yes. At Michaelmas,' she confirmed, baffled.

Brian fiddled with a pencil. 'I've spoken to the bishop,' he said. 'She's agreed to consider moving your priesting forward. To the Petertide ordinations, at the end of June.'

'But ... why?'

He cleared his throat. 'I asked her to. For ... personal reasons.'

Personal reasons?

She and Marco had talked about a summer wedding; neither of them wanted to wait any longer than necessary. Having to prepare for a wedding and an ordination within a month or two of each other seemed a bit much.

'I don't understand,' she said.

Once again he cleared his throat. 'I'm going to need a bit more help in the parish,' he stated. 'And it would make it much easier if you were a priest. You could take all the services, if necessary.'

As a deacon, there were quite a few things that Callie was authorised to do. She could preside at funerals, preach sermons, lead Morning and Evening Prayer. She could counsel parishioners, visit the sick. But she couldn't celebrate the Eucharist and consecrate the elements for communion. She couldn't perform weddings, or give absolutions or blessings. Those were privileges reserved only for priests.

At the recent Deacons' Week, one of Callie's fellow deacons had related a tragic story about her training incumbent's terminal illness, and a horrible suspicion now struck her. Personal reasons, he'd said. Why else would Brian be so anxious for her to be able to take the services? 'Brian, are you ... okay?' she blurted. 'You're not ill, are you?'

For just an instant he made eye contact. 'Oh, no,' he said. 'Nothing like that.' Then he looked down at his desk blotter. 'It's Janey,' he went on. 'She's going to need to take it easy for the next few months, the doctor said. And I'll need to be available to help her, as much as possible.'

Callie's kind heart went out to him. She and Jane had never become great friends, but this was something she wouldn't wish on anyone. 'Oh, I'm sorry. Is it serious, then?'

'Serious?' Again he made brief eye contact, shaking his head, before concentrating his gaze on his pencil, rolling it between his palms. 'Janey's not ill,' he said quietly, his voice dropping so that Callie had to strain to hear the next words. 'She's ... going to have a baby.'

A baby! Callie caught herself before echoing his words in astonishment. Jane was having a baby. And Brian was ... embarrassed. Clearly. 'That's wonderful,' she said heartily. 'Congratulations, Brian.'

Still he wouldn't look at her. 'Around Christmas. So it's very early days yet. But the doctor says that she'll need to be very careful.'

'At her age' were the unspoken words. Jane wasn't ancient, by any means, but she wouldn't see forty again. Her other children – her twins – were at university, virtually grown men.

'I explained the situation to the bishop,' he said. 'And I told her that as far as I was concerned, you were more than ready to be a priest.'

In spite of herself, Callie felt gratified. She'd been expecting a telling-off, not a commendation. 'Well, that's ... very kind of you, Brian. But what about my wedding?'

He raised his head and stared at her. 'Wedding? What are you talking about?'

'I told you. Marco and I want to get married. This summer. And we'd like you to take the service,' she added. 'Here at All Saints', of course.'

Brian sighed, then he smiled. 'Well, congratulations to you, too. And I'm sure it will all work out. One way or another.'

JULIAN ST CLAIR.

Felicity blinked rapidly, her mind flipping back more than thirty-five years. Golden hair, in a floppy school-boy fringe. The bluest of blue eyes. And a beautiful mouth that could charm her with its words – and make her dizzy with its kisses.

Julian St Clair.

With a trembling finger she touched the tiny thumbnail picture. It enlarged to fill the screen.

The golden hair, shorter, now shaded to silver at the temples; the blue eyes had tiny lines at their corners. But the beautiful mouth was unchanged, and, looking at it, curved in a smile, Felicity's heart skipped a beat.

She hesitated, but only for a moment, before touching the blue button. *Confirm.*

PETER HAD THOUGHT he might go to St John's, Lancaster Gate, for the Sunday morning service. But he'd had a gig the night before, playing at a wedding disco until the wee hours of the morning, so getting out of bed any time before noon on Sunday was out of the question – par for the course for a jobbing musician. Even the allure of the beautiful Father Michael wasn't going to make it happen, he realised.

Perhaps it was better that way, he acknowledged: apart from his sister's ordination at the cathedral, and his father's funeral, he couldn't remember the last time he'd set foot in a church. He wouldn't know what to do; he would stick out like the proverbial sore thumb.

Because Callie was a curate, Peter was aware that the popular conception that the clergy only worked one day a week was far from the truth. He also knew that their duties were not confined to the church premises, but he was an optimist by nature, and decided that a Monday morning trip to St John's might prove fruitful.

The church wasn't as easy to find as he'd expected. It was in fact some distance from the eponymous tube station, but eventually he spotted its tall Victorian spire in the middle of a traffic island. He made his way across the street, checked the notice board to confirm that he was in the right place, located the main door, and gave it an experimental tug.

The door was heavy, but it was unlocked. A further tug got him inside. He passed through the porch into the body of the church, blinking to adjust to the dim light which filtered through the stained glass windows.

To his unchurched eyes, it looked – and smelled – like a Catholic church: statues, candles, and a lingering waft of incense. Peter stood for a moment, trying to take it all in.

'Hello,' came a voice from somewhere to the side – a female voice.

Peter spun round.

'Sorry if I startled you,' said the owner of the voice, a young woman with cropped orange hair and a nose ring. She was carrying a tray with silver vessels on it.

'No, I just ... I didn't know there was anyone here.'

'I'm the sacristan,' the young woman stated. 'Just tidying up after the mass.'

Peter said the first thing that came into his head. 'Is this a Catholic church, then?'

The woman grinned. 'No. Though I can see why you might think so. We're good old C of E, of the Anglo-Catholic variety. Much spikier than the Romans. They're very down-market these days, you know, with guitar masses and spider plants on the altar. And lambswool ponchos instead of proper vestments.'

He was out of his depth here, so he merely shrugged.

'Can I help you with something?' she asked, shifting the weight of the tray.

'The vicar? Is he here?'

She shook her head. 'You've just missed him, I'm afraid. He doesn't generally hang about, once the mass is over. He likes to get to the gym early.'

Peter sensed a note of disapproval. 'He leaves you to clean up, then. Typical man.'

The woman set the tray down on a nearby pew, flexed her shoulders, and turned back to him, smiling. 'Actually, it's my job. Father Michael wouldn't know what to do with the vessels if his life depended on it. It will take him a while to learn the ropes round here.'

He felt an unreasonable thrill at the sound of the name, and couldn't resist repeating it, tasting it in his own mouth like a delectable sweet. 'Father Michael is ... new, then?'

'Yes, he's only been with us a few weeks,' she confirmed. 'He was sent to us after our ... troubles.'

It all came back to Peter then: the scandals of a few months ago, prominent in the national press. Murder. Disgrace. That was *this* church. 'Ah, yes,' he nodded.

She sighed. 'It was an awful time. Poor Leo. He didn't deserve any of it.'

'I'm sure.'

'So Father Michael has a big job ahead of him, picking up all of the pieces.'

That name again; Peter's skin prickled. 'I'm sure he'll do a good job,' he said.

His platitude produced an ironic smile. 'That's what the diocese is hoping, of course. Safe pair of hands and all that. He's fairly young, but he has a good track record – never put a foot wrong, apparently. They would have preferred a family man, after what happened with Leo, but Father Michael ticked all the other boxes.'

Peter felt his heart soar. 'He's not married, then?'

'No. And my gaydar tells me that the train isn't going to stop at that particular station.' The woman clapped her hand over her mouth. 'Sorry. I shouldn't have said that.'

If there was anything that Detective Inspector Neville Stewart hated more than paperwork ... he didn't know what it was. He only resorted to doing it when he had absolutely nothing else to do, and even then he required prodding from on high.

His boss, DCS Evans, deplored Neville's lack of attention to this necessary duty. On Monday morning he'd called Neville into his office and told him in no uncertain terms that until he signed off on the paperwork for the Frost case, he could expect no further proper assignments. 'Top priority, Stewart,' he growled. 'It's been over a week. Bloody get on with it!'

This was more than a prod, Neville realised: it was tantamount to a royal command. Begrudgingly he went to his desk, switched on his computer, and started compiling the necessary information.

After half an hour or so, his mobile phone rang, providing a welcome distraction. He pulled it out of his pocket. 'Stewart here.'

'Oh, hello. This is Andrew Linton.'

Neville had to think for a few seconds before the face materialised in his overloaded brain. Estate agent: fresh-faced, white-shirted. Exhaustingly upbeat. 'An inbred Jack Russell on uppers,' as his wife Triona had once described him.

He suppressed a sigh. 'Hello, Andrew.'

'Mr Stewart, is this a good time to talk?'

'As good as any.' Neville swivelled his chair around, literally as well as figuratively turning his back on the hated computer. 'What's up?'

'I'm afraid I have some rather bad news,' Andrew said in a voice so doleful that Neville scarcely recognised it. 'We've hit a snag with the sale of your flat.'

Neville closed his eyes and covered them with his free hand. 'Tell me.'

'The buyers? They've had a survey done? And they're not happy with the results.'

Oh, Lord. He should have known it was too good to be true, that someone would want to pay him such a vast sum of money for his grotty old flat.

'They said there's damp in the bathroom?'

'Damp? It's a bathroom, for God's sake!' Neville resisted the urge to push the disconnect button on the phone. What did the idiots not understand about running water?

'Well, yes. But it could be a deal-breaker. They're threatening to walk away.'

'We're supposed to exchange contracts next week,' Neville reminded him. 'They can't pull out now, can they?'

Andrew emitted a sound somewhere between an anguished groan and the yelp of a puppy which has just had its tail trodden on. 'Oh, yes, they can. Any time, up till the moment they sign the contracts.'

'Then what's the next step?'

'I'll talk to them,' Andrew said. 'I'll do my best. But I can't make any promises at this point. I thought I should warn you.'

'Keep me informed.' Neville ended the call, dropped the phone on his desk, and buried his face in his hands.

Triona was not going to be happy. Not one little bit.

WHEN THE SACRISTAN suggested a cup of coffee, Peter said yes.

'I'm going to make one for myself,' she said. 'As soon as I get the communion stuff back to the sacristy. You're welcome to join me.'

He followed her to a small room, where she quickly and efficiently washed the silver, dried it, and locked it in a wall safe, returning the key to her jeans pocket. 'I'm Willow, by the way,' she told him as she worked. 'Like I said, I'm the sacristan. I look after the silver and vestments. Get things ready for services, and clean up afterwards.'

'Is that, like, a real paying job?' he asked curiously.

She laughed. 'Oh, no. I work at a veggie café, afternoons and evenings mostly. Shift work. I suppose you could say that I do this for love, not money.'

Love. Now she was speaking his language. Peter wondered whether she, too, had already fallen in love with Father Michael. 'Have you been doing this for a long time?' he probed.

Willow led him out of the sacristy, locking the door behind them. 'A couple of years. It was Leo who drew me to this place. Leo was brilliant, no matter what you've read about him in the press,' she added with a frown. 'He brought a lot of people into this church. Young people, like me, who liked what he stood for. I mean, Leo really cared about stuff. About the environment, and about marginalised people. Social justice – all that.'

'And Father Michael doesn't?' Peter couldn't resist saying his name again.

'Too soon to tell.'

Willow took him to what was evidently the church hall, into a little kitchen, and set about the business of making coffee, spooning granules into mugs while the kettle boiled. 'The coffee isn't very good,' she admitted, 'but it's Fair Trade. Leo, of course.'

He was tired of hearing about the sainted Leo, and decided to change the subject. 'Why do you say it's too soon to tell about Father Michael? Has he done something to – I don't know – upset you, or someone else? Or,' he added, making an intuitive stab in the dark, 'is it the "gaydar" thing?'

'Not at all. I don't fancy him, if that's what you mean. And what he does in his private life is his own business.' She poured boiling water into the mugs and stirred. 'Milk? Sugar?'

'Black is fine.' Peter reached for the mug. 'Then what's bothering you about Father Michael?'

'He's not Leo,' she said with a wry, self-aware smile. 'That's not his fault, of course. And don't get me wrong. Leo wasn't perfect. But for me he got the balance just right. He was Anglo-Catholic, for sure, but social justice was more important to him than the number of candles on the altar. With Father Michael ... well, I have yet to be convinced.'

2

It was Saturday morning, and Brian's day off, so when Callie went into church to say Morning Prayer she wasn't expecting anyone else to be there.

Recently she had noticed that there seemed to be an unusual number of candles burning on the stand in the Lady Chapel, next to the statue of Our Lady. Every time she came into church – morning, afternoon or evening – there were several flickering flames. When she thought about it, she wondered whether perhaps Jane – or Brian – might be responsible; a few extra prayers for the well-being of their baby wouldn't go amiss.

This time, though, there was someone at the candle stand, and it wasn't either of the Stanfords.

It was a slender young woman. Little more than a girl, Callie judged – perhaps in her very early twenties, if that. She was fair-haired and strikingly pretty, with fine-boned features and huge china-blue eyes.

Those eyes were turned towards Callie, startled as an animal in a car's headlamps.

'Hello,' Callie said with a smile, trying to sound welcoming.

The smile was returned, tremulous and tentative. 'Is all right?' she asked, gesturing to the candle stand. 'Is all right to light candle?' Her voice was soft, its accent Eastern European.

'Yes, of course. That's what they're here for,' Callie assured her.

'I was not sure.' The girl hesitated, cast her eyes down for a second, then raised them back to Callie's. 'I am not ... how you say? Of the England Church?'

'Church of England,' Callie supplied automatically. 'Anglican.'

The girl tried the word. 'Anglican. I am not Anglican. I am Catholic.'

'That doesn't matter in the least.' She smiled again, in lieu of trying to explain that Anglicans – most of them, anyway – were a welcoming bunch.

'Thank you,' the girl said simply.

'I'm Callie, by the way. I'm the curate here.' She pointed to her dog collar.

The girl's eyes widened. 'You are priest?'

'Not yet,' Callie admitted. 'Soon, though. I'm a deacon now.'

'We have no women priests in Catholic Church.'

Don't I know it, thought Callie, sensing that the girl's words were informational rather than judgemental. 'One day, perhaps,' she ventured.

The girl seemed to ponder that thought for a moment, her brows drawn together, then she nodded. 'Would be good, I think. Women – I think they listen more better.'

'Well, if you ever need anyone to listen to you, that's what I'm here for.' She didn't mean it to sound dismissive, but she was aware that it was time for her to get on with things. 'I'm going to say Morning Prayer now,' she added, nodding towards the chancel. 'You're very welcome to join me if you like. Or not. Any time.'

'Thank you,' said the girl.

As Callie turned away, she caught the girl's final words. 'My name,' she said, 'is Zuzanna.'

FALLING in love with a priest in the Church of England was not a good idea. Peter Anson knew that. It was bad news, on so many levels. So he tried to put Father Michael Fairfax out of his mind. He distracted himself with other things, personally and professionally; he even made arrangements to see his mother, which was not something to be undertaken lightly.

As it happened, his visit to his mother took place only a few days after Callie had taken Marco to meet her for the first time.

At least, he reflected wryly, it gave Laura Anson something to talk about. He didn't have to worry about searching for suitable topics of conversation, or about fending off her attempts to talk up various young women of her acquaintance; she held the unshakable belief that he just hadn't yet met the right girl.

'I hope she knows what she's doing,' his mother said, frowning, almost as soon as Peter was through the door. 'I'm not sure about this at all.'

He anticipated all of her concerns, which – he suspected – largely boiled down to the fact that Marco Lombardi was not quite English enough for her. He might speak like a London-born native, but he was of Italian extraction; he was Roman Catholic.

'Mark seems a very nice young man,' she admitted. 'He couldn't have been more polite or well-spoken. He brought me a lovely box of chocolates from F&M, and some beautiful flowers.'

Peter looked round for a vase, just as Laura Anson sighed – what he always thought of as her martyr's sigh. 'I don't suppose Caroline told him that I was allergic to lilies. I had to give them to my neighbour. I mean, they were beautiful, but within minutes I was streaming. Literally streaming.'

'But the chocolates were all right,' he prompted.

'Oh, yes. A huge box. I really shouldn't eat them, you know.'

Peter tried again. 'Marco – Mark – is crazy about Callie,' he said. 'And he treats her really well. I think they'll be just fine.'

'But it's so ... sudden,' she frowned, lowering herself onto the striped silk settee. 'I mean, just a few months ago she thought she wanted to marry that other boy. The missionary one. She's hardly known this Mark for five minutes. I'm afraid she's rushing into it on the rebound.'

Peter sat down. 'Sometimes,' he said, 'you just know. When you've met the right person.' He experienced a little pang in the vicinity of his heart, but went on. 'I really think that Marco is the right person for Callie.'

'That may be,' she allowed. 'But they're in such a rush! They're talking about getting married in the summer! Surely they should wait for a decent period of time. Just to make sure.'

'Callie isn't getting any younger,' Peter suggested slyly.

For just a moment, Laura Anson looked uncertain. She drew her brows together and smoothed her skirt over her knees. 'Well, that's true,' she allowed. 'She's thirty this year. Thirty! It hardly seems possible! I know that young people are marrying later these days, but by the time I was thirty I was married and had two children.'

The deflection had been momentarily successful, but it didn't last long. She carried on, 'And he's a policeman! That's not exactly what one hopes for in a son-in-law. And I'm not sure about his family. Not sure that they're quite ... our sort. I mean, they run a ... *restaurant*?' She pronounced the word with evident distaste, wrinkling her nose.

Peter couldn't help grinning. 'It's not a house of ill repute, Mother. It's a restaurant. Actually a very *nice* restaurant.'

'An *Italian* restaurant.'

Now they were getting to the crux of the matter. 'Yes,' said Peter, deciding he may as well address it head-on. 'That's because they're Italian.'

DAYS HAD PASSED since Felicity had accepted the online friend request from Julian St Clair. She'd been expecting to hear something from him – a message, perhaps, or even a phone call.

Nothing.

She'd looked at his profile page on Facebook, of course. He'd put up very little information. His location was 'London'. No employment indicated, and no relationship status. Just the one photo. He had very few Facebook friends – half a dozen, including Felicity.

She hadn't thought about him for years – not really. Now, at odd times, she recalled, vividly, moments they'd shared. Then she would remind herself of all that had passed since then. Her life was perhaps not as exciting as Julian St Clair had once promised her it could be, but it was comfortable. It suited her. She had her beloved garden, and her lovely and immaculate home. She had Alan. She had Ben. What more could a woman want?

She was at the hairdresser's when the message came through, sitting under the heat lamp while her colour set. Her phone pinged. She retrieved it from her handbag and looked at the screen: a Facebook message from Julian St Clair.

In spite of everything she'd been telling herself, her heart thudded and her finger shook as she opened the Messenger app.

'Hi, Fliss,' she read. 'Long time no see. Can we meet up?'

Fliss: a seductive, sibilant whisper from the past. It unnerved her; it shook her resolve.

Felicity closed her eyes and took a deep breath, grounding herself. Then, with her index finger, she tapped out her reply, short and sweet.

No.

IT WAS after Peter left his mother's flat – exhausted with his efforts on Callie's behalf – that something quite unexpected happened. A sign, he would later tell himself. Something that was meant to be.

He'd thought about taking the Tube back to his flat, but it was only two stops, he was in no great hurry, and he reckoned that the exercise would do him good. Absorbed in his thoughts, he ambled through the streets of South Kensington, only half aware of his surroundings.

And then he saw him. Thrillingly, unmistakably – Father Michael, going into a nondescript storefront fitness centre on the other side of the street. Not in clericals, and with a black gym-bag slung over his shoulder. But it was him. No doubt about it.

Peter froze.

His first impulse was to dash across the street and follow him into the building. But even as his legs overcame their temporary paralysis and began to move towards the kerb, he realised that wouldn't do: he was dressed for coffee with his mother, not for the gym.

Time for a re-think.

Father Michael was just arriving. How long would he be there? Probably an hour, at least. Either Peter could lurk in the street for an hour or more, and waylay the priest on his departure, or he could nip home, change his clothes, and be back before Father Michael finished his workout.

He decided that the second course was the most sensible.

Reaching for his Oyster card, Peter dove into the nearby South Ken tube station, and was back at his flat within a few minutes.

Never having been a fitness fanatic, he didn't have proper gym clothes, but he quickly found something he thought would do: an old t-shirt, a pair of cut-offs, and trainers.

Back at the fitness centre a short time later, he quickly realised that he didn't look the part at all – not if you judged by the people who pushed past him as he hesitated at the door. And once he'd overcome his last-minute loss of nerve and entered its sacred portals, he found himself under scrutiny by the young woman at the desk just inside, with a logo on her chest and a supercilious expression on her face.

She looked him up and down, eyebrows raised. 'Card?' she demanded.

Peter shrugged.

'Membership card?' she enunciated slowly, as though speaking to someone with impaired hearing or reduced mental capacity.

'I don't have one. This is my first time.'

'Then you'll need to pay.'

He'd anticipated that; what he hadn't quite anticipated was the quantity of options with which he would be presented, and the amount of paperwork involved. No, he didn't want an annual membership. No, he didn't require the services of a personal trainer. No, he didn't wish to book a free assessment and induction session. No, he didn't need a schedule of the available classes. He just wanted to pay his money and be admitted to the premises.

Ten minutes later and ten quid poorer, he finally achieved that goal. Peter stepped through the glass doors and entered another world.

Lycra. That was clearly the uniform. No wonder the receptionist had scrutinised him so critically. He'd never seen so much lycra in one place – not even in a gay bar on retro night.

And these were people who meant business, intent on their workouts, oblivious of each other. Women with biceps and ponytails. Men with ...

Focused though he was on his search, once he'd passed through the room with cardio equipment, Peter couldn't help pausing at the entrance to the weight room, momentarily distracted by the male pulchritude on display. Not just on display, actually: flaunted. Muscles bulging under elaborate tattoos as their owners hefted impossibly large weights above their shaved heads, sculpted torsos quivering under tight lycra. The atmosphere reeked of testosterone.

He should have been excited by it, and yet ...

And yet there was something almost laughable about the primitive rituals being enacted before him. The weight room was large – large enough to comfortably accommodate several muscle-bound men and their equipment. But the men were clearly engaged in a territorial battle: pacing round the room, flexing their shoulders, moving equipment to suit their personal requirements, staking out their patch. Ignoring each other as they eyed themselves up in the mirrors which lined the room, admiring their own physiques.

They were much of a muchness, these men with their cropped heads, their waxed chests and their tattoos. Arms so muscled that their owners held them out at an angle as they paced, unable to lower them all the way to their sides. There was something grotesque about them, both in their self-absorption and in their exaggerated body shapes.

And, Peter reminded himself, this was all a distraction from his reason for being here. Wherever Father Michael was, if he was still on the premises, he wasn't in the weight room.

Backing out of the doorway, he scanned the cardio room – the rowers, the cycles, the treadmills, the cross-trainers – once again to make sure he hadn't missed anything, then went out into the corridor to search for other rooms as yet unexplored.

He found him at the water fountain, filling a plastic bottle. 'Sorry, I'm almost finished,' Father Michael said. A moment later he turned and regarded Peter with those electric – electrifying – blue eyes. His neutral expression shifted to puzzlement, then dawning recognition. 'Oh, hello,' he said, smiling. 'Haven't we met ...?'

IT WAS A WEDNESDAY EVENING, nearly the end of May. No more than a few weeks had passed, but for Felicity everything had changed. Although only a close observer would guess it to look at her, her whole world had been turned upside down.

She was sitting in a wine bar in a less than salubrious district of London. Alone at a table for two. Looking up every time the door opened, then looking down again. Twisting her wedding ring. Sipping a glass of chilled white wine. Fingering her pearls. Picking up her phone and peering at the screen. Smoothing a lock of hair back from her forehead. Glancing at the phone again.

She consciously slowed her breathing and turned her head to study herself in the crackly mirror which covered the adjoining wall. Not bad, she judged, especially in the murky, forgiving candlelight of the wine bar. Not bad for her age, at any rate.

And then suddenly he was behind her in the mirror, his hands on her shoulders, bending down to bring his face close to hers. 'Fliss,' he breathed caressingly as she twisted round. 'Fliss, you look wonderful.'

IT WAS a sunny Thursday morning when Jane Stanford went to the monthly gathering of the Deanery Clergy Wives group.

She knew from the start that she shouldn't have gone. The group was one of her chief outlets outside of the parish, and she usually enjoyed their get-togethers, but on this occasion she should have stayed home. She was running late as it was, due to a ferocious bout of morning sickness.

The meeting was being held at Christ Church vicarage, hosted by Barbara Grant, the vicar's wife. Barbara opened the door to Jane with a smile and an announcement. 'Ah, Jane, you're here at last. I've decided to do something special today. A little brunch, rather than just coffee and a bun.'

The smell of eggs wafted out of the door; Jane's stomach lurched. She should have made her apologies there and then, and gone back home, but it was too late to do that without more of an explanation than she wanted to give.

'I've invited Michael Fairfax to join us. You know – the new vicar of St John's.' Barbara lowered her voice to a whisper as she ushered Jane inside. 'After that unfortunate business with Leo, I thought we should make a special effort to welcome him to the deanery. Since he doesn't have a wife to join our little band.'

Barbara, Jane thought with a flash of irritation, tended to take rather too much upon herself. Her husband, Richard Grant, was now the Area Dean (after the unfortunate business with Leo), and Barbara seemed to feel that gave her special status in the deanery as well. Jane liked to think of herself as the quintessential old-fashioned vicar's wife; Barbara – half a generation older than Jane – was that as well, and now so much more. Beneath her fluffy, grandmotherly exterior Jane recognised a core of steel.

'Come on through to the lounge,' Barbara directed. 'You know most everyone, I think.' The clergy wives were arranged in a circle round the room.

Jane suppressed a frown. She'd been coming to these meetings for years; why wouldn't she know everyone?

'You remember Pippa Masters?' Barbara steered her towards a seat next to a very slender young woman with short silver-gilt hair. 'Our curate's wife.'

Jane remembered Pippa. Remembered, too, that Pippa's husband, Adam, had once been engaged to Callie Anson. Not a promising topic of conversation.

'And this is Michael,' Barbara announced unnecessarily, given that he was the only man in a room full of women. 'Michael, this is Jane Stanford. Her husband Brian is vicar of All Saints'.'

Michael Fairfax was, Jane observed, a very good-looking young man, with a charming smile. He turned that smile on her now, in a manner that suggested he knew exactly how attractive he was. With those laser-blue eyes, he was likely to stir the hearts of the women in his congregation – and not in a holy way. Perhaps, thought Jane a bit uncharitably, it would have been better – or at least safer, after the Leo fiasco – if the powers-that-be had appointed an unattractive middle-aged man with a wife and a tribe of children.

'It's very kind of you to join us,' Jane said, realising as she said it that she sounded patronising.

'It was very kind of Mrs Grant to invite me.'

One of the older clergy wives simpered at him. 'You must have much more important things to do.'

'Nothing could be more important.'

'Now that we're all here, I'll bring the food through,' Barbara stated.

She disappeared into the kitchen and returned a moment later bearing a steaming casserole dish. 'I've done something special. An American brunch casserole,' she explained. 'Eggs and sausages and mushrooms and bread and onions and so forth. All baked together.'

The smell was overpowering. Jane swallowed hard and closed her eyes, telling herself that it was all in her mind.

She couldn't remember having suffered with morning sickness at all with the twins. But that had been years ago – nineteen long years. Maybe her memory had blanked it out, or maybe this really was something new, a result of her advanced age.

Barbara kept talking as she spooned the casserole onto plates; Jane focused on the other woman's mouth. She'd never really noticed it before, but Barbara had extraordinarily full and sensuous lips, which seemed somehow incongruous – even indecent – for a vicar's wife of the extreme Evangelical persuasion. 'We had a lovely couple who came to stay with us last summer. Americans,' Barbara was saying. 'From a big church in Texas. She made this for us one day, and gave me the recipe. It's such a good idea – everything in one dish. And you can do it the night before and pop it in the fridge till morning! Ideal, really.'

Jane saw two of the older women exchange dubious glances, but Pippa Masters chimed in with enthusiasm. 'What a great idea. And it smells divine. I suppose you could put in just about anything you fancied, as well – Adam and I don't eat meat, of course, but I could use some tofu instead.'

The thought of tofu was the last straw. Jane's stomach gave her one final warning; she put her hand over her mouth, got up, and headed for the loo. Fortunately she'd been in the house before, and remembered where it was.

After her earlier bout of sickness, there was nothing left to come up, but that didn't mean her stomach didn't try. She felt wretched, miserable:

why, she asked herself, had it seemed a good idea to have a baby at her age? Why couldn't she have just left well alone? Been satisfied to be a granny to Simon's forthcoming child instead? She would be a laughing-stock to the clergy wives, that was for sure.

'Are you all right?'

Jane straightened up and turned round to see Pippa Masters hovering at the door, which she'd failed to shut properly in her haste to reach the loo.

'Not really,' she admitted.

'Morning sickness?'

Jane nodded reluctantly. She hadn't meant for anyone to know – not yet, anyway. But she couldn't really deny it. Not when her body was in open, visible revolt.

'Poor you.'

'I shouldn't have come,' said Jane. 'Now they'll all know. About the baby.'

Pippa Masters gave her a puzzled frown. 'Why wouldn't you want them to know?'

'Well, just because.' Jane shrugged.

'But motherhood is a woman's crowning glory,' stated Pippa. 'It's what women were made for. You should be proud that you're fulfilling your divine destiny. You should be shouting it from the rooftops!'

IT HAD BEEN QUITE some time since Neville Stewart had seen his mate Mark Lombardi. They'd been working different cases; their paths hadn't crossed at the station. So when Neville bumped into Mark in the corridor, late that Thursday morning, he was quick to suggest a remedy.

'Do you have plans for lunch?' he asked. 'Do you fancy a trip to the pub? Pie and a pint, maybe?'

'Sounds great,' Mark agreed. 'I don't have anything on till later this afternoon. It should be okay if I can stick to one pint.'

They tended to patronise a pub close to the police station, which had proximity to recommend it if nothing else. It was a bit scruffy, in need of a coat of paint and a good hoovering, if not a complete make-over. But the beer was to their taste – Guinness on draught for Neville, Peroni for Mark – and the food was no worse than what was on offer in the police canteen.

Neville went to the bar to fetch the beer while Mark scouted out an empty table – one not too close to anyone they knew. It wasn't that their conversation was likely to be particularly private, but they did have some catching up to do: these outings had once been a frequent post-work feature of their friendship, before Neville had become a married man and Mark had acquired new priorities as well.

What a difference a few months made, Neville reflected as he waited at the bar. Though some things never changed – the service here was still glacially slow.

Eventually, in possession of two pints, he made his way to the table. 'Here's your cat's pee,' he said, sliding the tall Peroni glass across the scarred wooden table.

'Cheers.' Mark lifted the glass and took a sip.

'Chicken and mushroom pie on the menu today. I went ahead and ordered, to save time.'

'So,' said Mark, when they'd settled in with their drinks. 'How is Triona?'

Neville sighed. 'Getting a bit ratty, to be perfectly honest. The baby is only a few weeks away now. She's feeling uncomfortable most of the time. Or so she says.'

There had been a period, in the middle of her pregnancy, when Neville had wished that it could go on forever. A time when Triona's naturally fiery temperament had mellowed, and her libido had increased. He looked back on those golden days – those few glorious weeks – with fond nostalgia. Now, along with the mother-to-be, he just wanted it to be over.

But not, heaven forbid, before the issue of where they would live was settled.

He'd thought it was sorted: his flat under offer, Triona's flat under offer, the purchase of the marvellous house in Ladbroke Square well in hand. To someone of Neville's naturally pessimistic disposition, it had seemed almost too good to be true.

And so it had proved.

Andrew Linton had managed to persuade the buyers of Neville's flat not to walk away, but they were demanding that a damp-proof course be installed, with the exchange of contracts delayed accordingly. And Triona's buyers were encountering some problems in their chain – Neville couldn't remember whether it was above or below them in the chain; the net result was the same. They weren't going to be moving any time soon.

He definitely didn't want to talk about it, with Mark or with anyone else. So he introduced a new subject.

'And Callie? How is she?'

Mark smiled. 'Oh, very well. Busy, as usual.' He leaned forward and dropped his voice. 'You know we're hoping to get married this summer.'

'Hoping?' Neville laughed. 'You'd better start doing something more than hoping, mate! You'd better start planning. Unless you want a last-minute wedding like we had. Which was fine, under the circumstances,' he added, just in case Triona had a spy at the next table, 'but your Callie deserves better than that.'

That elicited a slight grimace from Mark. He took a sip of his beer, then leaned further in. 'We're trying to sort a date. But it's my family,' he said. '*La famiglia*, as usual.'

'Not happy?'

'Well, it's Serena, really,' Mark admitted. 'My sister. We're ... not speaking.'

'That's serious.'

'She's never liked Callie. Because she's not Italian – there's no other reason. She's never made any effort to get to know her properly.'

Neville's own family had never been close; he'd always found it hard to understand why someone as intelligent as Mark Lombardi seemed to find it natural and even acceptable to allow his parents and sister to dictate his life. 'Tell her to stuff it,' he said with a shrug.

'That's basically what I've told her. And that's why we're not speaking. But now she's informed Mamma that she won't allow the girls to be bridesmaids.'

'What does your mother say?'

Mark sighed. 'She says it's breaking her heart, that her children won't talk to each other.'

'But she's okay about the wedding? About Callie?'

'She thinks Callie is wonderful.' He gave a wry smile. 'Or at least that's what she tells me. Mamma says that she wants me to be happy. And Pappa – he adores Callie. So do the girls. It's just Serena that's the problem.' Mark paused, shaking his head, looking down at the table, and continued haltingly. 'Well, actually that's not true. She's not the only problem. It's the wedding itself. I mean – where is it going to be? If it were up to me, we'd just ... go off and do it. To the register office, like you did. Not tell anyone – just grab a couple of witnesses off the street and do it.'

'But that's not an option?'

'Not for Callie.' He shrugged. 'She works for the church. For God, if you like. And it's important to her to be married in her own church. By her vicar. In the sight of God,' he added self-consciously. 'And I do understand that. But when I say "Anglican Church" to Mamma, she bursts into tears. As far as she's concerned, if it doesn't happen at the Italian Church, with Father Luigi presiding, it's not a real wedding.'

'And you're caught in the middle,' Neville analysed. Poor Mark – he wouldn't be in his shoes for a million quid. The poor bastard couldn't win.

'So you can see—'

Neville's mobile phone rang. He reached in his pocket for it and answered tersely. 'Stewart.'

'Guv,' said his sergeant, DS Sid Cowley. 'I've been looking for you.'

He rolled his eyes, foreseeing a premature conclusion to his lunch. 'I'm in the pub. What's up?'

'You know all those hotels in Sussex Gardens?'

Neville knew. There were dozens of them, all in a row: carved-up bits of formerly grand town-houses, now providing temporary lodging for transients. Tourists on a tight budget, who couldn't afford proper West End hotels. Foreign kids with back-packs. The police were regularly called there for matters involving drugs or hookers. 'What about them?' He quickly drained his beer glass, raising his eyebrows resignedly at Mark.

'Dead body,' said Sid Cowley. 'At the Regent Hotel. Probably drugs, or natural causes, but Evans wants us to check it out.'

3

After the Deanery Clergy Wives meeting, which she somehow survived, Jane Stanford went home to the vicarage and found it empty; Brian had left a note on the kitchen table to let her know that he had been called to visit a dying parishioner and wouldn't be home until later.

She was feeling a bit hollowed out, though not really up to eating anything, so she decided to take a nap. It was an indulgence which was not at all characteristic of her, but she told herself that she needed it and would surely feel better afterward. Brian kept insisting that she needed to look after herself and their baby; she was only following his instructions. She went upstairs to the bedroom, laid down on top of the duvet, and covered herself with a knitted throw. That way she wasn't quite in bed in the middle of the day, something she still found it difficult to justify to herself.

But she'd only just drifted off when the telephone jolted her back to immediate consciousness.

She stretched across Brian's side of the bed and reached for the phone on his bedside table. 'Hello?'

'Mum!'

Jane always smiled at the sound of Simon's voice. Though she would never have admitted to having a favourite, of the twins he was the one she thought of as being more like herself. 'Simon. How nice to hear you.' Now, she thought, might be the time to tell him about the baby.

'I have some news, Mum.'

At that, Jane felt a slight qualm. The last news he'd imparted to her, the *in utero* existence of her first grandchild, had not exactly filled her with joy. 'Yes?'

'I hope you and Dad are free tomorrow. Ellie and I are getting married!'

Now Jane felt as if she'd been kicked in the stomach. 'Tomorrow? Did you say *tomorrow*?'

'I know it's not a lot of notice, but I do hope you can be there.'

'But ... where?'

'The Randolph Hotel.' Blithely he imparted the details: Ellie's parents, the wealthy Dickinsons, had made the arrangements. As it was only halfway through Trinity term, the bride and groom couldn't really get away from Oxford for a wedding elsewhere, but in light of the baby on the way, the Dickinsons felt that they shouldn't wait any longer. So they'd pulled a few strings and booked a suite at the posh Randolph on very short notice. They had arranged everything, according to Simon. 'Eleven o'clock,' he said. 'With the wedding breakfast following. I know it's a bit early in the day, but you ought to be able to catch a train and get here in plenty of time. Just take a taxi from the station.'

So many questions she wanted to ask, but Jane was still breathless. 'A civil ceremony, then?' was all she managed.

'Yes, of course. The registrar is part of the package.' Belatedly he seemed to realise what was behind her question. 'It means that Dad won't be able to say any prayers, at least not at the ceremony. But he can do the Grace before we eat.'

She hadn't really expected them to get married at All Saints', not with Ellie's parents seemingly so involved in the young couple's decision-making, but it would have been nice if they could have been married in a church somewhere, with Brian taking or participating in the service. Brian would be disappointed, she knew. And it just didn't seem right that Simon's marriage wouldn't be blessed properly by God.

Then she thought of her other son. 'I assume that Charlie will be involved?'

'Yes, of course. He'll be my best man.' Simon chuckled. 'Old Charlie will have to miss a couple of lectures, which he moaned about, but I told him he didn't have any choice. And I've even convinced him to lay off the essay-writing tonight and go out with me for a bit of a stag night. Or at least a drink or two at the Bird and Baby. I don't want to overdo it, either. It's going to be a big day tomorrow!'

So they really were the last to know, Jane realised. Whatever was Brian going to say?

SUSSEX GARDENS MUST HAVE BEEN A VERY different sort of place in its heyday, Neville reflected as Cowley pulled the car up to the kerb. Its imposing rows of white-porticoed townhouses would have boasted a well-heeled and genteel population. Now they presented a jumble of tacky facades with signage indicating their current incarnations as so-called hotels. But if someone booked into one of them sight unseen, expecting the Ritz or the Dorchester, they were destined to be disappointed. 'Fleapits,' said Cowley with a disapproving sniff. 'Doss houses.'

They were close to Paddington Station, and they were cheap. Or cheap-ish, for London. That was all you could say for most of them.

The Regent, they discovered, seemed to have pretensions above most of its fellows. The name over the portico was proclaimed in gold letters, surmounted by a crown.

Inside, though, the lobby was as dreary as any of the others which Neville had had the misfortune to enter.

A man hovered behind the desk, an anxious expression on his face. He was perhaps in his early thirties, dressed in a cheap suit and open-necked shirt, with slicked-back hair, a wispy moustache and eyes like flint pebbles. 'You're the police?' he said.

Neville nodded tersely. 'DI Stewart, DS Cowley.'

'I'm the manager. Ronald Wicker.' There was a sheen of sweat on his high forehead.

'Tell us what happened, Mr Wicker,' Neville requested. He thought he could guess: most likely a fatal drug overdose in one of the bedrooms. It happened more often than people realised.

Wicker straightened his pronouncedly rounded shoulders. 'Housekeeping found her. It was past check-out time, so the cleaner used her pass-key to get into the room. She called me straightaway, of course.'

'And?'

He closed his eyes for just a second. 'She was dead. In her bed.'

'You were sure she was dead?' Cowley asked.

'Oh, yes. No doubt about it. And I checked for a pulse,' he added.

Compromising a potential crime scene, then, thought Neville unhappily. 'Gloves?' he asked without much hope, exchanging a look with Cowley.

'No time for that. I wanted to make sure there was nothing to be done.'

Too late to spend time worrying about crime scene integrity. 'Any evident cause of death?'

'Needles, or anything like that?' Cowley interjected.

The manager shook his head.

'And who is – was – this woman?'

Wicker's pebble eyes flicked away. 'She registered as Mary Smith.'

'Right,' Cowley said, with a snort of disbelief.

'Were you at the desk yourself when she arrived?' Neville queried.

'Yes. She signed in as Mrs Mary Smith, British nationality.'

'From?'

'No fixed address.' Wicker cleared his throat. 'We get quite a few guests like that.'

Cowley snorted again. 'I'll bet.'

'What day was this? I mean, how long has she been staying here?'

'Just since yesterday. Wednesday afternoon,' Wicker clarified.

'Did she book in advance?'

Wicker shook his head. 'No, she was a walk-in. Fortunately we had a vacancy. We don't always, you know. This is a very popular hotel.'

Neville caught Cowley's eye, but decided not to comment. 'And how long was she planning to stay?'

'She wasn't sure. Maybe two or three days, she said. She paid in advance for one night. In cash.'

No credit card, then. Neville sighed. 'I suppose you'd better take us up, Mr Wicker.'

CALLIE HAD SET ASIDE the afternoon for writing a sermon; Brian had bestowed on her the 'honour' of preaching on Whitsunday. She wasn't sure how much of an honour it was, really, but at least it was better by far than the poisoned chalice that was Trinity Sunday. At theological college they'd had a whole week of lectures on the pitfalls of Trinity Sunday sermons, with multitudinous examples of dodgy and theologically suspect analogies to the Holy Trinity, from apples (skin, flesh, pips) to H_2O (water, ice, steam). That would be Brian's problem, not hers.

But Callie had a problem of her own: her computer was playing up, randomly refusing to respond to commands. She really needed a new one, she realised. But how could she afford a new computer, with all of the expenses that a wedding would entail?

She looked at the screen and sighed. She'd just been on the phone with Marco, who had rung to urge her to start making some concrete wedding plans. 'Let's at least set a date,' he'd urged. And he was right. They needed to get on with it if they really were going to get married this summer.

Her phone rang again, and this time the caller display showed Brian's name. Fortuitous: she would make another attempt to set a wedding date, she decided.

But Brian had other ideas. 'Listen, Callie,' he cut across her before she'd had a chance to go beyond 'hello'. 'I'm going to have to be out of the parish for a couple of days, from early tomorrow. I know you can handle it – just Morning and Evening Prayer, and perhaps a hospital visit or two. I'll be back in time for the Sunday services.'

There went her day off, then, she thought fleetingly, before saying the right thing. 'Is it Jane? Is everything okay?'

'Jane? Oh, yes. She's fine. It's ... well, our son is getting married,' he said. 'Simon. In Oxford. Tomorrow. Jane thought we should stay over afterwards. Spend some time with Charlie, since we'll be there.'

Callie struggled to take it all on board. She had no idea that Simon was engaged, let alone on the brink of matrimony. 'Okay,' she said, then added quickly, 'Speaking of weddings, if you have your diary handy, perhaps we could look at dates for me and Marco. Something in July, maybe? Or August?'

'Not now,' he said. 'We can talk about that at our staff meeting. Next Monday.'

'But—'

'And if you wouldn't mind,' Brian added, 'I'd really appreciate it if you could call in at the hospital this afternoon. Mildred Channing's gone in for a knee replacement. And you know how she is.'

Callie knew all too well. Mildred Channing was one of those difficult parishioners who made even experienced clergy like Brian question their vocation as a parish priest. 'All right,' Callie said, instead of what she was thinking. Which was: *Nice one, Brian. Thanks so much.* And there went the time set aside to write her sermon, as well.

'You'll be fine,' Brian assured her, with far too much heartiness for Callie's liking.

THERE WERE NO NEEDLES, no visible blood. Just a woman, dead in bed. She appeared very peaceful, but she was – as the manager had indicated – very clearly dead.

But she wasn't the sort of woman Neville had been expecting in a hotel of this type. Not a young druggie, nor an elderly down-and-out.

She was middle-aged, probably in her fifties. Her blonde hair was, to Neville's inexpert eyes, professionally cut and styled – and probably professionally coloured, too. She was lying on her back, under a candlewick bedspread. There was nothing to indicate that she hadn't died of natural causes: perhaps she'd been sleeping, and had suffered a heart attack, an aneurism, a stroke. Whatever.

Neville sincerely and profoundly hoped so.

Perhaps her possessions would tell them something.

The manager was hovering by the door. Neville turned to him. 'Did she check in with any luggage?'

Wicker licked his lips. 'She had a case. She asked if there was someone to help bring it up, since there's no lift.'

'And was there?'

'I helped her myself.' He squared his shoulders. 'This isn't a large hotel, you know. I don't employ very many staff.'

Neville looked round the room. Needless to say, it was not only small but basic in the extreme, with a battered chest of drawers, an ancient wardrobe, and a simple bedside table. Thin, faded curtains covered an old sash window. A narrow door led to a minute ensuite, with a shower, loo, and tiny basin crammed into a space no larger than a broom cupboard. Not much scope for an extended search, then.

He did a cursory examination of the top of the bedside table. It held a plastic cup of water, a hotel key fob with a single key, a paperback novel, and a packet of tissues.

'I'll look in the chest of drawers,' he said to Cowley. 'You take the wardrobe.'

While Cowley turned to the wardrobe, Neville yanked on the handles of the top drawer; it slid out with a protesting squeak. Inside were two pairs of knickers, neatly folded, and an unopened packet of tights.

'Whoa, Guv,' said Cowley, with a low whistle. 'Her case is in here. And it's proper Louis Vuitton. Leather and all.'

BEST TO GET it over with, then, Callie decided with resignation. There might yet be time to work on the sermon when she got back from the hospital.

She slung her bag over her shoulder, with a twinge at Bella's look of reproach. 'I won't be long,' she promised the dog, bending over and scratching behind her floppy ears. 'You can have your supper when I'm back.'

In spite of herself, Callie found herself humming as she walked towards the hospital. It had turned into a lovely day, warmer than she'd expected. And she realised that her visit to the hospital might give her an opportunity to see her friend Frances Cherry, the hospital chaplain. With one thing and another, it had been ages since she and Frances done much more than chat briefly on the phone, and she missed her. Maybe they could have a cup of tea in the hospital cafe and catch up.

First things first, though.

She asked at the enquiries desk for the whereabouts of Mildred Channing, and was directed towards a far-flung ward. As she walked the long, sterile corridors, she mentally prepared herself for the negativity she was likely to encounter, beginning with Mrs Channing's disappointment at being visited by the lowly curate instead of the vicar.

Her expectation was spot-on, as Mildred Channing, lying back against her pillows, narrowed her eyes at Callie in disapproval. 'I was expecting Father Brian,' she said stiffly. 'Father Brian *himself*.'

Callie gave her her sunniest smile. 'I'm afraid Father Brian wasn't able to come. You'll have to make do with me instead.'

'Fobbing me off,' the old woman muttered, turning towards her bedside table. She grabbed an empty plastic cup and held it out towards Callie. 'Can you get me some fresh water, then? I've asked and I've asked. But those people act like they don't even understand me. I certainly don't understand *them*. Foreigners, all of them. But surely they understand plain English, even if they can't speak it?'

Glad for an opportunity to escape, even briefly, Calle took the cup and went in search of water.

She filled the cup in a nearby lavatory, but was stopped by one of the nurses before she got back to the ward. The woman appeared to be Filipino, with a round face and black eyes. Her English, though, was as clear and precise as Callie's. 'Is that for Mrs Channing?' she queried.

'Yes. She asked me to get it for her.'

'I'd appreciate it if you didn't give it to her. They're going to be taking her down for some pre-op tests soon, and they don't want her to drink too much water beforehand.' The nurse smiled. 'I've told her several times. But she doesn't seem to take it on board.'

Callie was mortified. 'I'm sorry. I didn't know.'

'Not your fault,' the woman assured her. 'She's a crafty one, is our Mrs Channing. She has ways of getting what she wants. By fair means or foul.'

Callie couldn't help laughing, then gave the nurse a rueful smile. 'I'm not looking forward to telling her that she can't have it,' she confessed.

But she was spared the necessity, as a porter with an empty wheelchair came down the corridor at that moment, headed for the ward. 'That will be for Mrs Channing,' the nurse said. 'Why don't you come back tomorrow, after she's had the op?'

As soon as they were out of the hotel, Cowley turned to Neville and put it bluntly and succinctly. 'So what was a posh bird like that doing in a dump like this?'

'And pretending to be Mary Smith?' He shook his head. 'I don't like it. Not one bit.'

It had been easy enough to ascertain that the woman's name was as fictitious as it sounded. Her handbag – good quality leather, with a designer label – had yielded up some valuable information, including a driving license issued to a Felicity Chapman. The photo was recognisable as the dead woman, which was good enough for Neville. Her date of birth indicated that she was fifty-six years old, and her postal address was given as Devizes.

'Where the hell is Devizes, anyway?' Cowley grumbled.

Neville shook his head again. 'Not a clue,' he admitted. 'Let's go back to the station and talk this one through.'

'Or the pub?' suggested Cowley, pointing his thumb hopefully at the establishment on the corner they were approaching.

Neville considered the fact that he'd already had one beer, at lunch with Mark. But that had been a couple of hours ago now, and he really could use another at this point. 'Oh, why not.'

It was an old-fashioned pub, dark and invitingly cool on a day which had unexpectedly turned quite warm.

'My shout, Guv,' said Cowley with a magnanimous flourish. 'Your usual, I assume?'

Neville sighed. 'Better make it a half, Sid.' He was going to need all of his faculties for this one. He chose a table in a corner, slid onto the padded banquette at the back, and waited for Sid to join him with the drinks.

Was it a suspicious death, or one attributable to natural causes? The police doctor, Colin Tompkins, had been unwilling to commit himself at the scene, when he and the SOCOs had arrived a short while after Neville and Cowley. 'We'll know in due course,' he'd said, with his usual taciturnity. 'She's dead. Dead is dead. It doesn't matter to her how it happened.' That wasn't helpful, as far as Neville was concerned. It might not have made any difference to the dead woman – or indeed to Dr Tompkins, who was happy to carve up corpses no matter the manner of their death – but it was bloody important to Neville. If she'd popped off with a heart attack, or a burst aneurism, he could wash his hands of this one in short order. If she'd topped herself, though, or someone had helped her along, then the ball was firmly in the police's court. Detective Superintendent Evans was going to want to know; he wouldn't be fobbed off with Colin Tompkins' shilly-shallying.

Cowley appeared, Neville's half in one hand, a pint of lager in the other, and the corner of a packet of pork scratchings gripped between his teeth. He slid the glasses onto the table and released the packet to land in front of Neville. 'Here, Guv. Don't say I never gave you anyfing.'

Neville frowned. He'd once rather enjoyed pork scratchings, along with the cigarettes he'd considered essential to the pub experience, but that all now seemed part of a long-distant past. He'd quit smoking even before the ban on lighting up had changed pubs beyond recognition, and Triona had subtly managed to influence his taste in foods. Pork scratchings no longer appealed to him. He pushed the packet towards Cowley. 'No thanks, Sid. Help yourself.'

'Don't mind if I do.' Cowley ripped the packet open and tipped its contents onto the scarred wooden table. 'The wife won't let you eat pork scratchings, eh?'

'It has nothing to do with Triona,' Neville said tersely. Though of course it did. He knew that marriage had changed him, in spite of his determination that it wouldn't. But maybe, he reflected, change was no bad thing. Sid could stand to make a few changes.

'So, this bird,' Cowley resumed, after a gulp of lager. 'Dead posh, right? I mean, she had a Louis Vuitton case, and a Coach bag! My sister would kill for one of those. Either one. I mean, she's got a fake Louis Vuitton – she got it down the market for a tenner. But that bird's bag was no fake. It was the real deal, or my name's not Sid Cowley.'

'Your point being?'

'Like I said, Guv. She didn't belong in a minging dump like that. She should of been at the Ritz. Or the Savoy. You know what I mean. You know I'm right.'

Neville knew exactly what he meant. And he didn't like the implications of that realisation: there was something suspicious about the circumstances of this death which made it more rather than less likely that they were going to end up investigating it.

AS FAR AS Frances Cherry was concerned, her job as a hospital chaplain was all about connecting with the human beings – patients, families and staff – who needed her pastoral care: spending time in the wards, the waiting rooms and wherever there were people who needed to talk. But the National Health Service saw things somewhat differently, and insisted upon accountability and documentation. That meant that Frances had to spend more of her time than she would have liked on her computer, making notes about every visit and each encounter. Just in case.

On Thursday afternoon, that's exactly what she was doing when there was a knock on the door of her office.

'Come in,' she called.

The door opened a crack to reveal her friend Callie Anson.

'Oh, it's you!' Frances' frown transformed to a delighted grin.

'Sorry to disturb you,' Callie apologised.

'You're not disturbing me in the least!' Frances came from behind her desk and enfolded Callie in a hug.

'Do you have time for a cup of tea?'

'Absolutely.' Frances was already reaching for her handbag. 'I can't bear another moment in this office. Let's go to the caf. My treat.'

Frances always felt a bit protective of Callie, and in a way responsible for her. They'd met when Callie's father was a patient, and dying; Frances, the hospital chaplain, had inspired Callie to embrace faith, then nurtured a dawning realisation of a calling to the priesthood. Half a generation older than Callie, she was both mentor and friend. Their busy lives meant that they weren't often able to spend time together, but Frances was always glad to see her young friend.

'What brings you here today?' she asked as they traversed yet another long corridor. 'I'm sure it wasn't just to see me.'

'Pastoral visit. Not one I was looking forward to, and you're the reward I promised myself for being virtuous and doing it,' confessed Callie.

'It wasn't that Mildred Channing, was it?'

'How did you know?'

Frances groaned. 'I've been to see her. She told me that her vicar was coming to visit her, thank-you-very-much, and sent me packing.'

'And I turned up instead.' Callie chuckled. 'She wasn't best pleased that Brian didn't come himself.'

'She seemed a thoroughly miserable human being, if that isn't being too uncharitable.'

'Oh, she is. And nothing – but nothing – makes her happy. Sort of like my mother, only ten times worse!'

Frances threw up her hands in mock horror. 'Good Lord. I'd think you were exaggerating, if I hadn't had the pleasure of her company myself.'

'Though you were probably spared one of her rants on being surrounded by incomprehensible foreigners. It's one of her favourite subjects.'

'Humph.' Frances grimaced. 'I don't know who she thinks would be emptying her bedpans otherwise.'

They reached the cafe and joined the queue. 'Live dangerously,' Frances urged. 'Have a scone. Or some cake.'

'Oh, I shouldn't.' Callie patted her waistline. 'I've been doing too much comfort eating lately as it is.'

Frances turned and gave her a searching look. 'Does this perchance have anything to do with a wedding dress?'

'I wish.' Callie sighed and shook her head.

'Okay. You're going to tell me everything,' Frances declared firmly. She grabbed a tray, ordered the tea, paid at the till, and led the way to an empty table. 'Start talking,' she said, as soon as they were settled in their chairs.

Callie shook her head again. 'I don't want to burden you with my problems.'

'Don't be silly. What are friends for? Tell me what's going on.' Frances tried to remember the last time they'd had a proper heart-to-heart, and realised guiltily that it had been at least a couple of months – the last time must have been in the hot tub when they'd enjoyed a spa day together, back before Easter. They had a lot of catching up to do.

'Well,' Callie said, 'it's Marco's family, really. Or his sister, to be precise.'

'She's been a problem since the beginning, hasn't she?' Frances flipped open the lid of the metal teapot and gave it a brisk stir.

'Serena has never liked me,' Callie confessed. 'But she and Marco had a tremendous row when he told her we were going to get married. They're not speaking.'

'That should make it easier, then. Just ignore her and get on with it.' She poured the tea and slid a cup across the table to Callie.

'I'm trying to do that. But I haven't even been able to pin Brian down long enough to set a date for the wedding. Every time I bring it up, he changes the subject. It's almost like he doesn't want to do it! And Marco and I ... we really would like to get married this summer.'

'This summer? As in ... *this summer*?' Frances stared at her incredulously.

'July or August, we were thinking.'

'Then you'd better get busy. Do you have any idea how long it takes to plan a wedding?'

'Not really,' Callie admitted. 'I know that people usually book the church about a year in advance. But I was hoping that it wouldn't take that long, if we kept it sort of low key.'

'Ha.' Frances blew on her tea and took a sip. 'I'd offer to do it myself, but I don't have a church.'

Callie sighed and stirred her cup. 'I want to get married at All Saints'. It's my church.'

'Then you've got to set a date, if you have to lock Brian into his study with his diary until he comes up with one.' She reached across the table and squeezed Callie's hand. 'But there *is* something I can do. I can take you shopping for wedding dresses. Shall we say one day next week?'

4

Detective Chief Superintendent Idris Evans didn't bother to get up from behind his desk when Neville entered his office, but he looked up from a pile of papers and grunted in acknowledgement.

'Sir,' said Neville, then waited as his boss took his time, leafing through a couple of sheets of paper, pushing them aside, and folding his hands in front of him.

'Stewart.' Evans fixed his piggy eyes on him and thrust out his already prominent jaw. 'Let's cut to the chase, shall we, boyo? The woman in the hotel. Ours, or not?'

If only he could give a simple, definitive answer. 'I don't know,' Neville admitted, then when Evans narrowed his eyes, he ventured a reluctant opinion. 'Probably.'

'Damn it, Stewart, we've got enough on our plates right now without this.'

Neville couldn't disagree with that statement, nor did he know why he was being blamed for it. No one would have been happier if the dead woman had had a needle sticking out of her arm. 'We'll have to wait for the postmortem,' he said apologetically. 'But just to be on the safe side, I've sealed the room and called in the SOCOs.'

'Fill me in, then.' Evans leaned back in his chair, linking his hands behind his thick neck.

Trying to make it as concise as possible, Neville began. 'No obvious cause of death. She was just ... dead. In bed.'

'Then why aren't we assuming natural causes?'

'There are some ... anomalies, I guess you'd say.' He ticked them off on his fingers. 'It's a down-market hotel, but the dead woman was definitely not down-market – she was what Sid Cowley called a 'posh bird'. Nicely dressed, good quality luggage. She registered under a false name, and paid in cash. And the hotel manager is a dodgy bloke called Ronald Wicker who was definitely hiding something.' It wasn't until he said it that he realised that was one of the things that had been bothering him: Ronald Wicker had bent over backwards to be helpful, but all of Neville's instincts told him that he was keeping something back, if not being downright untruthful.

Evans sighed. 'Who was she, then?'

'Her driving license says she was a Felicity Chapman, aged fifty-six, from somewhere called Devizes. Wherever the hell that is.'

'Wiltshire,' Evans informed him. 'Denise has a sister near there.' Denise, Neville well knew, was the second Mrs Evans, much younger and far more attractive than the previous model. 'You have an address?'

Neville nodded.

'Then I guess you'd better get on to the next-of-kin, hadn't you?'

He stared at his boss incredulously. 'You want me to go to bloody ... Wiltshire?'

'Don't be daft,' Evans snapped in a sing-song voice; he always sounded more Welsh when he was annoyed. 'You don't have to go there yourself. Not yet, anyway. But you'll need to liaise with the local force and have them notify the next-of-kin. And keep me informed.'

'Yes, sir.' Neville realised that he was being dismissed, and turned to go.

'And,' Evans added as he reached the door, 'I'd check into Ronald Wicker, if I were you. That name rings bells, somehow.'

Callie walked home quickly from the hospital, conscious that she didn't have much time to spare before Evening Prayer in church. Not that she expected Brian to be there today, to look askance at her if she were late, but she didn't want to take chances. And punctuality was a virtue she favoured, just on general principle.

All thoughts of punctuality went out of the window, though, when she slipped through the small side door which led directly into the chancel. A quick glance confirmed that Brian was not in his stall in the chancel, but the church was definitely not empty. Issuing from the direction of the adjacent Lady Chapel was the unmistakeable sound of sobbing – loud and uncontrolled. Without even thinking about it, Callie headed in the direction of the sobs.

The candle stand by the statue of Our Lady was ablaze with light, every pricket filled. And kneeling at the foot of the statue was the source of the noise: the same fair-haired girl Callie had surprised in the Lady Chapel a few weeks before, gazing up intently at the face of Our Lady with her raised hands clasped in supplication as she cried her heart out.

Hesitant to interrupt, Callie stood irresolutely at the chapel entrance for a moment, trying to remember the girl's name. Zuzanna – that was it.

She took a step into the chapel, and the girl turned with a startled gasp.

'Zuzanna? Are you okay?' It was a stupid question, Callie realised immediately. Of course she wasn't okay. She wanted to take the girl in her arms and comfort her, but was that the proper pastoral thing to do? If only Frances were here – or even Brian – to ask for advice ...

Zuzanna choked back a sob. 'No, am not okay.'

Callie held out her arms and the girl flung herself into them, wetting the shoulder of her clerical shirt with tears. She rubbed the girl's back and made soothing noises which transcended the language barrier; after a few moments Zuzanna's sobs subsided, and eventually she pulled away and covered her face with her hands.

'I am sorry,' she sniffled. 'Sorry to bother you, Miss curate Callie.'

'Just Callie.'

'Callie. Miss Callie. Am sorry.'

'No need for that. Is there something you'd like to talk to me about?' Callie suggested. 'Remember, I told you that's what I'm here for.' She steered Zuzanna towards a pew and sat down next to her, resisting the impulse to put her arm round her shoulders.

Zuzanna fumbled in her pocket and brought out a damp tissue, pressing it to her eyes as she visibly struggled for control. 'I see terrible thing,' she said at last. 'Woman is dead.'

Callie's heart lurched. Whatever she'd expected, it wasn't that. 'You saw a dead woman? Where?'

'In hotel. Where I work.' Zuzanna gestured vaguely in the direction of Sussex Gardens. 'I go in to clean room, see? I use key.

'And?'

'Woman is in bed. I think sleeping, maybe too much drink? But—' Here she was overwhelmed by emotion again; a sob escaped and she gulped it back.

'She was dead?'

Zuzanna nodded. 'I go closer. I say something like sorry to bother, then I see. She is dead.'

Curiosity struggled with horror and came out on top. 'What did you do?' Callie couldn't help asking.

'I scream. I scream much. Manager come then. Mr Wicker, he come. He tell me go home. But – I come here. I come, light candles. Say prayers.' She turned her head and looked up at the statue. 'I tell Our Lady.'

PC Grace Long climbed into the passenger seat of the police car; her guv, Sergeant Tom Burton, liked to do the driving.

He also liked to do the talking. Confident in his superior experience and rank, he tended to treat Grace in what she often felt was a somewhat condescending manner. She'd grown used to it.

Burton punched an address into the GPS and waited a moment for it to give him the first command. 'So,' he said as he pulled out of the car park and turned left onto the A361, heading away from the Devizes town centre, 'I suppose you'd like to know what this is about.'

'I would,' she agreed.

'I've been on the phone with a bloke from the Met. A Detective

Inspector, no less. They've got a body on their hands – a woman found dead in a hotel room in London. They're not sure yet whether it's a police matter – whether she died from natural causes or not, and they won't know till the postmortem, tomorrow morning.' He turned his attention to the GPS screen.

'And he rang you because ... ?'

'She lives ... lived ... round here, see? We have to notify the next-of-kin.'

Oh, great. Grace felt like she needed a bit more preparation for what was commonly agreed to be pretty much the hardest job a police officer had to carry out. 'And who is that?'

'We don't know, do we? Won't know till we get there. We'll have to play it by ear, like.'

This was the height of the rush hour; the traffic leaving Devizes meant that their progress was slow. Tom hummed to himself; Grace closed her eyes and thought about the dead woman. Who was she? How old? Had she left behind a husband and, perhaps, young children? Or parents, who'd never expected to outlive their daughter?

After a few minutes, once they'd left the town behind, the GPS directed them to turn left off the main road onto a less-travelled side road. Then they turned again into a cul-de-sac, and Tom slowed down as the GPS announced, 'Arriving at destination, on right.' He pulled the car to the kerb in front of a substantial red brick house, set back from the road.

This wasn't exactly what one would describe as a neighbourhood or a housing estate, but neither was it a solitary country house. It was more a cluster of large detached houses, surrounded by generous plots of land. Grace, who had lived just a few miles from here for all of her life, had never been there before. The children who grew up in these houses would have gone to public school somewhere, rather than to the local comprehensive with her, and the adult inhabitants were unlikely to have attracted the attention of the police for any reason. These solid houses spoke of a modest sort of privilege and respectability, rather than flamboyant wealth. Their owners were people who got on with their comfortable lives, secure and serene.

But, she reminded herself, a woman who had lived in this house was dead. Dead in a London hotel room.

Tom Burton got out of the car and slammed the door, as if in defiance at the tranquility of the surroundings. 'Let's do this,' he said.

The house had a name, not a number, on the wrought iron gate which blocked the entrance to the drive. 'Kennet House,' Grace read.

Her guv opened the gate, marched up the long drive to the front door and put his thumb on the bell; she trailed behind him a few steps.

'Coming,' called a voice from within.

The heavy wooden door swung open to reveal a middle-aged man with a quizzical expression. Dark hair, greying at the sides. Spectacles. And, incongruously, he was wearing a flowered pinny over his clothes. 'Can I help you?' he said. Posh voice, Grace noted. Educated. And polite.

Grace was grateful, this time, that her guv liked to do the talking.

'Sergeant Burton, PC Long,' he said, flashing his warrant card. 'We're here about a Mrs Felicity Chapman, of this address. Would she be your wife, sir?'

The man's quizzical expression deepened to a frown. 'Yes. But I'm afraid she's not here. Is this something I can help you with instead?'

Burton shifted his weight from one foot to the other. 'Could we come in, sir? We need to have a word with you.'

'Of course.' The man opened the door wide and stepped aside. 'I'm Alan Chapman, by the way.'

They followed him through a spacious hallway into a large room which Grace would have called a lounge; she suspected that Mr Chapman would have called it something else – a living room, a sitting room perhaps, or even a drawing room.

'Felicity's not here,' he repeated, indicating his pinny with a sheepish smile. 'As you can see. You caught me in the middle of making my own supper.'

'And where do you believe Mrs Chapman to be, then, sir?'

Alan Chapman frowned again, displaying more puzzlement than irritation. 'Where do I believe her to be? What an odd question. She's in London, if you must know. For the Chelsea Flower Show. She goes every year – wouldn't miss it,' he added. 'Felicity's a very keen gardener.'

Grace held her breath as Burton charged ahead. 'I'm sorry to have to tell you this, sir, but your wife is dead. Her body was found this afternoon in her room at the Regent Hotel in Paddington.'

Chapman smiled and shook his head. 'I'm afraid you're mistaken, Sergeant. That's not possible.'

'I'm afraid it's true, sir. She was identified through her driving license.' Burton crossed his arms across his chest and waited.

'But ... how? Paddington? An hotel? You must have the wrong person. Felicity always stays with our son. Ben. He has a flat near Sloane Square. One of those mansion blocks, you know. Very convenient for Chelsea.'

He was babbling, Grace realised. Trying to process the information, and failing. In shock, most probably. She should offer to make tea, but she didn't want to leave.

'Why don't you ring your son, then, sir?' Burton suggested. 'He can confirm whether Mrs Chapman is with him, or not.'

IT HAD BEEN a couple of days since Mark Lombardi had seen Callie, and he was missing her. They didn't have any firm plans to meet up before the weekend, but when he got back to his flat after work on Thursday, he realised that he didn't want to wait any longer. He would offer to cook her a meal, Mark decided. And perhaps, if they were discreet about it, he'd even manage to stay the night. After all, tomorrow was her day off, and he'd booked a day off for himself tomorrow in anticipation and hope.

He showered and changed into fresh clothes, then rummaged in the kitchen cabinets for a few things to take along. Shoving them into a carrier bag, he pulled out his mobile and rang her.

Callie answered after a couple of rings 'Marco?'

'Are you free, *Cara Mia*? I thought I could come by and cook for you. I have some of those lovely dried porcini.'

There was a slight hesitation on the other end. 'I'm ... not sure, Marco. I'd love to see you – you know I would – but ... I really need to work on my sermon for Sunday. Brian's been called away, and he's left me in charge.'

'But tomorrow's your day off,' he reminded her.

'Not this week, it isn't.'

'That's a bit rotten of Brian,' he said indignantly.

Callie sighed. 'He couldn't help it. His son is getting married tomorrow. In Oxford.'

'Well, he must have known about that a long time ago.'

'I don't think he did, actually. I think it's caught him on the hop.'

'It's not fair on you.' Or on me, Mark said to himself, knowing that he was being petulant in his disappointment.

'I'll try to carve out some time tomorrow, if I can,' she promised. 'Tomorrow evening, maybe. I'll ring you, okay?'

'Okay,' he agreed with a sigh, putting the packet of porcini back in the cabinet.

WHILE ALAN CHAPMAN rang his son, Grace went to the kitchen to make tea.

She was aware that she ought to resent being consigned to the traditional female role, but Grace honestly didn't mind. She knew that she was good at doing practical things, and that included making tea at the appropriate moment.

The kitchen was as spacious as the other rooms she'd seen. It was, Grace believed, what was known as a farmhouse kitchen, though it bore very little resemblance to the cluttered kitchen in the farmhouse where she'd lived all her life, replete with muddy boots and dog beds.

This kitchen was immaculate, with surfaces gleaming and a few clean dishes slotted into the drying rack by the sink. A fragrant pot of stew bubbled away on the top of the Aga. Grace found a wooden spoon and gave the pot a stir to keep it from catching, then she located the electric kettle and switched it on.

She was impressed: Alan Chapman was obviously a tidy man. She didn't know how long his wife had been away from home, but if, say, her own father had been on his own for any period of time, it wouldn't have taken very long for the kitchen to resemble a disaster area, above and beyond the usual clutter. Dirty dishes, burnt saucepans, filthy worktops – she could imagine it all too well.

The teabags were in a canister by the kettle, and a variety of Emma

Bridgewater mugs hung from hooks on the Welsh dresser. Grace picked three at random – one with spots, one with hearts, and one with black labradors – and put them on a convenient tray, along with a jug of milk from the fridge and a matching sugar basin from the dresser.

'Ah. Good girl,' Tom Burton said as she carried the tray into the lounge.

He was sitting now. So was Alan Chapman, who sagged onto a comfortable-looking sofa, his face grey and his arms limp. He was still wearing the pinny.

'Plenty of sugar for Mr Chapman,' Burton directed as Grace poured the tea.

She complied, then tried to give the mug to Alan Chapman. He looked at her blankly and made no effort to take it, so she put it on a coaster on the table beside him.

Alan Chapman blinked, then shook his head. 'She's not there,' he said flatly. 'Felicity isn't at Ben's.'

'Could you tell us what your son said, sir? Exactly?' Burton urged, with a sideways glance at Grace.

Grace got out her notebook and opened it to a blank page.

'She sent him a text message. Yesterday. The day she ... left. She said that her plans had changed, and she wouldn't be coming to stay.'

'Was that the last message he had from her, then?'

Chapman nodded. 'That's what he said. He just assumed that she was at home. Here. So he didn't worry.'

'And did Mrs Chapman text you, at all, over the last couple of days?'

'No.' He shook his head. 'I don't use a mobile phone, Sergeant. It's beyond me – I'm too old for that sort of thing.'

Just like her own dad, thought Grace as she wrote 'no mobile'.

'But Mrs Chapman did?'

'Yes.' He pressed his fingertips together and contemplated them. 'She finds it ... found it ... useful for keeping in touch with Ben. Text messages, and ... Facebook, I believe it's called.'

'Is Ben your only child?' Grace asked; Burton swivelled his head and glared at her.

'Yes. Just Ben. Felicity and Ben are ... were ... very close,' he added softly.

Having already gained Burton's disapprobation, Grace decided to risk another question; in for a penny, in for a pound, as her dad would say. 'Is Ben married?'

Chapman shook his head. 'He has a ... partner. That's what he calls it.' His mouth twisted in a wry smile. 'Felicity hates ... hated ... that word. And I can't say I think much of it myself. Danielle, she's called. They live together. Felicity hated that, too. She's ... she was ... very old-fashioned in a lot of ways. She thought they ought to get married. And of course she was hoping for grandchildren. Sooner, rather than later, she always said. While we were still young enough to enjoy them.'

That was, Grace realised, the largest quantity of words that Alan Chapman had strung together since they'd arrived. She shot a quick look of triumph at Tom Burton.

He ignored her and pressed on. 'So you hadn't heard anything from your wife since she left home yesterday? She didn't ring you?'

'No.' Chapman reached for the mug of tea and took a sip. He grimaced, either at its sweetness or its temperature, Grace surmised.

Burton leaned back in his chair. 'Tell me about yesterday, then. When did your wife leave home? How did she go? What did she take with her? Did you see her or talk to her before she went?'

After a few more tentative sips of tea, Chapman replied slowly and patiently. 'I don't know what time she left, or what she took with her. I was at work. She was here when I went in the morning, and gone when I got home.'

'Did she leave a note?'

He shook his head. 'No, why would she? I knew she was going.'

'Would she have driven to London, sir?' Burton asked.

'No. No reason to, when there's a direct train from Pewsey. There's no long-term parking there, so she would have taken a taxi to the station. It's only a few miles,' he added.

Grace wrote 'taxi' and 'Pewsey'. 'That's the mainline train, then,' she said. 'Into Paddington.'

NEVILLE HAD BEEN on to the Wiltshire police headquarters about the notification of next-of-kin, and had deputised Cowley to look into Ronald Wicker. Deciding that there was nothing else he could usefully do at his desk, and aware that he would need to be at the mortuary for the postmortem early the next morning, he shut down his computer and went home.

These days, he was never quite sure what he would find when he got home. Triona's moods were unpredictable at the best of times, but now that she was well into the third trimester of her pregnancy ...

The second trimester, when Triona had been uncharacteristically sunny and upbeat, had suited Neville down to the ground. If he could have frozen that period in time, he would have done so gladly.

Now, though, he always felt as if he were walking on eggshells. Some days she was cheerful and positive. But mostly she was grumpy, tired, and fed up with being pregnant.

He unlocked the door of the flat and pushed it open with a called greeting. 'Hi – I'm home!'

No greeting in return, and no cooking smells. That didn't bode particularly well.

'Triona?'

Suddenly, terrifyingly, his mind jumped back nearly ten years. Back to that evening he'd come home from work to discover that, without any warning, Triona had walked out of his life. It had taken him nine years to find her again.

Panicking, his heart pounding, Neville called her name again as he rushed towards the bedroom.

Triona was in bed, her wild dark curls fanned out on the pillow. She looked very pale, and blinked at him as she struggled into a sitting position. 'What's wrong? Is the flat on fire or something?'

'No, I just ...' He tried to stop the words from tumbling out, but they came anyway. 'I thought you were gone,' he blurted. 'I thought you'd left me.'

'Don't be daft,' she snapped. 'Isn't a pregnant woman allowed to take a nap?'

'Yes, of course.' Now he felt foolish; she'd managed to wrong-foot him, without even trying. Neville took a deep, calming breath. 'But you're okay?'

She managed to lever herself up on the pillows, making a face. 'Well, not really,' she admitted. 'This afternoon I felt ... odd. When I was at work. I started having some pains. Contractions.'

The sense of panic returned, but with an entirely different focus. 'Contractions! The baby's coming? But it's weeks too early!'

'That's what I thought,' Triona admitted. 'I rang the midwife. She assures me that it's only Braxton Hicks.'

Neville had dutifully been to all of the antenatal classes with Triona; he knew what Braxton Hicks contractions were. 'That's all right, then,' he said, relieved.

'Easy for you to say, Stewart. I'm the one who feels like crap. And I'm the one who's going to be pushing this great lump of baby out in a few weeks' time.'

At least she was smiling – sort of – when she said it. 'What can I do for you? A cup of tea?' Neville suggested, searching his memory banks for what they'd said in the antenatal class. 'A back rub, maybe? Or we could practice your breathing exercises?'

'I've been practicing my breathing exercises all afternoon, thank you very much.'

'Would you like something to eat, then?'

'Toast,' she said. 'Toast with Marmite.'

Neville pressed a kiss onto her forehead, then escaped to the kitchen.

The loaf in the bread bin was beginning to go mouldy, so he picked out the two least manky slices and pinched off the blue bits round the edges. He slotted them into the toaster, then tried to find where Triona had hidden the Marmite.

Once he had her settled in for the night, he decided, he'd nip out to the corner shop and get a fresh loaf of bread. His stomach rumbled, reminding him that he'd scorned Cowley's pork scratchings some hours earlier. A guilty take-away was in his future, then: not a curry, of course – which would be detectable by Triona's acute nose even the next morning – but maybe he could get away with something from the chippie. He could murder a sausage and chips about now ...

Neville's salivary musings were interrupted by the simultaneous ping of the toaster and the bleat of his mobile phone.

Sid Cowley, the display told him.

He pincered the hot toast onto a plate with one hand and thumbed the green button on his phone with the other. 'Sid?'

'Guv, I've been checking up on that Wicker cove – like you asked me to.'

'And?'

Cowley gave a little chuckle. 'Bent as a nine-bob note. Just like you fought.'

'He has form?'

There was a pause; Neville could hear an indrawn breath and knew that Cowley was taking a drag on his cigarette.

'Yeah. Minor stuff, mostly. He's done some time, but mostly just nicking cars and that sort of lark. But here's the fing, Guv.' Again he took a drag. 'He's part of a family of minor East End villains. The Garveys. His mum's a Garvey, and it's her brother what owns the Regent Hotel. He's a bloke called Frank Garvey – and he's got form a mile long. So that means our boy Ronnie Wicker is working for his crooked uncle.'

Neville smiled; his instincts had been right. 'Good work, Sid,' he said. 'Keep digging. Wicker wasn't being straight with us. He's hiding something – I'm sure of it.'

5

Callie didn't sleep very well on Thursday night: apart from her worries about the unfinished sermon, and her guilt at putting Marco off, she couldn't stop thinking about Zuzanna.

She didn't feel she'd handled the situation very well, or given much help or even comfort to the distressed girl. Finding a dead body wasn't something in her own experience; she could scarcely even imagine the horror of it. She'd listened, she'd made soothing noises. She'd made sure that Zuzanna knew she was welcome to talk to her at any time. But at the end of the day, Zuzanna had melted away, back to wherever she lived. Would she see her again? Was there anything more she could do?

Tossing and turning in the early morning light, she gave up trying to sleep, and instead took a brisk shower. After that she felt a bit more focused, made herself a cup of coffee, and spent an hour or so at the computer working on her sermon.

It was still very early, but as she worked Callie became aware that Bella was sitting beside her desk, fixing her with an expectant stare.

She looked at her watch: still an hour before Morning Prayer. 'Oh, all right,' she capitulated. 'We'll go for walkies, then.'

She grabbed her jacket from the hook by the door, and clipped on

Bella's lead. 'I'm warning you,' she said to the dog as they went down the flight of stairs, 'it's too early for all of your mates to be out. If you think you're going to see them, you're going to be disappointed.'

It was a clear morning, and after the warmth of the previous afternoon it seemed rather chilly; Callie was glad to have the jacket.

Their customary route from her flat above the church hall to Hyde Park took them past the west doors of the church. Callie glanced towards the doors, then stopped in her tracks. The doors were shut, as they should be, but at the foot of them huddled a forlorn figure: it was Zuzanna, sitting on the ground with her back to the doors, her eyes closed. She looked terribly frail, her face pale and her eyelids blue, her arms wrapped round her slender body with nothing but a flimsy cardigan to keep her warm.

'Zuzanna!' Callie hurried to her side, dragging Bella behind her.

The girl opened her eyes and smiled. 'Miss Callie. I know you come.' She spotted Bella and her smile became a delighted grin. Bella rushed to her, tail wagging; the girl reached out and stroked her. 'Nice doggie.'

'She's called Bella,' Callie said automatically, adding, 'but what are you doing here? How long have you been here? You must be freezing!' Had Zuzanna been there all night, then?

'Not so long. I did not know church was locked.'

All thoughts of a dog walk abandoned, Callie reached out her free hand to help her to her feet. 'Let's get you inside,' she said. Not the church this time, though. She would take her back to her warm flat.

SINCE TRIONA HAD MOVED in with him a few months ago, Neville had stopped setting an alarm. By nature a morning person, she was always up before he was, and she would make sure that he was awake when he needed to be.

But on Friday morning, in spite of the fact that her maternity leave wasn't due to start for another week, Triona didn't get up.

Neville discovered this fact when his mobile rang. He surfaced out of an amorphous dream to find Triona sleeping beside him, the phone bleating insistently on the bedside table, and sun streaming through the window.

'Bloody hell,' he said, reaching for the phone.

It was Colin Tompkins. 'Just wondering where you were,' said the pathologist. 'I'm about to begin.'

The postmortem.

Bloody hell. This time he didn't say it aloud. 'Sorry. Sorry, mate. I ... err, I guess I overslept.' Neville ran his hand over his stubbly chin and tried to calculate quickly how long it would take him to be where he needed to be. 'I'll be there in about an hour. That's the best I can do.'

'I'll just carry on, then.' The pathologist, always a man of few words, hung up.

Neville threw the phone onto the bed. Just what he needed: to be wrong-footed at the beginning of what was almost certainly not going to be a straightforward case. Evans would not be amused. Maybe, with any luck, Evans would punish him by taking the case away and giving it to someone else ...

Triona turned over in bed and opened her eyes. 'What's wrong?'

She looked terrible, he saw; her colour was bad, and there were dark shadows under her eyes. Instantly contrite, he sat down next to her and took her hand. 'I've overslept, that's all. How are you feeling?'

'Like crap.' She grimaced and rubbed her enormous bump. 'It hasn't been a good night. I'm not going to make it to work today.'

Sympathy for her warred with his own urgent need to get to the mortuary. Neville took a deep breath and made the decision to be a good husband. 'Okay. What can I do for you?'

'A cup of tea. Then you can find my phone so I can ring the office. And then,' she said, squeezing his hand, 'you can bugger off and go to work. I'll be okay. It's only Braxton Hicks.'

'SORRY, SWEETIE,' Callie said to Bella. 'Maybe a bit later.' She settled Zuzanna on the sofa, tucked a fleecy throw round her thin shoulders, then went to switch on the kettle. 'Tea?' she asked over her shoulder. 'Or would you rather have coffee?'

'Tea, please. No milk.'

The girl hadn't moved by the time she returned a few minutes later. Callie put the mug of steaming black tea into her cold hands.

'Thank you, Miss Callie,' said Zuzanna, wrapping her hands round the mug with a sigh.

Callie fetched a mug for herself and sat down across from the girl. 'Don't you have to go to work this morning?' she probed.

Zuzanna shook her head. 'I go to work. But Mr Wicker, he say go home. Police will come, he say. Police will ... ask. Ask questions.' She shrugged. 'Many questions, maybe.'

Of course they would. And quite rightly, if this was a murder investigation. 'But you don't have anything to hide. Why shouldn't you answer their questions?'

She shrugged again. 'Mr Wicker say no. He say they trick me, maybe. Make me say things.'

Callie was indignant on behalf of the police. 'They wouldn't do that!'

'Maybe.' Her head drooped and she looked down into her tea, eyes welling.

Trying to avoid a repeat of last night's tears, Callie decided that some distraction was in order. 'I don't know very much about you, Zuzanna. Tell me – where do you come from? How long have you been in London?'

The girl raised her head. 'I come from Poland. Last year. With my sister. Krysia. We come together to work.'

'Do you live together, then? You and your sister?'

She nodded. 'Yes. We have room. Bed-sit, is called.' Her mouth quirked in a small smile. 'Two beds, one chair. We can sleep, we can sit. But most of time we work.'

'What sort of work does your sister do?'

'Krysia, her English is more better than me. She work in cafe. Sometimes in bar, too. Me, English not too good. Work in housekeeping is best.'

'Do you like your job, then?' Callie asked, then wished she could take back her words as Zuzanna's face creased in pain.

'Like job? No. Is bad job,' she stated. Haltingly, yet with conviction, she proceeded to tell Callie what it was like to work in housekeeping in a downmarket tourist hotel.

The hotel had thirty-two rooms and one other cleaner. That meant that Zuzanna was responsible for cleaning sixteen rooms each day, seven days a week. No benefits, no sick leave. Half an hour – unpaid – for lunch. Demanding and ungrateful hotel guests. Disgusting messes to clean up after, often – things she couldn't bring herself to describe, even if she'd had the vocabulary. It was strenuous work, requiring physical stamina and the sort of strength it was difficult to imagine the slender young girl possessing. And Mr Wicker was a slave-driver of a boss, without humour or compassion. 'I hate it,' she concluded, scowling. 'I hate job. I hate Mr Wicker.'

Callie was appalled. 'Can't you find a better job somewhere else? Maybe at one of the big hotels?'

Zuzanna shook her head emphatically. 'Big hotel is more worse. I work at big hotel first. Last year. Rich people more worse.' She went on to explain that the patrons of the hotel where she'd worked had expected far more – spotless rooms, and extra touches which meant more work for the housekeeping staff. And far too often they demanded other perks as well, especially when the cleaner was as pretty as Zuzanna. She'd had her bottom pinched, her breasts groped, and worse; when one guest had tried to haul her into his bed, she had slapped him. That had got her fired without a reference. She had considered herself fortunate that Mr Wicker had taken her on after that.

Colin Tompkins was stripping off his gloves as a breathless Neville arrived at the mortuary.

'Okay, what can you tell me?' Neville blurted.

The pathologist shrugged. 'Not much to say, really. Healthy middle-aged female. Nothing interesting going on internally. No disease, no abnormality. I suppose you're going to ask me about time of death.'

Neville nodded, though that wasn't the foremost question in his mind.

'At least twelve hours before I first saw her yesterday afternoon. Possibly more – say fourteen to eighteen hours. That would put it at

Wednesday evening, or some time Wednesday night.' He shrugged again. 'Stomach contents, rigour mortis, the usual. It will be in the report.'

All very interesting, if you were into that sort of thing. Which Neville wasn't. There was really only one thing he wanted to know at this point, and his urgency rendered him as terse as the pathologist. 'Cause of death?' he demanded. 'Bottom line – was she murdered?'

Colin Tompkins showed his teeth in what passed for a smile. 'Forceful suffocation,' he said. 'So – yes. She was murdered.'

CALLIE GUILTILY STOLE a quick look at her watch. Absorbed as she was in Zuzanna's story, she was aware that it was nearly time for Morning Prayer, and she would be letting Brian down if she was late.

'I need to go to church,' she said. 'I won't be long. Half an hour at the most. You stay here, okay?'

As she walked the short distance back to the church, she looked round and realised that Zuzanna had opened her eyes to something she had never thought about before.

Her parish. The parish of All Saints', Paddington, for which Brian – and she, as his 'curate' – had been entrusted 'the cure of souls'. It was a physical entity, with specific geographic boundaries; it was home to many of the people who came to services at the church, who counted themselves a part of the church family in one way or another. But it was also home to countless others who were somehow invisible, going about their daily lives and their business unobserved and uncared-for.

Dozens of small tourist hotels lined the streets of her parish, each one of them employing people like Zuzanna: men and women who were far from what they considered to be home, lonely and isolated in a city whose language was not their own and whose natives regarded them as commodities or – worse – as nuisances.

They, Callie told herself, were their flock – hers, and Brian's – just as much as those well-heeled parishioners who turned up on a Sunday morning or for a Thursday lunchtime concert. Why had she never given them a thought until a girl called Zuzanna turned up and started lighting candles?

She got through the words of the service as quickly as she could, mentally apologising to both Brian and God.

Then she hurried back to her flat.

'Sorry,' she said as she opened the door. 'I hope you—'

Callie stopped as she sensed the the truth, even before she saw the abandoned throw on the empty sofa.

Zuzanna was gone.

MARK LOMBARDI HAD a rare lie-in on Friday morning. He'd arranged to have the day off, in anticipation of spending it with Callie. But that was clearly not going to happen, and Mark – usually a sanguine and optimistic person – was indulging in the uncharacteristic pastime of feeling very sorry for himself.

He'd woken quite early, when his flat-mate used the shower. It was a sunny morning; his thin curtains did little to block the light. Mark turned over, buried his face in his pillow, and tried to get back to sleep. He'd just about managed it when the flat door slammed: that would be Geoff leaving for work.

For a while longer he stayed in bed, just for the principle of the thing. A day off should be enjoyed, not just endured. But he was in no mood to enjoy a solitary lie-in, any more than the prospect of a day spent on his own without Callie.

What was he going to do? Once upon a time he would have gone to the family restaurant and made himself useful there, but that wasn't currently an option – not as long as he and Serena weren't speaking to each other. He could cook himself a nice meal, but then he'd eat the lot and get fat and Callie wouldn't want to marry him.

Assuming she did want to marry him. He wasn't so sure at the moment. She seemed to keep finding excuses not to set a date, and already the summer was looming. Was she having doubts, second thoughts? What was the big deal? Why couldn't they just—

His mobile phone rang, and he could tell by the ring-tone that it wasn't Callie. He grabbed it from the bedside table.

'Mark, mate? It's Neville.'

He sighed, guessing this wasn't a social call. 'What's up?'

'Listen, I know you're off today, but I need you.'

Concisely and without wasting time, Neville filled him in on what had transpired since their pub lunch was interrupted.

A woman was dead in a hotel room: that much Mark knew already.

The woman had a driving license which identified her as Felicity Chapman, aged fifty-six, from Devizes in Wiltshire. Her next-of-kin – a husband – had been notified by the local constabulary. The husband had known that she was in London, but not her actual whereabouts in a rather seedy hotel; he hadn't heard from her since she left home. She had died some time on Wednesday night by forceful suffocation. She had probably been killed where the body was discovered, as there was no evidence that she had been moved. She had not been sexually assaulted or engaged in recent sexual activity. DCS Evans had assigned Neville as the SIO.

A family liaison officer was urgently needed, and that was where Mark came into it.

'You want me to go to Wiltshire?' he asked incredulously.

'Good Lord, no. I may have to go there eventually,' Neville said, his reluctance obvious in his voice, 'but there's a son. In London. He'll need to do the formal identification of the body. And I need someone I can trust, to take him there.'

Why not? Mark asked himself. He had nothing better to do. And it was gratifying to know that Neville Stewart trusted him to do a good job. 'All right,' he agreed.

Neville sighed 'Thanks, mate. I'll owe you one. I don't mind telling you that this one could turn out to be a real bugger.'

To be summoned to the inner sanctum of the *Daily Globe*'s editor, Rob Gardiner-Smith, was an honour which was not accorded to Lilith Noone as often as she thought was warranted. She usually received her assignments from someone farther down the food chain from the boss, so she was gratified when the call came from the editor himself.

He looked up from his computer as she entered his office and uttered a single word. 'Immigrants,' he said.

'Immigrants?' Lilith did a quick mental review of her recent stories, but nothing in particular came to mind. Yes, she knew that immigrants were a hot topic with the red-top newspapers, including the *Daily Globe*; readers seemingly couldn't get enough stories about the evil foreigners who were invading to steal jobs and claim benefits. It wasn't her area of expertise.

'We've pretty much done it to death.' Rob Gardiner-Smith spread his hands in an eloquent gesture. 'We need something new, Lilith. Something beyond all of those stories we've been running about petty crime and stretched resources. Something beyond same old, same old.' He tilted his head to the side and looked at her, eyebrows raised.

It wasn't often that Lilith was at a loss for words; she wished she knew what he wanted her to say. 'And ... ?'

'And I'm hoping you can come up with something that will grab people's attention. Something they can relate to. Something ... *juicy*.'

'Me?'

He favoured her with a rare smile, possibly tinged with irony. 'If there's anyone who can do juicy, it's Lilith Noone,' he stated. 'Look at all of those toothsome murders you've served up for our loyal readers. A murder – now that would be ideal.'

'A murder?' She realised that she wasn't presenting at her best and most confident; giving herself a mental shake, Lilith returned his smile with a dazzling one of her own. 'I'll see what I can do,' she promised.

AFTER HIS CONVERSATION with Mark Lombardi, confident that he'd put the formal identification of the body into safe hands, Neville rounded up Sid Cowley, and they headed back to the Regent Hotel.

'Have you managed to dig up any more dirt on our friend Ronald Wicker?' Neville quizzed his sergeant as they dodged through the road works on Praed Street.

'Ronnie's a rum cove, all right,' Cowley confirmed. 'Definitely one to keep an eye on.'

'But nothing specific?'

'Not as regards the Regent Hotel, no.' He tapped his nose. 'But I just have this feeling about him, Guv. He's hiding something.'

That echoed Neville's own gut feeling, but he realised that a cautious approach was called for. 'For the moment,' he warned, 'we've got to handle him with kid gloves. We don't want him to clam up and refuse to co-operate, or actively obstruct our investigation. Which he could do, quite easily. We've got to keep him on side. Let him think that we trust him.'

Cowley scowled. 'I'd like to put the fear of God into him, Guv.'

'So would I. But not yet.'

'Give him enough rope to hang himself, eh?'

'Exactly.'

They turned off Praed Street towards Sussex Gardens. 'What's the deal with the SOCOs, Guv?' Cowley asked. 'Have they finished with the crime scene?'

Neville had taken a quick look at the preliminary report from the Scenes of Crime officers, and he filled Cowley in. 'The room is still sealed. They may need to go back,' he said. 'Obviously the body's been removed, and they've done all the usual stuff. Photos, fingerprints, and a pretty good search of the room. But depending on how things go, a more detailed search might be required.'

They were in luck when it came to parking the car; a delivery van was pulling out of a space just a few doors down from the Regent Hotel, so they slotted into it.

'Time for a fag before we go in?' Cowley suggested hopefully, patting his pocket.

Neville glared at him. 'Not a chance. Let's get this over with. And remember, Sid – kid gloves.'

They found Ronald Wicker behind the desk, just like the previous day. An expression flickered across his face when he saw them, quickly suppressed; Neville couldn't decide whether it was fear, calculation or something else.

Wicker didn't wait for them to speak. 'Gentlemen,' he said. 'Officers. I respectfully request – no, I demand – that something be done about this ... situation.'

'And what situation is that, Sunshine?' Cowley responded, strolling towards the desk.

'Sid,' Neville warned, sensing that things could go wrong very quickly if he didn't take control. He looked at Wicker. 'What would you like us to do for you, Mr Wicker?'

'The room. They've sealed it. They can't even tell me when they're going to release it. And I can't afford to have a room off the rack for the weekend! It's Friday, for God's sake! I need every room in the hotel. I've already had to turn people away.'

'I'm sorry,' said Neville, hiding his scepticism at the vaunted popularity of the Regent Hotel. 'I can see your difficulty, Mr Wicker. But surely you can see ours as well. We have a murder on our hands.'

'Murder?' Wicker's eyebrows rose and his pebble eyes widened.

'Yes, murder. And the sooner we can find out who did it, the sooner you can have your room back,' Neville went on smoothly. 'So I'm certain that you're prepared to give us your full co-operation in this matter, in the best interest of all involved. Including you, Mr Wicker.'

'Yes, of course.' He swallowed hard; his Adam's apple bobbed. 'How can I help you, Detective Inspector?'

Neville put his elbows on the counter and leaned towards Wicker, who took a step backwards. 'First of all, you can bring me the chamber maid – if that's what you call her – who found the body. We'll need to interview her as soon as possible. Then I'd like to interview all of your other employees, and we'll need to take the fingerprints of everyone who works here – including you, Mr Wicker – for purposes of elimination.'

Wicker's eyes flicked away. 'The cleaner. Who found the body. I'm afraid there's a problem there. She's rung in sick this morning. I've had to bring in a back-up.'

Alarm bells went off in Neville's brain, but he managed to speak calmly. 'Then you'll need to supply me with her address and her telephone number. We'll go to her, if necessary.'

'I ... don't have that information.' Wicker looked up at the ceiling, then down at the counter – anywhere but at Neville.

Cowley took a step forward. 'I don't buy that for a minute, Sunshine.'

'What is her name?' Neville asked quickly, with a warning look at Cowley.

'Susie, I call her.' Wicker drummed his fingers on the counter, took a deep breath, and went on. 'Zuzanna. She's Polish. I mean, it would be a waste of your time to talk to her. Her English is rubbish. I was in the room a few seconds after she found the body. There's nothing she could tell you that I can't.' By the time he reached the end of that speech, he seemed to have regained his confidence; he squared his shoulders and looked Neville in the eye.

6

Jane had never been in a hotel as posh as the Randolph. Yes, she'd had tea once or twice in the restaurant of such an establishment, as a special treat, but she'd never before penetrated into the gilded heart of five-star luxury.

The day had not begun auspiciously for the Stanfords. Their plans had necessarily been made at the last minute and in haste: they would catch an early train from Paddington to Oxford, take a taxi to Charlie's rooms in college, and change into their wedding finery there. They'd rung and booked a guest room at Charlie's college for the night, so they would be able to leave their case there, even if their room wasn't yet available. Then they could accompany Charlie to the wedding venue.

But in the midst of their early, hurried packing, Jane had suffered her worse bout of morning sickness yet. There was no question of an early train.

In the end they barely made it onto a train that would get them to Oxford a bit after ten. Jane rang Charlie from the train with the revised plan: they would have to go straight to the Randolph and hope that there would be a room somewhere where she could quickly change her clothes and make herself presentable. Brian would be all right; he was already wearing his clericals and dog collar, which were always acceptable if not elegant.

Not that, realistically, Jane was aspiring to elegance herself. If only she'd had a few more days to think about it, she might have put together something suitably smart, or even sprung for a new frock. Under the circumstances, she'd had to settle for the best her wardrobe had to offer: a dress and jacket ensemble she'd splurged on five or six years ago when they'd been invited to a reception at the bishop's palace, and not had occasion to wear since. She would, Jane knew, end up looking like a respectable vicar's wife rather than the mother of the groom. That would have to do.

The taxi pulled up in front of the Randolph. Brian paid the driver; Jane clambered out of the taxi, dragging their case behind her.

There was an iron-and-glass canopy stretching across the pavement from the gothic arch of a door to the street. Three shallow steps, red-carpeted and flanked by brass railings, led up to the entrance. At the top of the steps stood a young woman with a clip-board. She was immaculately dressed, made-up and coiffed, with impossibly high heels. Jane looked enviously at the shoes; they were beautiful, obviously very expensive, and even if Jane could have afforded to buy them, she couldn't have worn them in a million years – one step on those towering heels and she would have fallen flat on her face.

Jane put her head down and tried to scurry past, but the young woman stretched out a hand – freshly manicured, of course – to detain them. 'The Stanfords?' she said.

Astonished, Jane stared at her. 'Yes. How did you know?'

The woman smiled. 'Your son asked me to look out for you. He did mention the dog collar.' She made a small hand gesture; a man in a uniform with shiny gold buttons stepped forward and reached for the case.

Jane yanked it back and tightened her grip on the handle. 'But we're not staying here. I just need a place to change my clothes.'

Consulting her clip-board quickly, the woman looked up and gave her another professional smile. 'Room 54 has been booked for you, Mrs Stanford. By Mr and Mrs Dickinson. We've made sure it would be ready for you now, before the ceremony. Edward will show you to your room.'

'IF THIS ZUZANNA – the cleaner – rang in sick,' Neville said, 'that means she has a phone, and you have the number. If you won't give it to me now, I'll have to obtain your phone records. Why don't you just save us both some time and write down her number for me? And her address, while you're at it.'

A sheen of sweat had appeared on Wicker's high forehead. 'I'll ... see what I can do. Give me a few minutes, mate.'

'And your other employees?'

'Yes. All right.' He nodded his head. 'I'll tell you what, Detective Inspector. If you come into the staff lounge, I'll bring them to you.'

Wicker led them down a cramped flight of stairs and ushered them into a small room with a revolting patterned carpet, rendered even more bilious in the glare of the fluorescent strip light. Then he disappeared while Neville surveyed the room. It featured a length of chipped formica counter with a rusty fridge beneath and microwave and kettle on top, plus a beat-up table and an assortment of mismatched chairs. 'God, this is depressing,' he said. 'I can't imagine anyone spending time in here by choice.'

'Maybe that's the idea, Guv. No one would be tempted to bunk off work to relax in here.' Cowley looked dolefully at the 'No Smoking' sign which was tacked to the wall.

A few minutes later, Wicker returned with a small, dark woman he introduced as Angel. 'She's Filipino,' he said. 'Her English is as rubbish as the Polish girl's. But she's a good cleaner. And,' he added, 'she's on the clock, with quite a few more rooms to clean today, so I'd be much obliged if you could keep it short.'

Neville quickly discovered that Wicker hadn't been joking about the woman's English language skill. It was rudimentary, and that was being generous, taking into account her reliance on expressive hand gestures.

In the course of what passed for an interview – sitting round the beat-up table – Neville managed to discover only that Angel had not, as far as she knew, seen the woman in question; that room was not her responsibility. She did not know Zuzanna well, as communication between them was hampered by mutual lack of skill in their only common language, English. Yes, they had sometimes shared a quick sandwich or a cup of coffee here in the staff lounge, but Angel would not describe Zuzanna as a friend. 'Good girl,' she said, nodding. 'Good cleaner. Works hard. I like her. But we not friends.'

Wicker poked his head round the door. 'If you're done, I have Les here. Les Fielding. He works in the kitchen.'

Realising that they were unlikely to get much more helpful information out of Angel, Neville allowed her to go, and gestured the young man to take the chair she'd vacated.

He was not a promising specimen: sallow, spotty, and with a vacant expression. Neville judged that he was little more than sixteen.

'Les is me sister's lad,' Wicker volunteered before he departed.

'So Mr Wicker is your uncle, then,' Neville clarified.

'Yeah.'

'And you work in the kitchen?'

'Yeah.' He ducked his head, seemingly as reluctant as his uncle to look them in the eye.

'Tell me about your job.'

'Breakfast,' the boy said. 'We serve breakfast.'

If this was the chef, heaven help the poor hotel guests. Neville caught Cowley's eye and suppressed a grin. 'You cook, or you serve? Which one?'

'Bofe. Everyfink. Me and one ovver cove, Terry. Cook, put da food out, clear da tables, wash up.' His Cockney accent was even more pronounced than Cowley's.

Felicity Chapman hadn't arrived at the Regent Hotel until Wednesday afternoon, Neville reminded himself, and by Thursday morning she was dead, so she would have been spared the experience of a breakfast prepared and served by young Mr Fielding. There was no reason he would have encountered her, or remembered her if he had done. Without much hope, he asked, 'The woman who died. A blonde woman, on her own – you didn't happen to see her at all, did you?'

'Nah. Never seen her.'

Cowley made an involuntary sound of disgust and rolled his eyes in Neville's direction. He drew his finger across his throat in a gesture that Neville interpreted to mean that they were on to a loser and should give up before they wasted any more valuable time.

He tended to agree, but decided it was worth just one more attempt. 'Do you know this Zuzanna? The cleaner? Ever talk to her?'

'Susie, ya mean?' He shook his head. 'Nah. She's a looker, all right, but she wouldn't give me da time ov day. Besides, she's got a bloke. And he'd break me arm if he saw me talkin' to her.'

Neville sighed. 'Okay. Thanks for your help. We'll need to take your fingerprints a bit later.'

That got Les's attention. He looked straight at Neville for the first time, grinning. 'Like on da telly? Wicked!'

The boy scarpered off quickly. His uncle must have been waiting outside the room; he sidled back in with a scrap of paper in his hand. 'Here,' he said, proffering it to Neville. 'She's called Zuzanna Dabrowska. This is her mobile number. I can't find her address.'

Neville took the note and stuffed it in his pocket. 'Thanks. Now we'll see the other bloke who works in the kitchen. Terry, he's called?'

Wicker shrugged his shoulders and looked down at the floor. 'Terry's gone,' he stated. 'He finished breakfast service, and said he wasn't feeling well. So I told him he could clear off.'

'You seem to have a lot of sick employees,' Cowley observed sarcastically.

Neville had been thinking the same thing – convenient, or what? – but preferred to keep his suspicions to himself for the time being. He shot Cowley a warning look, then turned back to Wicker. 'Who else works here, then?'

'That's the lot. Two cleaners, two in the kitchen. And me. If we need anyone else, I call in a temp.' He spread his hands and gave Neville a disingenuous smile, baring his teeth. 'I told you yesterday, Detective Inspector. We're a small operation.'

By the time Callie and Bella made it to Hyde Park, the sun was shining and the morning was warming up nicely. Consequently people were in a good mood; they smiled and nodded at her, exchanging weather-related pleasantries, sometimes stopping for a little chat if they were regular dog walkers who recognised the two of them. Bella would sniff her canine chum while

Callie passed the time of day with the owner. Callie usually wore her clerical collar when she walked Bella, on the basis that it was a good thing for women in ministry to be visible in public. Sometimes, she'd observed, it seemed to put people off, but there were other occasions when she'd had meaningful discussions with folks who would not necessarily have sought out a church. Today, apart from the dog- and weather-based conversations, she was able to offer some helpful advice to a young woman with an enormous pram who wanted to know how to go about getting her baby christened.

So when she eventually arrived back home, her intention to ring Marco was subsumed by her guilt at having been too long away from her computer and Sunday's sermon. She gave Bella a rawhide chew to keep her occupied, then went back to work on her Whitsun sermon.

Absorbed, she wasn't at all sure how much time had passed when her doorbell rang.

Bella rushed to the door, her tail wagging, and Callie followed, trying to imagine who it might be. She didn't think she had any appointments, and wasn't expecting a delivery. Marco, maybe? Or her brother?

On the other side of the door was Zuzanna, and behind her a young man, perhaps in his mid-twenties. In contrast with Zuzanna's blond fairness, the man was black-haired and brown-eyed. He was burdened with a large rucksack and carried something bundled in his arms.

'Miss Callie, I am sorry,' Zuzanna began, looking like she might be ready to cry.

Callie opened the door wider. 'Come in,' she said. 'No need to be sorry.'

'This is Tariq,' Zuzanna said as they came into her flat. 'He is my ... my boyfriend.' She gave Callie a self-conscious smile.

'It's good to meet you.' Callie extended her hand to the young man, who awkwardly shifted his bundle before he was able to shake it.

He spoke for the first time. 'Zuzanna has told me about you. You've been very kind to her. Thank you for that.'

His English, Callie realised with some relief, was much better than Zuzanna's, and only slightly accented. 'I haven't done anything special,' she demurred.

'You were there when she needed someone to talk to.'

That was her job, Callie wanted to say. But instead she smiled at the young couple and ushered them into her sitting room. 'Can I get you something to drink?' she offered. 'Tea? Coffee?'

Tariq spoke for both of them. 'No, thank you.' He put his burden down in the corner and shrugged off his rucksack. 'If you don't mind.'

'Of course not. Make yourselves at home.'

The two of them sat on the sofa, close together, while Callie perched on a chair. Zuzanna stroked Bella, who settled at her feet, then leaned back and snuggled into Tariq's encircling arm. Seeming to take courage as well as comfort from him, she addressed Callie with a boldness she hadn't previously displayed. 'Tariq, he need place to stay,' she said. 'Just tonight, maybe. Or maybe longer. He stay here, Miss Callie? On your floor, maybe?'

Callie looked over at Tariq's belongings and realised that the bundle he'd carried was a sleeping bag.

She didn't even think about it – about the consequences, about what Brian would say. About what Marco would say. She responded from her heart, and from her instincts. 'Yes, she said. 'Yes, of course.'

MARK LOMBARDI WAS WAITING at the mortuary when Ben Chapman arrived. He was in no doubt that the young man who strode through the door was the one he was there to meet: he was tall, well-dressed in a City suit and an expensive-looking silk tie, and he had the confident air – reinforced somehow by the heavy tortoiseshell-framed spectacles he wore – of one who was not intimidated by even such a setting.

'Mr Chapman?'

'That's right.'

'I'm Sergeant Mark Lombardi, and I've been assigned to act as your Family Liaison Officer in the matter of your mother's death.'

Ben Chapman shook his head. 'I'm certain there's some mistake here, Sergeant. A big mistake. I don't believe for one minute that my mother is dead.'

'That is what we're here to establish,' Mark reminded him. 'In the absence of your father, who is I believe in Wiltshire, you are here as next-of-kin to identify the body.'

'Or not.'

'I suppose it's possible that a mistake has been made,' Mark conceded. 'Anyway, thank you for coming.'

'I'm a busy man, Sergeant. Let's get this over with, shall we?'

No tension-easing chit-chat, then. No preliminary cup of tea. 'All right, Mr Chapman. It's this way.' He led the way into the viewing room which had been prepared in advance, the covered body on a gurney.

The attendant met them with a sad smile. 'Thanks, Ray,' said Mark.

'No problem.' He pulled back the sheet from the face.

Mark's eyes were on Ben Chapman rather than the body. The man gasped, paled visibly, and reached out an instinctive hand for some sort of support which wasn't there.

While Ray re-covered the face, Mark took Chapman's arm and led him to a folding chair at the side of the room. 'Sit here,' he said. 'Would you like some tea? Water? Something else?'

The man was trembling; he buried his face in his hands as he sank onto the chair. 'No. Nothing.'

Mark spoke gently. 'It's your mother, then?'

Ben Chapman nodded.

'TELL ME WHAT'S HAPPENED,' said Callie.

Zuzanna spoke quickly. 'Mr Wicker, he tell Tariq to go away.'

Wicker – the hotel manager. 'Away from the hotel?'

She nodded.

Callie was confused. Maybe, she reasoned, Tariq was hanging round the place and distracting Zuzanna from her work. But Zuzanna wasn't at the hotel: she'd been sent away earlier.

The young man tightened his arm round Zuzanna's shoulders and explained the situation to Callie. He worked at the hotel, in the kitchen. That was how he and Zuzanna had met, and where they'd fallen in love. But that morning, after he'd cleaned up at the end of the breakfast shift,

Wicker had told him to clear off and not come back until he contacted him.

He pulled a phone out of his pocket. 'Mr Wicker said he would ring me in a few days, when things had calmed down. When it was safe to come back.'

'I don't understand. Why can't you go home?'

The young man gave her a grave smile, infused with sorrow. 'I have no home,' he said simply. 'Mr Wicker allows me to sleep in a store room at the back of the kitchen. That' – he pointed to his sleeping bag and rucksack – 'is my home. It is all I have. Mr Wicker told me to pack it all up and take it away.'

'You can't stay with Zuzanna?'

The girl shook her head vehemently. 'My sister. Krysia. She would not allow. She not even know about Tariq.'

'But why haven't you told her?' Callie spoke impulsively, without thinking. A second later she realised the answer to her question, even before Zuzanna opened her mouth to reply.

'Tariq is not Polish. Tariq is not Catholic. Tariq is not ... Christian. Krysia, she would not like him. She would not allow.'

Tariq took Zuzanna's small pale hand in his olive one and squeezed it. 'I'm Syrian,' he said. 'I'm Muslim. But I love Zuzanna very much. I want to marry her.'

Zuzanna's smile, in spite of everything, was radiant. 'You see, Miss Callie? You see how it is?'

Callie saw all too well. Romeo and Juliet had nothing on this pair. After all, unlike this star-crossed pair – and herself and Marco, for that matter – Romeo and Juliet were both Italian, and both Roman Catholic. The friar had no problem marrying them.

'Miss Callie, I tell Tariq you will do wedding for us.'

Never had Callie been gladder that her status as a deacon did not allow her to perform marriages. 'I can't,' she said quickly. 'Not that I don't want to. But I can't marry people until I'm a priest.'

'You said you would be priest soon,' Zuzanna reminded her. 'Soon. Then you will do wedding?'

SID COWLEY LIT up a fag as soon as they were out of the Regent Hotel. 'What a piece of work,' he pronounced. 'He's hiding something – there's absolutely no doubt in my mind.'

Neville couldn't disagree with that pronouncement. 'He isn't very keen on us talking to his employees, for a start.'

'Ring her,' Cowley urged. 'Ring that Polish cleaner.'

'I'll do it when we get back to the station. I need to check a few things first.' He unlocked the car and climbed into the driver's seat. 'Speaking of phones, Sid, something just occurred to me. The dead woman – did she have a mobile? I don't think there was one on the bedside table, was there?'

Cowley scratched his head. 'No. But there was one in her handbag, I'm pretty sure.'

Neville put that on his mental list of things to check up on at the station. 'You were so busy drooling over the bag – Coach, wasn't it? – to worry about little things like a phone.'

'I found her driving license, didn't I?'

'You did,' he admitted.

Running through his priorities on the short drive back to the station, Neville made some decisions, and they involved delegation. 'Okay, Sid,' he said as he pulled into the car park. 'Here's what I want you to do. First, put out that fag.'

Cowley gave him a reproachful look, opened the car door, tossed the cigarette on the tarmac and ostentatiously ground it out with his heel.

'Then go and find that bag. If there's a phone in it, bring it to me in my office. Or ... no, wait. If it's unlocked and useable, bring it to me. If you can't easily get into it, take it to the techies and see what they can do. Then you can make the arrangements to get everyone at the bloody Regent Hotel fingerprinted – and get DNA samples, while they're at it. Check with the SOCOS to see what sorts of prints they've come up with at the crime scene. Or anything else we ought to know, for that matter,' he added. 'I need to make some phone calls.'

Callie decided it was time to change the subject – away from weddings. 'Mr Wicker,' she said. 'Why would he send you away? Why doesn't he want you to talk to the police?'

The two young people looked quickly at each other, then down. Neither one of them spoke, and neither would meet Callie's eyes.

'What aren't you telling me?'

The silence stretched, uncomfortably, into a great many seconds. Finally, reluctantly, Tariq raised his head. 'I must trust you,' he said. 'I will tell you. It is because I am ... not legal.'

'Not legal?'

'I did not enter this country legally,' he amplified. 'It is better if you don't know all of the details, but I came from Syria. I had to leave. It took many weeks, many months. And reaching England – it is not easy. They don't want us here,' he added with a flash of bitterness. 'But I came. I got here to London. No passport, no papers – no way to get work. I need work to live.'

'What sort of work did you do in Syria?' Callie asked.

He gave her a bittersweet, twisted smile. 'I was an English teacher. Can you believe that, Miss Callie?'

'I wondered why your English was so good.'

Tariq looked gratified. 'I learned English at school, studied it at university. Everyone wants to learn English, so it was a good job. But no one in London needs a Syrian English teacher. Even if I had papers, even if I were legal.'

'But Mr Wicker gave you a job?'

'I asked around. Someone told me to try the Regent Hotel. They said that Mr Wicker wouldn't be too picky, wouldn't ask too many questions.'

'Mr Wicker pay Tariq very bad,' Zuzanna interjected, frowning.

Tariq squeezed her hand. 'Nothing on the books, so he can get away with it. He gives me a roof over my head – of sorts – and feeds me three meals a day.'

'Food very bad, too,' stated Zuzanna. 'Cheap food.'

'Every week he slips me a few quid in cash. And that's it. That's my life.'

Callie was appalled. It must have showed on her face.

'It's not ideal,' Tariq said with a philosophic shrug. 'But it's better than living on the streets. And it's better than living in Syria – trust me on that.'

'But that man Wicker – he's exploiting you! And he was only thinking of himself when he sent you away. He just doesn't want to get caught doing something illegal.' Callie's sense of justice kicked into action, followed rapidly by indignation. 'You shouldn't let him get away with it!'

He shrugged again, and spread his hands in an eloquent gesture. 'What can I do?'

Callie thought about Marco, and about his other friends in the police. Decent people, all of them, working to see the right thing done. 'My fiancé is a policeman,' she said slowly. 'You could talk to him. I'm sure that something—'

'No!' Zuzanna jumped up from the sofa and interrupted her. 'No! No police!'

'But he could give you advice. He could—'

'No police!' She was crying now, already on the verge of hysteria. 'Police not understand. Police, they would send Tariq back to Syria!'

Callie reached for a box of tissues and held it out wordlessly. Zuzanna grabbed one, pressing it to her face as her shoulders shook with emotion. 'Please! Please, Miss Callie! No police! You must promise.'

'But ...'

'Promise!' Zuzanna took a step closer to her and stretched out an imploring hand. 'We trust you, Miss Callie. You must promise, no police.' She waited.

'All right,' said Callie reluctantly. 'I promise.'

THERE WERE important phone calls to be made, but first things first.

Neville grabbed his office phone and rang Triona's mobile; she picked up after three rings. 'Thanks for nothing, Stewart,' she snapped. 'You just woke me up.'

'Sorry. I just wanted to see how you're doing.'

Triona sighed. 'I'm feeling a bit better, I suppose. But washed out. All I want to do is sleep.'

'No more contractions, then?'

'Not since last night.'

Neville let out a breath he hadn't realised he was holding. 'I'll let you get back to sleep, then. And I'll see you tonight.' He added, almost self-consciously, 'I love you,' then pushed the button to end the call before she had a chance to reply. Or not.

His next call was to Mark Lombardi's mobile. Mark answered immediately. 'Did you get my voice message?'

'No,' Neville admitted. 'I didn't even check.' He wasn't very keen on mobile phones. The one he had was rather antiquated and not easy to use; Neville tended to keep it switched off and didn't check his messages as often as he knew that he should. 'What did it say?'

'Only that I've been at the mortuary with Ben Chapman and he ID-ed his mother's body. Didn't want to believe it, and he didn't take it very well. Now I'm awaiting further instructions from you.'

'Where is Chapman now? Are you with him?'

'He's gone back to work. I tried to tell him he should go home, but he wasn't having it. Apparently the financial stability of the planet depends on him being at his desk,' Mark added ironically.

Neville rubbed his cheek, discovering a small patch he'd missed during his hasty morning shave. 'Well, mate,' he said, 'it sounds like you've done all you could at this point. You've given him information on how to contact you?'

'He said he didn't need a Family Liaison Officer. But he did take my card. Reluctantly.'

'And you know how to reach him, as well?'

'Yes.'

'Then I'd say you can leave it till tomorrow, unless he rings you later. Give him a follow-up call tomorrow. Or show up on his doorstep, if you think that would be more effective. I'll try to keep you posted about what's going on at this end. Not much, so far,' Neville added ruefully. It's early days. We know who she was, we know how she died. And that's about it. So if I were you, I'd just go ahead and enjoy the rest of your day off.'

'Ha,' said Mark. 'Cheers, mate.'

Neville put down the phone, then fished in his pocket till he found the scrap of paper he'd been given by Ronald Wicker. He smoothed it out on his desk. 'Zuzanna Dabrowska,' he said aloud, practicing, then reached again for the phone.

He was disappointed but not surprised when, after a few rings, he was told by a mechanical voice, 'I'm sorry, but the person you called is not available. Please leave a message after the tone.'

7

PC Grace Long couldn't stop thinking about Felicity Chapman, dead in a London hotel room. Admittedly, the case was a huge – and rather exciting – departure from the usual routine activities which filled the days of a junior police officer in rural Wiltshire. But something about it had reached her on a deeper level.

After the visit to Alan Chapman, mindful of the sensitive and confidential nature of the case, she hadn't said anything about it to her father or her brother. She'd been quiet through tea, and had retired rather earlier than usual to her room, the better to be alone with her own thoughts.

Propped up in bed, she'd tried for a while to read the crime novel she had from the library – it was an old one by Ann Cleeves, and up till tonight she'd been utterly absorbed in it. But she'd found her mind wandering again and again away from Vera in Northumberland to Felicity Chapman, dead in a London hotel room. Eventually she'd given up on Vera and retrieved her notebook, reading and re-reading the notes she'd made during the interview with Alan Chapman.

On Friday morning she'd hoped to discuss the case with Tom Burton. Tom, though, wasn't at his desk in the morning, and she wasn't able to catch up with him until lunch-time, when she spotted him in the canteen. He was hunched over the usual Friday fare – fish and chips – and looked up reluctantly as she arrived beside him.

'Is there any news?' Grace asked eagerly.

'News? What sort of news?'

'About Felicity Chapman.'

Burton frowned and shoved a chip in his mouth. 'Why would I have any news? It's not our case, sweetheart.'

'But we were ... involved.'

He shook his head. 'We did what we were asked to do. End of. It's nothing to do with us.'

Grace felt like stamping her foot. Instead she pulled out the chair across from him and sat down, fixing him with a stare which her father would have recognised as dangerous.

He ate another chip, hacked off a piece of fish, and conveyed it to his mouth.

Grace continued to stare at him silently.

'What?' he said eventually, swallowing.

'Would you ring him, please? The officer at the Met?'

'What for? I told you – it's nothing—'

'To do with us,' she finished for him. 'I know that. But aren't you even curious? You said they'd know more this morning, after the post-mortem. Whether she was murdered or not. Did you talk to him last night? After we visited Mr Chapman?'

'I reported back to him, yes. And that was it.'

Grace simmered with frustration; she grabbed a chip from Burton's plate and nibbled on it. 'What's his name?' she asked.

He shook his head. 'Oh, no, sweetheart. I'm not telling you that. I'm not having you poking your nose into something that's none of our business.'

'Then would you just—'

He heaved an ostentatious sigh and reached for his mobile. 'If I do, will you drop the subject?'

'I promise.' With the index finger of her right hand, she crossed her heart. But it was not the only thing crossed: under the table, out of Tom Burton's view, Grace crossed the fingers of her left hand.

After a couple more routine phone calls, Neville suddenly realised that he was famished: last night's supper had been sketchy at best, and he hadn't had time for breakfast. There were still other calls to be made, but the grumbling of his stomach could no longer be ignored.

It was Friday, which meant fish and chips would be on offer in the station canteen. Neville was partial to fish and chips, so it wasn't a difficult decision to make his way to the canteen. In the queue he spotted Sid Cowley, presumably on a similar mission. Ignoring the glares of those behind Cowley in the queue, he slipped in beside him.

'Hey, Guv. Any news?' Cowley greeted him.

Neville ticked the calls off on his fingers – minus the one to Triona, which was none of Cowley's business. 'The body's been formally ID-ed by the son. The Polish cleaner isn't answering her phone, which is a nuisance but frankly no surprise. The coroner is planning to open the inquest on Tuesday, after the Bank Holiday. And,' he added, 'I've liaised with the press department on information for the web site and the routine press release. They suggested a news conference, but I think it's early days for that yet. We don't have enough to go on to even think about it at this stage.'

Cowley nodded his agreement.

'And how have you been getting on? With the phone and the SOCOs?'

'I found the phone,' Cowley confirmed. 'In the handbag, where I fought it was. It's a smart phone, but not a top-of-the-line one.'

Hence Cowley's lack of interest in it during the initial examination of the handbag, Neville intuited.

'Unfortunately, it needs a passcode to get into it. So I did what you said, Guv – I took it to the tech department and handed it over to Danny Duffy. He said it shouldn't be too hard to crack it. He ought to have the results by Tuesday.'

Neville scowled. 'Tuesday?'

'This *is* Friday afternoon, Guv,' Cowley reminded him. Danny's a nine-to-five bloke. Unlike us, he gets the weekend off. And like you said, Monday's a Bank Holiday.'

'Bugger.'

'But unlike me, I'll bet he doesn't have a hot date lined up for tonight.' Cowley cracked his knuckles and gave Neville a smug, anticipatory grin.

They'd reached the serving counter. 'Fish and chips, me darlin',' Cowley said to the girl behind the counter.

'Make that two,' Neville added, salivating in spite of himself. 'Plenty of salt and vinegar on mine.'

They paid at the till, collected their cutlery, and took their trays to a recently vacated table.

Neville gobbled a chip, burning his fingers, his tongue and the roof of his mouth. He swore and reached for a glass of water.

Cowley grinned. 'Do you want to hear about the SOCOs?'

When he was able to speak again, Neville glared at him. 'Of course I do.'

'They're sending someone to the Regent this afternoon to collect prints and DNA off the staff, like you requested.'

'Good. And?'

'And what they've got so far at the crime scene is a shedload of fingerprints. Which won't be any help to us,' he added, stating the obvious, 'until they've got something to compare them to.'

'Stewart?'

Neville's heart skipped a beat as he turned his head and looked up at the scowling face of Detective Chief Superintendent Evans, standing beside their table. 'Yes, sir?'

'I've been looking for you, boyo. You're not an easy man to find. And your phone is switched off.'

'Sorry, sir.'

'I figured I'd find you here, eating fish and chips.'

Neville was sure he'd seen a small smile, quickly suppressed; that gave him the courage to reply in kind. 'Yes, sir. And I can recommend them. They do very good fish and chips here on a Friday.'

'I'll leave you to it, then.' Evans narrowed his piggy eyes. 'But when you've finished, I'll be waiting to see you. In my office.'

THE WEDDING WAS OVER. Simon and Ellie were now joined – if not in holy matrimony, as Jane and Brian would have wished – at least in legal matrimony. Ellie could now rejoice in the title of Mrs Stanford; their baby would be born into a recognised family unit.

Ellie, Jane admitted to herself, had cleaned up very well indeed. Jane had always – privately – thought her an unprepossessing little thing, skinny and charmless, but today she glowed from within; swathed in satin and lace, she was every inch the radiant bride. Her long, straight hair had been coaxed by the means of some skilful hairdresser's art into a confection of upswept curls, and her makeup emphasised her rather pretty eyes. Her smile of pure joy owed nothing to either art or artifice. But it might, Jane told herself, have had something to do with that tiny life which was growing within her, too small as yet to spoil the lines of her wedding gown.

Jane's hand went to her own abdomen, smoothing down her dress, suddenly self-conscious. In a few months she wouldn't be able to hide her pregnancy, and she was going to have to get used to that.

After the official photographs, the wedding party was ushered into a small private dining room for the wedding breakfast. Jane had somehow imagined that she would sit with Brian and Charlie, but of course she was reckoning without the strict wedding protocol which dictated such matters. The smartly-dressed young woman with the clip-board was efficiently directing people to their seats. Brian was quickly paired off with Georgina Dickinson, while Jane found herself partnered at the other end of the head table with Hugh Dickinson. 'Bride's father? Groom's mother? Right here,' said the young woman, pointing to the calligraphied place cards.

The union of Simon and Ellie had happened with such indecent speed that this was the first time Jane and Brian had met the Dickinsons. All they'd really known about them, filtered through Simon, was that they were wealthy and lived in Northamptonshire. The mental images Jane had conjured up for herself proved to be not far off the reality: Georgina Dickinson was sleek, beautifully turned out and rather formidable, while her husband had a nice smile and a kindly manner. It was obvious that Ellie – their only child – was the adored centre of their world, for whom they would have done anything.

Hugh pulled out Jane's chair with a courtly bow. 'Mrs Stanford, what a pleasure it is to meet you at last,' he said. 'I blame myself, of course. We should have met months ago, when it became obvious that our children had a future together.'

'Please, call me Jane.'

'And you must call me Hugh.' He favoured her with a twinkly smile. 'We should have invited you and your husband for a weekend in the country. We'll have to remedy that soon, so we can get to know each other.'

'Our weekends are rather ... occupied,' Jane said. 'Church, you know.'

'Of course. How silly of me!'

They chatted for a few minutes; Jane learned that Hugh Dickinson had not inherited his wealth, as she had imagined, but was a self-made man, running his own business. Somehow that made him seem less remote to her world – more like a regular person than a pampered aristocrat – and she found herself liking him far more than she'd expected.

'And what about you?' he said. 'I've been doing all the talking, which is unforgivable. And rude. Do tell me about yourself, Jane.'

Jane was glad that they were interrupted at that point by a server with the first course, which proved to be a bowl of pale-coloured creamy soup, garnished with something exotic. 'This looks lovely,' she said.

'It's vegetarian,' Hugh told her. 'The entire menu is. That's what Ellie – and Simon, of course – wanted. The Randolph didn't half give me a hard time about that. They have standard wedding menus, and at such short notice ...' He shook his head, bemused. 'But they allowed themselves to be persuaded.'

At a price, of course. But money clearly meant nothing to Hugh Dickinson, when it came to his daughter's happiness.

'So,' he said. 'You were telling me about yourself.'

Jane immediately felt awkward, defensive. 'I'm just a vicar's wife,' she said, staring down at the soup. 'Nothing else to say, really. I've never worked outside of the home.'

'It's a fine vocation, I'm sure. And you have the two boys?'

'Yes. The twins.'

Hugh glanced down the table to make sure that everyone had been served, then lifted his heavy silver soup spoon. 'It must have been quite a challenge, raising twins.'

Jane's sigh was heart-felt. 'Sometimes. Yes.' The challenges, on a vicar's stipend, had been largely financial – something she wasn't sure Hugh Dickinson would have understood.

'Did you ever wish you'd had more?' He turned a candid face towards her and confided softly, 'We didn't plan for Ellie to be an only child. It just ... happened that way. I sometimes wonder how things might have been different if we'd had more children.'

'I always wanted a daughter,' Jane heard herself telling him, to her horror. To cover her embarrassment, she looked down into her soup and spooned some into her mouth.

'Well, now you have Ellie! We'll allow you to share her.' He chuckled. 'And by the end of the year, who knows? We both might have a granddaughter to spoil rotten.'

FELICITY CHAPMAN HAD BEEN MURDERED. Suffocated, in fact. In a London hotel room. Tom Burton, true to his word, had rung the SIO at the Met, and he had confirmed it.

Grace Long was supposed to be writing up a report on the successful investigation of a quad bike theft, but she just couldn't concentrate. She sat at her desk, pulled out her notebook, and read through her notes again.

'Taxi,' she said aloud, when she reached the end. 'Pewsey.'

The taxi driver would have been the last person in Devizes to see Felicity Chapman.

She picked up her phone and googled 'Devizes taxi'. A long list popped up, many of them as far away as Swindon.

'If I were going to take a taxi to Pewsey,' Grace said to herself, 'wouldn't I use the taxi firm closest to my house?' She tapped the map and enlarged it, found three firms within the town, and rang the nearest one.

'Hello,' she said when the dispatcher answered. 'This is PC Grace Long of the Wiltshire Police, making a routine enquiry. Did one of your drivers by any chance pick up a Mrs Felicity Chapman at Kennet House, Devizes, on Wednesday morning and take her to Pewsey Station?'

After a couple of minutes on hold, she received a negative answer.

Undaunted, she tried again, repeating the same words to the next-nearest dispatcher. This time she wasn't even put on hold.

'That would be Maggie,' the dispatcher said. 'Mrs Chapman always asks for Maggie.'

'Maggie?'

'Some people prefer a woman driver.'

Grace pumped her fist. 'Can I talk to this Maggie?'

'Sure. She's out on a job at the moment, but I can have her ring you when she's finished.'

'That,' said Grace, 'would be perfect.'

LILITH NOONE WAS FEELING FRUSTRATED. On the one hand, she was flattered and pleased that Rob Gardiner-Smith had challenged her to find a juicy story involving immigrants. But so far she'd been entirely unsuccessful.

She'd made phone calls to all of her usual inside sources, with no result. She'd checked the Metropolitan Police's online news section repeatedly, to no avail. There were murders there, of course, but none of them could be described as 'juicy"; the desired link to immigrants was likewise elusive.

On Friday afternoon she had another go on the Met's news section, scanning for newly-added stories. The one titled 'Hotel death investigation launched' didn't sound particularly promising, but she clicked on it anyway. The name 'Detective Inspector Neville Stewart' jumped off the screen at her; she leaned forward and read the story with an increasing sense of elation.

'A murder investigation has been launched following the death of a woman in the Paddington area. Police were called to the Regent Hotel in Sussex Gardens on Thursday afternoon. The woman was pronounced dead at the scene.

'The 56-year-old woman has been formally identified by next of kin, but the name is being withheld. A post-mortem examination has taken place; cause of death has not been disclosed at this time.

'Detective Inspector Neville Stewart, the Chief Investigating Officer, is asking for help in contacting a material witness, hotel housekeeping staff member Zuzanna Dabrowska. If anyone knows the whereabouts of Miss Dabrowska, they are asked to contact DI Stewart as a matter of urgency.'

Behind the bland police-speak in which these news stories were always couched, Lilith's instincts told that she was on to something. Detective Inspector Neville Stewart, her old adversary and sparring-partner. And Zuzanna Dabrowska? In immigrant if ever there was one …

LOOKING over her shoulder to make sure that no one was watching – especially Tom Burton – Grace strolled out of the police station and headed for the car park.

The taxi dispatcher had been as good as her word; Maggie had rung her back, and had suggested meeting at the Rule Britannia mobile transport cafe, located in a lay-by on the A361.

Grace knew the place; she drove by it twice daily on her way into work from the farm and back again. But she'd never stopped there – she'd never had reason to. She spotted the over-sized – if somewhat tatty – union jack flapping in the breeze, indicated and pulled into the lay-by, parking behind a huge lorry.

The taxi was there already, in front of the lorry. As Grace headed for the red-white-and-blue-painted caravan, the taxi door opened and a petite woman in jeans and a donkey jacket got out.

'Hi, I'm Maggie,' she said, extending her hand.

Grace shook it. 'I'm Grace. PC Long, I suppose I should say. Thanks for meeting me.'

'No problem.' It was a local voice, with a warm west-country burr.

She'd always considered herself a good judge of character, and it didn't take Grace more than a split second to decide that she liked this woman with the spiky greying hair. Her lined, un-made-up face spoke of a life which had not been an easy one, but her smile was spontaneous and genuine.

'Can I buy you a cup of coffee?' Grace suggested.

The smile was turned up a notch. 'I've been stopping here for years, and trust me – the coffee is best avoided.'

'How about tea?'

Maggie nodded. 'The tea is strong, but it won't kill you.'

They went to the serving hatch. 'Two teas, please,' said Grace. While she paid and collected the two mugs, Maggie claimed a rickety table which had just been vacated by the lorry driver.

'Now,' said Maggie, accepting one of the mugs and spooning in a generous amount of sugar, 'how can I help you?'

Grace followed suit with the sugar, which seemed a good idea given the robust colour of the tea. 'It's very kind of you to meet me,' she repeated. 'I just wanted to ask you a few questions about Felicity Chapman. I believe you took her to Pewsey station on Wednesday morning?'

Immediately the other woman looked wary, then took a few seconds to frame a reply. 'Why don't you ask *her*?'

Oh, God, Grace said to herself, hoping her dismay wasn't showing on her face. Maggie didn't know that Felicity Chapman was dead. And why would she? Nothing had been in the press, as far as Grace was aware.

Berating herself for her stupidity, she chose her words very carefully. 'I'm really sorry to have to tell you this, Maggie, but Mrs Chapman is dead. She died in London. And I'm ... involved ... in the investigation.'

The blood drained out of Maggie's face; in an instant the lines on her face appeared deeper, almost graven into the skin, and she seemed ten years older. 'No,' she choked. 'She killed herself, didn't she?'

'SID, I'M SORRY,' Neville said as he put the car in gear and drove out of the station carpark. It was at least the tenth time he'd repeated it, not counting the number of times he'd said it to Triona over the phone.

'But doesn't that Welsh bastard realise that the rest of us have lives, too? I mean, he's heading home tonight to Denise and his bloody kids.

No chance of him going off to bloody Wiltshire on a Friday afternoon, is there?'

Neville didn't even offer the usual token protest when Cowley rolled down his window and lit up a fag. 'It's not my fault. I don't want to do this, either,' he said.

'Then why didn't you talk him out of it? Why didn't you say we'd go to bloody Wiltshire on Monday morning?'

He repeated what he'd said before. 'Evans thinks it's important that we interview the husband in person.'

'Then why can't the husband bloody well come to London?'

Neville sighed. 'It's not just interviewing him, is it? We can take a look at the house, get the lay of the land.'

'But she didn't die in that house.' Cowley took a drag on his cigarette, then expertly flicked the ash out of the window as he exhaled. 'She died in London, in case you forgot.'

'How could I forget? If she'd died in Wiltshire, we wouldn't be involved.' Blissfully unaware of Felicity Chapman's existence, in fact. Neville was tired of defending Evans' decision – to Sid, to Triona. In his rational mind he understood it: understood why it was important to get a feel for where the victim had come from, and the sort of life she'd lived, if they wanted to get to the bottom of her death. But that didn't make it any less inconvenient on a Friday afternoon, fighting all of the traffic fleeing London for the Bank Holiday weekend. According to the GPS, the drive to Devizes shouldn't take more than two hours, in optimal conditions; he had no idea how long it would take on a Friday afternoon. And then they'd have to drive back. Sid was going to miss out on his Friday night hot date, no matter what. And Triona would be waiting at home to give Neville a face-to-face tongue-lashing. He sighed again and pulled into Marylebone Road.

GRACE HAD DISPENSED HALF a packet of tissues to Maggie before the tears were under control.

'I'm that sorry,' said Maggie at last. 'You must think I'm a bit daft, carrying on like that.'

'Not at all.'

'It's just that ... well, it's a shock. I saw her on Wednesday, and ... she killed herself, didn't she?'

'No, she didn't. She was ... murdered.' Grace wasn't sure how much else she was authorised to tell her, so she opted for caution and stopped with that.

'My God!' that brought on a fresh round of tears.

Grace handed her another tissue. 'But I'm going to make sure that we catch the person who did it,' she stated.

Maggie dabbed at her eyes, took a deep breath, then had a gulp of tea. 'It must seem strange to you, me being so upset about ... a passenger.'

'The dispatcher said that Mrs Chapman always asks ... asked ... for you. So you must have known her ... a while?'

'A few years. And you probably won't understand this, but she wasn't just a passenger. You wouldn't reckon that someone like her – the sort of *lady* who wouldn't even think about going out of the house without her pearls – would have anything to do with the likes of me. But she did. She talked to me. Woman to woman, like.' She ducked her head, as if she were embarrassed, and looked down at her tea mug.

Grace didn't find it that hard to believe: she'd already realised that Maggie was the sort of person who just naturally drew others to her. 'Do you feel that you can tell me what she talked about?' she suggested.

Frowning, Maggie looked up. 'It doesn't seem right to talk about it,' she said slowly. 'But if it will help you catch the bastard who killed her ...'

Grace wanted to get out her notebook, but decided that might inhibit Maggie. She would just have to rely on her memory.

Over the next quarter of an hour, she absorbed a story which went a long way towards explaining the other woman's deeply lined face.

Up until about ten years ago, Maggie had lived an unexceptional life. A local girl, she'd worked for years at the Wadworth brewery, along with her husband Steve. Their marriage – as far as she was concerned – had been a happy one, though childless.

And then she had discovered that Steve was having an affair with a much younger woman – one who also worked at the brewery, and who was carrying his child. The resulting divorce was a messy one, and

Maggie had lost not just her husband and her home but her job and livelihood.

In desperation, she'd taken a job as a taxi driver, and found that she enjoyed it. She was also good at it, and attracted repeat passengers who always asked for her, and often tipped her generously.

It had been several years since she'd first driven Felicity Chapman to Pewsey to catch a train. They'd clicked instantly, she told Grace, and over the ensuing time they'd had quite a few conversations – some frivolous, some serious. 'Mrs Chapman – she didn't really like to drive,' Maggie said. 'She'd ring and ask me to take her to the hairdresser, or the supermarket, or even into Bath to the shops. Not just to the station. And we'd just ... talk.'

Over the course of these talks, Maggie had confided in Felicity Chapman about the history of her marriage breakdown. And Mrs Chapman had started asking questions. 'How did you find out he was having an affair?' she'd quizzed her. 'Did you suspect it for a long time?'

'I told her it was a bolt from the blue,' Maggie said to Grace. 'Then she told me that she suspected her husband was maybe having it off with someone. Nothing concrete, just lots of little things that didn't add up, like. Home late from work, taking a shower as soon as he got home – that sort of thing.'

'And that was ... how long ago?'

'A few months, maybe. After that we talked about it a lot. In some ways, she was desperate to find out. But in other ways, she didn't really want to know – you know what I mean?'

Grace thought she did, and nodded.

'Her life was ... comfortable. Her husband's a solicitor. She didn't have to worry about money. She had a beautiful home, with a wonderful garden. She was mad about that garden. And she was potty about her son. Ben, he's called. She wanted to know the truth, but she didn't really want to rock the boat. At least that's how it seemed to me, if I'm honest.'

'So did something happen?'

Maggie nodded. 'It was that morning.'

'Which morning? Wednesday?' Grace felt a prickle of ... something. Apprehension, excitement, premonition?

'Yeah, Wednesday. She was packing her case to go to London. For the

Chelsea Flower Show, like. So she was in the bedroom, and her husband was getting ready to go to work. He put on his jacket, and a paper fell out of the pocket. She picked it up.' Maggie closed her eyes and covered them with her hand.

'And?' Grace urged her.

After a moment Maggie continued. 'She looked at it. It was a note. Something about looking forward to sleeping in his bed while his wife was gone, sort of thing.'

'Oh my God.'

'So that was it. She knew the truth, and her husband couldn't deny it. He admitted he'd been having it off with his secretary – just a young thing, apparently. Like Steve.' Her mouth twisted in a bitter smile, then she continued. 'They had an almighty row, she said. Screaming and the lot. Then he went to work, and she ... well, I collected her, like we'd arranged, and took her to Pewsey to catch her train.'

'And she told you all this on the way to the station?'

Maggie nodded. 'She was that upset. Crying, and all. Said she didn't know what she was going to do. That's why I thought ... why I thought she must of killed herself.'

8

It had been a long afternoon for Callie. She had done all of the things that Brian would usually have done on a Friday afternoon, including a round of hospital visits. She'd been to see Mildred Channing, whose temper – and temperament – had not been improved by her knee replacement. This time Callie hadn't sought out Frances, and actually hoped that she wouldn't run into her; the dilemma in which she'd suddenly found herself was so overwhelming that she didn't want to risk being in a position in which she would say anything she would later regret, even to a close and trusted friend like Frances.

When she got back to church for Evening Prayer, Callie was relieved to find that she was on her own in the stalls. She went through the motions of reading the Office, without her brain or her heart really engaged. While the words – familiar enough not to need any help from either heart or brain – came out of her mouth, her thoughts went round and round in circles.

She was, to put not too fine a point on it, harbouring fugitives. Fugitives from the law. One an illegal immigrant, the other a person whom the police were undoubtedly most anxious to talk to.

And she'd promised not to tell.

Was she doing the right thing? Was it defensible, in any context?

But hadn't Jesus instructed his followers to look after those who weren't able to look after themselves? To feed the hungry, clothe the naked, take in the stranger?

Take in the stranger. That was exactly what she was doing.

What would Marco say, if he knew what she'd committed herself to? She couldn't tell him; she'd promised not to.

And what about Brian? Was she obliged to tell him? Perhaps even the bishop?

Blessed are they ...

Do unto others ...

When she reached the end of the Office, she went down on her knees in her stall and buried her face in her hands. 'Help me,' she said aloud. 'Dear Father in heaven, help me to do the right thing, whatever it is and whatever it may cost me. Thy will be done, in this as in all things. Lighten our darkness, we beseech thee, O Lord; and by thy great mercy defend us from all perils and dangers of this night; for the love of thy only Son, our Saviour Jesus Christ. Amen.'

Then she composed herself, got up from her knees, locked the church, and with some reluctance headed back to her flat to face the situation in which she'd somehow found herself embroiled.

She went up the stairs, unsure whether she should call out or not. In the end she said, 'I'm back' as she opened the door with her key.

The sitting room was empty. The rucksack and the sleeping bag were still in the corner, but there were no human occupants, and not even Bella was there to offer her customary greeting.

'I'm here. In the kitchen,' came the voice of Tariq.

BACK AT THE Devizes headquarters of the Wiltshire Police, Grace sat in her car in the car park for a very long time, thinking about what Maggie had told her. The affair, the screaming row.

It would all have made perfect sense if Felicity Chapman had killed herself – if she'd checked into that hotel in London and swallowed a bottle of sleeping tablets, or slit her wrists in the bath.

But she hadn't killed herself: she'd been suffocated.

Grace pulled out her notebook and fingered it, thinking hard. Remembering.

Alan Chapman had been so convincing as the disbelieving, grieving husband. Shocked and stunned by his wife's death. She had certainly been taken in by him, and so had Tom Burton.

Was there any way, she asked herself now, that he could have killed his wife? Could he have followed her to London, furious after their row and guilty over his infidelity, and murdered her? In the midst of another heated argument, perhaps? Then returned home and met them at the door the next evening with his all-so-believable simulation of surprise and grief?

That had been Maggie's parting verdict. 'I'll bet he did it, and all,' she'd said. 'That husband of hers. I don't know how, if I'm honest, but who else had a good reason to kill her?'

It was time for Grace to go home. Past time, actually: her father would be wondering where she was, and when tea was going to be on the table. But she'd come this far; she couldn't just file it away and talk to Tom about it tomorrow.

Tom might still be at his desk, she told herself. He was a bit of a workaholic at the best of times, and his wife was away at the moment so he wouldn't be in a rush to get home.

She pulled out her phone and sent her brother a text. Her father – frustratingly – refused to use a mobile phone like normal people, but at least her brother could convey a message. Maybe he'd even make tea, if they were both hungry enough. 'Delayed. Home l8r,' she texted, pocketed her phone and went back into the police station.

Grace was in luck: Tom was indeed still at his desk, tapping something into his computer. He looked up as she approached.

'You still here? Your dad'll be wanting his tea, won't he?'

'He can wait a few minutes. There's something I need to talk to you about.' She took a deep breath. 'Mrs Chapman,' she said. 'I was thinking—'

Tom waved his hand, as if he were flicking away a troublesome fly. 'That's your problem, sweetheart. You think too much. Just leave it, will you?'

'But—'

'No buts, Grace. Go home.'

Tom's mobile rang; he picked it up, looked at the screen, pressed a button and turned away from her as he put it to his ear. 'Yes, all right,' he said after a few seconds. 'I'll wait here till you arrive. No problem. ... Yeah, I'll take you there. Not easy to find if you don't know the area.'

Grace knew instantly, intuitively, that he was talking to the London police officer in charge of the case. He was coming here – of course he would. He would need to talk to Alan Chapman. And Tom would be going with him.

'Let me come,' she said as soon as Tom finished the call and put his phone back on the desk.

Burton gave a deep, long-suffering sigh. 'You promised to drop it, remember?'

'But—'

'But nothing, Grace. Look, this is just routine. No need for you to be involved in any way.' This time he flicked with both hands, a clear gesture of dismissal. 'Go home, sweetheart. Give your dad his tea, like a good girl.'

CALLIE FOLLOWED TARIQ'S VOICE – and her nose – into the kitchen. Glorious smells were wafting through the open door, spicy and sweet, unfamiliar and intriguing.

Tariq was standing by the cooker; Bella, at his feet, stared up at him in rapt attention. He waved a wooden spoon in greeting. 'Hello, Miss Callie.'

'Tariq – what are you doing?'

'I am making dinner for you, Miss Callie. To thank you for your very kind hospitality.' With the spoon he indicated a number of plates lined up on the worktop, then the pot simmering fragrantly on the hob. 'Mezze. And other things. Food from my country.'

'But ... where did you get the food?' she asked, bewildered. The last time she'd looked in her fridge, it hadn't contained anything that looked – or smelled – like the delights now on view.

Tariq grinned at her. 'Like you British say, I popped out to the shops.

The Edgware Road – many Middle Eastern shops there. I could get everything I needed.'

'And ... Zuzanna?'

'She's gone home. To her bedsit. She wanted to stay, but she knew that her sister would be expecting her.'

Callie hadn't thought about food all afternoon; suddenly she was ravenous. The smells in the kitchen were truly intoxicating. 'Is it ready to eat?' she asked hopefully, her mouth watering.

'Mostly ready. The lamb will take a few more minutes. Here.' Tariq picked up a plate and held it out towards her. 'Try this. Warak inab – stuffed vine leaves.'

She picked up one of the little parcels with her fingers. It virtually melted in her mouth, tasting as delicious as it looked. 'This is amazing,' she said.

Between them, they carried all of the little plates to the table, then Tariq gave the pot on the hob another stir. 'First we eat mezze,' he suggested. 'Then the lamb will be ready.'

They shared the plates of hummus, flat bread, falafel, borek, baba ganoush, fattoush and warak inab with little conversation other than moans of delight from Callie as she tasted each one. Eventually Tariq dished up the lamb. 'This is called bamia,' he told her. 'Lamb, okra, tomato, garlic, and coriander.'

'Heaven,' she pronounced after the first rapturous bite. 'I didn't think I cared much for okra, but this ...'

He smiled. 'My mother's recipe.'

'Your mother is a genius, then. And so are you. Where on earth did you learn to cook like this, Tariq?'

'From my mother, of course.' Tariq smiled again. 'She was unusual, my mother. Not like typical Syrian women, who think that men have no place in the kitchen. She could see that I was interested in food, so she taught me. Then when I went to university, I had a job in a restaurant to help pay for my schooling. I learned much from that, working in a kitchen every night.'

'And now ...'

'Now I work in Mr Wicker's kitchen.' He gave an ironic laugh. 'At the Regent Hotel. Making breakfast from cheap and horrible ingredients from the cash and carry for people who cannot afford to stay at a better place.'

'What a waste of your talents,' Callie said with feeling.

Tariq grinned at her. 'But Mr Wicker, he doesn't know what I do at night. I go to the shops on the Edgware Road and buy lovely things, as much as I can afford. I cook for myself. In his kitchen.'

'And for Zuzanna?'

'Only a few times,' he admitted. 'When her sister has an evening shift, and doesn't know that Zuzanna has gone out.'

'Lucky girl.'

'I am not sure she likes it very much,' Tariq confessed. 'It is very different from what she is used to.' He smiled. 'When we are married, Miss Callie, I will learn to cook Polish food. For my Zuzanna.'

Callie noted the way his face softened as he said her name, and this made her like him even more than she did already. He was clearly deeply in love with the girl for whom Callie had – in spite of herself – developed protective feelings. But their future marriage was one of the subjects she was determined to avoid. 'My fiancé is Italian,' she said. 'He's a wonderful cook, like you. His family have a restaurant.'

'He is called Marco?'

'That's right.' She looked at him quizzically across the table; wondering how he could have known that. She was sure she hadn't mentioned Marco's name.

'I am sorry, Miss Callie.' Tariq lowered his head. 'I should not have heard, but I could not help it. He has been ringing while you were away, leaving messages on your answering machine.'

Callie sighed and put down her fork. 'I'd better check.'

Reluctantly she got up from the table, went over to the little black box and pushed the playback button. There were three messages from Marco, more or less repeating the same thing: 'It's Marco. Ring me when you can.'

After that, though, there was one more message – this time a plummy woman's voice. 'Miss Anson, this is the bishop's secretary. The bishop would like to see you. Could you please ring back to make an appointment at your earliest convenience?'

GRACE SAT in her car in the car park. Patiently, at first, though increasingly frustrated as the moments ticked by. The nine-to-five staff had long since gone home and there was minimal activity to observe. She resisted the temptation to get out her phone and play a game or check her e-mails, lest she get distracted and miss something.

And then, suddenly, it happened. A car pulled into the car park: a silver car with a distinctive yellow-and-blue checkerboard paint job and a Metropolitan Police logo on the door.

It stopped not far from where she was parked. The doors on either side opened and two men got out. Plain clothes, obviously. Both quite good-looking, if one were inclined to notice such things; Grace, after all, was a young unattached woman, not insensible of male pulchritude and living in a town where that quality was in regrettably short supply, and she *did* notice such things. The one nearest to her was tall and young – perhaps mid-to-late twenties – and from the way he moved it was obvious that he quite fancied himself. Grace decided that she preferred the one in the battered tweed jacket, who was shorter, maybe ten years older, attractive in a way that was still a bit boyish, yet ... weathered – as if he'd been round the block a few times, seen everything, and could take whatever life happened to throw at him. Her preference hardened to certainty as the younger one pulled out a packet of cigarettes and lit up.

If there was anything that Grace loathed, it was men who smoked. Her mother had died of lung cancer – caused by second-hand smoke, which somehow made it worse. Her mum had never smoked herself, but Grace's dad was a chain-smoker, and years of living with him had literally killed her.

Her father didn't smoke any more. And Grace wouldn't have touched a smoker with a barge pole. Not even a good-looking one. The very thought of kissing a bloke whose mouth tasted like an ashtray was enough to turn her stomach.

With her windows shut, Grace couldn't quite hear what the two men were saying to each other. But she was soon able to figure it out, as the older one gestured at the younger one's cigarette. The younger one frowned, said something, then dropped the cigarette on the tarmac and ground it out ostentatiously with the toe of his very fashionable shoe.

Grace reached for the door handle. But before she could get out of her car Tom Burton appeared, headed in the direction of the two Londoners. He shook hands with them and escorted them towards his car, fishing in his pocket for the keys.

Sighing, Grace pulled out her phone and sent her brother another text. It looked like she was going to be here for a while.

LILITH NOONE HAD a few enemies in the Metropolitan Police, not least among them DI Neville Stewart, but she also had a few friends. Most of them were people who had no scruples about sharing a bit of information, especially when a discreet exchange of cash was involved.

She wouldn't have been daft enough to ring them at work, during office hours, so she waited until Friday evening to contact one of her reliable sources.

After identifying herself, she went straight to the point. 'What can you tell me about this woman who died in the hotel?' she asked.

'I thought I might be hearing from you. Usual arrangement?'

'Usual arrangement. Maybe a bit more, if it's good enough.'

She had her notebook in front of her, and scribbled as her source talked.

The woman was Felicity Chapman, aged 56. She lived in Devizes, Wiltshire. She'd had a husband called Alan Chapman and a son named Ben, who lived in London and who had identified his mother's body. She had died some time on Wednesday evening at the Regent Hotel, Sussex Gardens, and her body had been discovered the following afternoon by the chambermaid, a Zuzanna Dabrowska, current whereabouts unknown and sought urgently by the police. The manager of the hotel and other employees had been interviewed. The postmortem indicated that the cause of death was forceful suffocation and a full murder investigation was underway, headed by Detective Inspector Neville Stewart.

Nothing there, apart from the names and the cause of death, that Lilith didn't already know or might have guessed. Slightly disappointed, she looked over the notes she'd just made and tried again. 'That's it? Nothing else?'

'Well.' There was a pause on the other end of the phone. 'This isn't official, mind. Not on the computer. I'm not even sure that DI Stewart has twigged to it. But the word on the street – in the neighbourhood – is that the hotel manager, Ronnie Wicker, is a bit dodgy. Not above employing the occasional illegal, off the books as it were. If you know what I mean.'

That was more like it. Lilith grinned to herself and made a note. 'Thanks,' she said. 'I think that's worth a bit of a bonus.'

CALLIE HAD EATEN until she was certain that she couldn't manage another bite. 'Thank you so much for that,' she said to Tariq. 'Everything was wonderful.'

'There is one more thing to eat.' He must have seen the dismay on her face, and added, holding his finger and his thumb about an inch apart, 'Just a little. And some mint tea?'

She nodded. 'Shall we take it into the other room, where it's more comfortable?'

'You go, Miss Callie. I will bring it to you.'

Callie went into the sitting room, noting that Bella had remained in the kitchen – where the food was – rather than following her. She flopped on the sofa and rubbed her stomach with both hands, already regretting her over-indulgence.

A few minutes later Tariq, Bella at his heels, carried in a tray and placed it carefully on the coffee table. 'We usually serve mint tea in glass cups,' he said. 'But you have only mugs. So this is not authentic. I am sorry.'

'My fault, not yours.' She accepted a mug from him and sniffed the heady, astringent mint fragrance.

'And baklava.' Tariq held out a plate of tiny pastries.

In spite of herself, Callie couldn't resist; she took one and gobbled it in one bite. Nuts, cinnamon, honey, flaky pastry. 'These are divine, Tariq. You're not going to tell me you made these, as well?'

'No.' He shook his head apologetically. 'I did not. I bought them. I can make baklava, but it takes much time. And it works better with two people – one to handle the filo pastry, and one to spread the filling.'

'Your mother,' she intuited. 'You used to make it with your mother?'

'Yes.' He gave her a sad smile, then turned his head away and looked off into the distance. 'Many times, my mother and I made baklava.'

Homesickness, then, thought Callie, before the sudden realisation that perhaps there was more to it than that. 'Do you want to tell me about your mother?' she asked cautiously.

Tariq hesitated for a second, then nodded. 'One moment.' He went to the flat's external door and fastened the security chain, then returned and settled cross-legged on the floor next to Bella. 'Sorry. I feel I must be very careful. I talk only to Zuzanna about ... my life before London. But I trust you, Miss Callie.'

'BELIEVE ME, Detective Inspector. He was gobsmacked about his wife's death. Kept insisting we'd made a mistake.'

Neville, in the passenger seat, turned his head and regarded Tom Burton. Burton lived up to every stereotype Neville held about provincial police: pudgy, florid of complexion, and with a pronounced regional accent. Still, he had to believe that the man was competent at his job. 'Did he say whether he'd talked to her or heard from her since she left for London?' he asked him.

Burton scratched his head. 'He said not. He doesn't use a mobile, mind. He didn't seem to think it was unusual that he hadn't heard from her – he just assumed she was at the son's, as planned.'

Cowley snorted from the back seat. 'Not worried that his missus was off with another man, then.'

'Oh, no. Not at all,' Burton replied earnestly. 'At least he didn't seem to be. Mind you, I didn't ask him. I didn't even think about that.'

Neville looked over his shoulder and shot him a frown. 'Why would you say that, Sid?'

'Well,' Cowley said with a shrug, 'she was pretty well preserved for her age. You saw her, Guv. Not a bad looker. I've been finking about it, and was finking maybe she had a bit on side. Why else would she be in that sort of a hotel? A ron-day-voo, innit?'

Cowley had a point, Neville admitted to himself. Why hadn't he considered that possibility? Colin Tompkins had said that there was no evidence of sexual activity at the time of the murder – immediately before or after – but that didn't mean something couldn't have happened at another time.

Sid's theory would explain a lot – not least the sleazy hotel – and it might point them in the direction of a motive and a suspect.

'We'll ask Mr Chapman about that,' he resolved.

'We're almost there,' Burton said, turning left off the main road.

'MY MOTHER – SHE'S DEAD,' Tariq said starkly. 'My father too.'

Callie went cold, but forced herself into professional mode. 'Do you want to tell me about it?'

'A bomb. It fell on the house. A direct hit. They were all killed – my mother and father, my three brothers, my little sister. In the night, in their beds, they were killed. And the house – gone.'

She'd seen the horrific videos on the evening news, and at the time she'd felt moved by them. But nothing she'd seen on the screen had stricken her to the heart like his few simple sentences. 'Tariq, I'm so sorry.' She knew it was inadequate; it was all she could manage. 'You weren't there when it happened?'

'I am ... was ... the eldest. I did not live there then.' He bent over Bella and stroked her ears. 'But that was not the end of it, Miss Callie. The next day the school was hit. The school where I worked. I was lucky – I was not there that day. I was burying my family instead.' His mouth twisted.

'Oh, Tariq!'

He began again immediately, relentlessly, as though having once started he was unable to stop. 'The day after that, though. I went back to the school. I did not know, see. I did not know that the school was gone. And while I was away ...' His voice failed him for just a second, then he carried on. 'While I was away, a bomb hit my house. My wife was killed, and my baby daughter Amira. She was not yet one year old.' Tariq swallowed; Callie could see that his eyes were swimming with unshed tears. 'The medics, they said that they died instantly. They did not know what hit them. That is a comfort.'

Callie was gripping the handle of her mug so tightly that her nails were digging into her hand. 'But that's—'

'I should have been there with them,' he stated. 'I should have died with them. But I did not. Perhaps it was not Allah's will for me to die that day. But I could not stay. In three days – just three days – I had lost everything. Family, home, job. All gone. Nothing to hold me there. I knew I had to go.'

'So you came to England.'

'The journey – it was very hard. Many died on the way. I did not.' His head drooped; he blinked away the tears. 'Maybe some day I will tell you the rest, Miss Callie. About the journey. Not today. That is enough for today.'

'Have you told Zuzanna all of this?' Callie couldn't help asking. 'About your wife and baby? Does she know about that?'

He raised his chin and looked her in the eye. 'Of course,' he said simply. 'Zuzanna is ... what I think in your language is called my soul mate. I tell her everything.'

'How does she feel about you having a wife? Is she ... jealous?'

Tariq shook his head. 'I don't think you understand, Miss Callie. My wife – Rima – it was arranged. My parents, her parents. They fixed it up.'

'So ...'

'Don't get me wrong, Miss Callie,' he went on earnestly. 'I loved Rima – she was my wife. We shared a life. We had a child together. Of course I loved her. But it was not the same as the way I feel about Zuzanna.' Tariq pressed both of his hands to his heart. 'Zuzanna ... she is everything to me. My gift from Allah. With her love, she has made a broken man whole again. She has given me back my life, given me a reason to be alive.'

Callie suddenly became aware of footsteps on the stairs up to her flat. A second later, there was a tap on the door. 'Callie?' came Marco's voice. 'Are you there, *Cara Mia*?'

She looked at Tariq.

'No,' he mouthed soundlessly, shaking his head.

The options available to her raced through Callie's mind in a split second, none of them palatable. She could sit here silently and pretend not to be in; maybe Marco would just go away. But he did have a key. If he let himself in that would be worse. The security chain was on, though – it would keep him from getting in, but he'd know she was here.

Bella rushed to the door, wagging her tail vigorously.

Simultaneously, Tariq jumped up from the floor and headed for the kitchen.

'Callie?' She could hear his key in the lock now.

'Coming,' she called, putting down her mug, following Bella to the door. She turned the handle and opened it as far as the security chain would allow.

'*Cara Mia*! Are you—'

'I'm sorry, Marco. I'm ... not well,' she said through the gap in the door. She could see him standing there at the top of the stairs, holding a bag, and all she wanted to do was open the door wide and fling herself into his arms. Bring him in, tell him everything.

'What's wrong?'

'I have a migraine,' she improvised. 'I was ... resting.'

Marco frowned. 'Let me in, then. I'll look after you.' His beloved face now had an expression of intense concern. 'I thought I'd surprise you. Bring you some nice things to eat. But if you're not well, I'll just sit and hold your hand. Put cold compresses on your head, or whatever you want me to do.'

Callie forced the next words out of her mouth, hardly believing that she was capable of such treachery and deceit. 'Sorry, Marco. I appreciate it, but I think I'd rather be alone right now. I just need to sleep it off.'

Sick at heart, she closed the door and secured the lock, knowing that she would be haunted by the hurt on his face for a very long time.

FOR THE DRIVE back to the Devizes police headquarters, Neville claimed the back seat and allowed Sid to sit in the passenger seat beside Burton.

It had been an interesting interview, and he wanted a few minutes to think about it before the long trip back to London.

Alan Chapman seemed to have remained in a state of bewilderment – almost disbelief – over his wife's death. He'd said that he could think of no reason why she might have been in the Regent Hotel, or why she had cancelled her plans to stay with their son. When Neville had asked him about the possibility that there might be another man involved, Chapman's denial had been vehement – and convincing, he admitted to himself. 'Another man? In London? Don't be ridiculous. I mean, Felicity had a perfect life here. Just the way she wanted it. Her garden – she loved it. If she could have changed anything about her life, it would have had to do with Ben. She would have liked to have Ben living closer, to have him married, to have grandchildren to spoil. But another man? No chance.'

'You would characterise your marriage as a happy one, then?' Neville had followed up.

Had there been just the slightest hesitation before the emphatic 'Yes, of course!'?

Marriage. It was a funny thing. There were moments, and then there were ... moments. Could any marriage, Neville asked himself, be characterised as truly happy? Or was it just him who found the whole institution baffling at times?

His mobile vibrated and he pulled it out of his pocket. Triona.

'Stewart,' she said breathlessly. 'Wherever you are, could you get back here? I feel ... awful. I don't think this can be Braxton Hicks. I'm going to go to hospital.'

His heart lurched. 'I'll be there as soon as I can. A couple of hours, tops.'

They were almost back to where their car was parked, thank God. 'Just leave us here,' he directed Burton, and to Sid he said, 'You can drive back. I might need to be on the phone.'

Burton dropped them off and drove away – probably anxious to be home with his family.

Neville went round to the passenger side of the car, but before he could open the door, a voice called out 'Just a moment, please!'

He looked round to see where the voice had come from and whether it was directed towards him.

A young woman was climbing out of a car nearby – one of the few left in the nearly deserted car park – and was definitely looking at him.

She was in uniform: white shirt with epaulets, black trousers, thin black tie. Tall, with ginger hair pulled back into a regulation bun. Not beautiful, but she had a lively face. An interesting face.

'Sorry to bother you, Sir,' she said as she approached. 'I'm PC Grace Long. Wiltshire Police. And I have something to tell you that you might want to know about.'

9

Not surprisingly, it was pretty much a sleepless night for Callie. For one thing, she was acutely conscious of the young man sleeping on the floor in the other room. She wasn't accustomed to having anyone else in her flat at night; those weeks last winter when her brother had stayed with her had been profoundly disruptive, both physically and mentally. She had offered to make up the pull-out sofa bed for Tariq, but he'd insisted on using his sleeping bag on the floor. 'It's what I'm accustomed to,' he'd explained.

And Marco.

She had lied to Marco. Deliberately lied to him, for the first time. There had been a few occasions when she'd failed to tell him the entire truth – for his own peace of mind, of course – but she'd never before told him an outright falsehood.

How was she going to make it right? Would he ever be able to understand? Could he forgive her? She knew she'd been backed into a corner, hadn't had any other option, but would Marco ever accept that? Would he even want to marry her now?

Miserably she tossed and turned, wishing desperately that she'd never got involved with Zuzanna. Why hadn't she just minded her own business, that day she'd first come across the girl lighting candles in the church? If she had, Marco would probably be sleeping here beside her right now, and they'd both be happy.

But Zuzanna *was* her business. It was her calling, she reminded herself. The life she'd chosen – or had it chosen *her*? The role of a Deacon was to serve others – and to serve sacrificially. Putting others' needs before her own.

She thought back to her ordination – how she'd prepared for it, studied the words of the service and thought about the vows that she would make. She'd taken those vows seriously; they were engraved in her memory, on her heart. The bishop had said, 'Will you strive to make the love of Christ known through word and example, and have a particular care for those in need?'

And she had said, in unison with the other ordinands, 'By the help of God, I will.'

She had sworn it; she had meant it.

After that, the bishop had laid hands on her, and had changed her from what she'd been before into a person whose function was to serve. The bishop had prayed over the new deacons with the words, 'May they follow the example of Jesus Christ your Son, who washed the feet of his disciples, and set the needs of others before his own.'

That was what she was doing.

And it was too late to turn back now.

She must have fallen asleep eventually, because the sound of a flushing toilet startled her awake. *Peter* was her first thought, before she remembered. Not Peter. Tariq.

But it turned her thoughts to her brother, and Callie realised that she hadn't seen him for several weeks. He hadn't even rung her. That, for Peter, was highly unusual, and a possible cause for concern. Peter going quiet on her was never a good sign, even if it might be a welcome respite. What, she asked herself, was he up to now?

IT WAS BRAXTON HICKS, after all. False alarm.

Triona was embarrassed and apologetic, which rather let Neville off the hook when it came to the row he'd dreaded – the one about the trip to Devizes.

She'd been to hospital in a panic; they'd sent her home with the assurance that Braxton Hicks really did mimic the early stages of labour. An easy mistake to make, especially in a first pregnancy.

Now she was asleep, and Neville was awake beside her.

He wished he'd been in less of a hurry to get away when he'd talked to PC Grace Long. The things she'd told them about Felicity Chapman, about the relationship between the dead woman and her husband ... The girl's account turned everything he'd believed about this case on its head, but he'd been in such a rush to get back to London – back to Triona – that he'd scarcely had time to question her.

If PC Grace Long was to be believed – and why shouldn't he believe her? – Alan Chapman had lied to them. Alan Chapman, the picture of a mild-mannered, bewildered, bereaved husband, had not had the perfect marriage he had portrayed to them. There might not be another man involved, as Sid had suspected, but it seemed that there was another woman in the picture. And that woman had been the source of a furious row – a row which was the last interaction between Alan Chapman and his dead wife.

Unless ...

Was there any possibility that Alan Chapman had killed his wife?

Could he have followed her to London, or somehow tracked her down there and suffocated her to death? In the midst of another row, perhaps?

According to PC Long, that was the theory of the taxi driver – someone who knew the dead woman well.

It seemed improbable, but wasn't the murderer almost always a person close to the victim, rather than a random stranger?

And who else was in the picture at the moment as a likely suspect? Precisely no one.

One thing was certain: they would be going back to Devizes, and sooner rather than later.

Neville turned over, sighed, and willed himself to go to sleep.

LILITH HAD BEEN UP HALF the night, digging around on the internet. Finding out all she could about Ronald Wicker and his family – not a pretty picture, that. She'd also been learning an eye-opening amount about the London hotel industry. It was, she discovered, not a world in which the British-born played much of a part. The industry seemed to rely on an unlimited supply of young immigrants, keen for employment and not shy of work that was back-breakingly difficult and shockingly under-paid. Work that, to put not too fine a point on it, no self-respecting Brit would touch with a barge pole, even while complaining loudly that immigrants were stealing their jobs.

That was the sort of hypocrisy that sold newspapers, Lilith knew better than most. Disingenuous it might be – if not downright dishonest – but it was grist for the mill of the *Daily Globe* and so many others like it.

Rob Gardiner-Smith wanted a juicy story about immigrants. Something front-page-worthy. If Lilith wasn't badly mistaken, she was on to something here. She wasn't sure yet what it would be, but she knew where she was going to be headed in the morning.

TO NEVILLE'S SURPRISE, it was Sid Cowley who rang him first, early on Saturday morning.

'Your sprog been born yet?' Cowley queried.

'No,' he said tersely. 'False alarm.' In spite of himself, he was touched that Sid had asked – had even remembered.

'What time are we leaving, then?'

'Leaving?'

'For Devizes. To nail that lying bastard.'

Neville had had plenty of time to think about it, during the night. 'Not yet,' he said. 'I'd like to talk to the son first, I think. Find out what he knows, what he's willing to tell us.'

With any luck, Ben Chapman ought to be at home on a Saturday morning. Neville made arrangements for Cowley to meet him at the younger Chapman's Chelsea flat, then he rang Mark Lombardi and asked him to join them. Mark was the only one who had met Ben Chapman, and his presence as FLO might prove to be very useful.

The traffic shouldn't be too bad on a Saturday morning, Neville told himself as he set out. But he had reckoned without the Chelsea Flower Show; the closer he got to Chelsea, the slower his progress. Maybe he should have taken the Tube – but that probably wouldn't have been any better. During this particular week in May, Sloane Square was truly the centre of the universe, not least on the Saturday.

And where the hell was he going to put the car?

Ben Chapman lived in Sloane Gardens, very close to the Sloane Square tube station. On impulse and without a better plan in mind, Neville followed his GPS and turned into the road, just as a BMW was pulling out of a space.

'Thank you, Jesus,' he breathed, easing his car into the vacancy.

Sloane Gardens, Neville discovered, was an impressive enclave of gabled mansion blocks constructed all of a piece in red brick, one floor below street level and four stories above. He hoped, as he got out of the car and surveyed the road, that Ben Chapman didn't live on the top floor.

'Hey, Guv.' Cowley was lounging against the iron railings of one of the mansion blocks, smoking a cigarette. 'High rent district, for sure. The son must be loaded.'

'You're pretty bright-eyed this morning,' Neville observed. 'Does that mean you were back in time for your hot date last night, or not?'

'Not so hot, after all. She promised more than she delivered.' Cowley shrugged. 'Never mind. Win some, lose some.'

'Plenty more fish in the sea.'

Cowley grinned. 'Like that PC Long, eh? Bit of all right, I fought. I do have a weakness for ginger birds, to be honest.'

Not to mention blondes and brunettes. So that was it. 'No, Sid,' Neville said firmly. 'Don't even think about it.'

'She wasn't wearing a ring. I reckon I may be in with a chance. Unless she's a lezzie?'

Just ignore him, Neville told himself, frowning.

By the time Callie got up, showered and dressed, and went through to the sitting room, Tariq had stashed his sleeping bag in the corner and was perched on the sofa, Bella at his feet, looking at the screen of his phone.

He put down the phone as she entered. 'Good morning, Miss Callie,' he said. 'Bella and I, we are doing well this morning. I hope that you are also.'

'Yes, thanks,' she fibbed. 'Would you like some breakfast? Cereal? Toast?'

'Whatever you are eating.'

'I have to go over to the church in a few minutes to say Morning Prayer,' she explained. 'I usually have something when I get back.'

'I will wait for you.' He gave her a twisted smile. 'I wonder who has prepared breakfast at the Regent Hotel this morning? If it is Les only, I feel sorry for the guests.'

Callie made a quick getaway, slipping into the church through the side door and into her stall, thankful once again that she had no congregation. Once again she rattled through the set words of the Office, then went onto her knees to pray.

'Help me,' she said simply, into the silence of the empty church. 'Help me.'

This was too much for her to deal with on her own, she now realised. Was that what God was telling her? That she needed help? Help of a practical kind, as well as emotional support and wise advice?

Frances.

The name came into her head, like an immediate answer to prayer.

Frances Cherry was the wisest person she'd ever known. Frances would listen and not judge. Frances would know what to do.

Mark Lombardi arrived in Sloan Gardens after a few minutes, and before they went into the mansion block Neville filled him in on what they'd learned from PC Grace Long. 'So it puts the husband in the picture, no matter how unlikely,' he explained. 'I don't honestly see how he could have come to London, tracked her down in that doss house of a hotel, and killed her. But he's not been honest with us, and that makes me suspicious.'

'But you're not suspicious, of Ben, the son?'

'That remains to be seen. What do you make of him?'

Mark shook his head. 'Not a particularly likeable bloke, honestly. Quite full of himself and his own importance. But I'd stake my reputation on the fact that his mother's murder was a huge shock to him. Either that, or he deserves an Oscar for his performance yesterday.'

'Chapman – the husband – told us that the boy and his mum were close,' Cowley put in.

'Well, let's go and see what we can get out of him,' Neville suggested, leading them up the three shallow steps to the front door of the huge red brick edifice.

He buzzed the doorbell, identified himself, and a moment later the door released.

To Neville's relief, Ben Chapman's flat was on the first floor rather than the third. They climbed the flight of stairs; a woman was waiting for them at the door to the flat. 'I'm Danielle Fisher,' she said, unsmiling. 'Ben's partner.'

'Detective Inspector Stewart, Detective Sergeant Cowley, Family Liaison Officer Lombardi,' Neville responded tersely, pulling out his warrant card.

'Detective Inspector, is this really necessary?' she demanded. 'Ben is in shock. I realise that you need to find the person who did this terrible thing, but it certainly wasn't Ben, and he doesn't know anything that can help you.'

'We'll be the judge of that,' Neville stated, taking an instant dislike to Danielle Fisher.

She was a woman in her late twenties, with the sort of figure a catwalk model would envy – thin-hipped, flat-chested. Her dark hair was a Kate Middleton-like length and cut, pulled back into a loose ponytail. She did, in fact, quite resemble the Duchess of Cambridge, but without any of the duchess's smiling charm in evidence in her sour expression. And her eyes, Neville decided, were just a fraction too close together.

Reluctantly she opened the door wide enough to admit them. 'I'll give you ten minutes,' she said.

They found Ben Chapman in the front room of the flat: a spacious, high-ceilinged room with a bay window overlooking the street. Its decor was modern, chic, neutral – not at all in keeping with the period of the building. Chapman, in chinos and an open-necked blue oxford shirt, was sitting on a pale sofa, his hands hanging between his knees and a vacant look on his face as he glanced up at the intruders. Danielle crossed the room and stood protectively behind him, putting her manicured hand on his shoulder. 'Ben,' she said, 'these policemen want to talk to you for a few minutes.'

He raised his chin and glared at them through his tortoise-shell spectacles. 'And I want you to get your asses out of here and find the bastard who killed my mother.'

'Mr Chapman, we're going to do everything we can,' Neville said in his most conciliatory voice. 'We'd just like to ask you a few questions. To help us.'

Ben Chapman gave a reluctant nod.

'The last contact you had with your mother,' Neville began, careful not to make assumptions or to put words in the man's mouth. 'Was ... when?'

'Wednesday. She sent a text.'

'We were expecting her to arrive that morning,' Danielle amplified. 'To stay for a few days. For the flower show.'

Neville wished that Danielle would go away, but knew that wasn't going to happen. 'Were you planning to be here when she arrived? Either of you?' he asked.

She shook her head. 'We were both at work. Felicity had her own key. She came up to town fairly often – not just for Chelsea – and that was the easiest arrangement. She could come and go as she pleased.'

Neville made a mental note to check on whether the key to the flat had been in the dead woman's handbag. 'Mr Chapman, could you possibly show us the text on your phone?'

An iPhone was on the table beside him; Chapman picked it up, punched a few buttons, then silently handed the phone to Neville.

'Change of plan,' Neville read aloud. 'Not coming after all.' The message was time-stamped at 10.14 on Wednesday, he noted. 'And what did you assume had happened?' he asked.

Ben Chapman shrugged. 'Maybe she just changed her mind. The weather wasn't so great on Wednesday, you might recall. I don't think Chelsea is much fun in the rain.'

'Or she might not have been feeling well,' Danielle contributed.

'Did Mrs Chapman suffer from poor health?' Neville asked.

Ben lifted his head and met Neville's eyes. 'No,' he stated, frowning. 'Ma was very ... fit. In the old-fashioned sense of the word. She gardened. She went to the gym. She looked after herself.'

'But she was ... you know. At that sort of age,' Danielle put in. 'Hot flushes. That sort of thing. So it could have been ... hormone-related.'

Cowley grunted; Neville shot him a warning look before carrying on. 'Okay. I'd like to ask you a few questions about your parents' marriage. Were you aware of any ... problems?'

Ben sat up a bit straighter, glaring at Neville. 'There was nothing wrong with my parents' marriage! End of story.'

'They were very happy,' Danielle added primly. 'I mean, they were married for over thirty years, weren't they? They wouldn't have stayed together that long if they weren't happy.'

Thus spoke a true millennial, Neville said to himself; 'Till death us do part' didn't seem to come into it for this generation. If it didn't work out – married or not, for whatever reason – you cut your losses and moved on. Suddenly feeling quite old, he chose his next words carefully. 'So you're not aware ... whether ... either of them perhaps had another relationship?'

'That's ridiculous!' Ben half-rose from his seat; Danielle put both hands on his shoulders and gently pushed him back down again.

'And why do you say that?'

He seemed at a loss for words; after a few seconds of sputtering he managed, 'Ma – she was devoted to my father. She adored him. And he ... well, you've met him, haven't you? You've talked to him. Can you imagine him having an affair?'

Neville couldn't, frankly, imagine it, but he had credible reason for believing that it was nevertheless true. He refrained from saying so.

'He wouldn't have the time. He wouldn't have the imagination,' Ben added. 'Even if he wanted to. And why would he want to?'

'Why would any bloke have an affair?' Cowley interjected. 'Lots of reasons, mate. Variety is the spice of life, innit? Somefing different. Someone younger. Excitement. The frill of the chase. The kick you get from doing somefing dangerous, and maybe getting caught. And maybe just great sex. Simple as.'

Everyone turned and stared at him. Danielle was the first to speak. 'I think,' she said quietly, 'it's time for you all to leave.'

FRANCES CHERRY WAS ENJOYING a rare lie-in on Saturday morning. Even more rare, she was alone in the vicarage: her husband Graham, a parish priest, was off for the whole day on a PCC away-day, at a retreat centre somewhere in Hertfordshire. Before he left, fairly early, he'd brought her a cup of tea, given her a kiss, and admonished her to make the most of her day off. 'Don't get sucked into anything you don't want to do,' he'd said. 'Go shopping, if you fancy it. Have a manicure. Watch an old film on the telly. Whatever pleases you. I'll be home in time to make the spag bol.' Graham's spaghetti bolognaise was a long-standing Saturday night tradition in the Cherry household, and one that Frances much enjoyed.

She slept a bit, but once she'd sat up in bed to drink her tea before it got too cold, she started thinking about how she'd like to spend her day. She really ought to ring Triona Stewart, she told herself – just to see how she was doing. She hadn't seen her in a while. Triona's pregnancy was far advanced now; she was only a few weeks away from her due date.

Frances felt personally invested in Triona's pregnancy: she had known about it very early on, even before Neville was aware that he was going to be a father. She had given shelter, counsel and moral support to Triona during the difficult first weeks of her marriage. She had even, in a roundabout way, been responsible for the events that brought Triona and Neville back together again after years of estrangement.

So perhaps she should ring Triona, and see if she needed help with anything practical, like shopping for baby things. Or, considering how organised Triona was, everything practical was undoubtedly under control and she might, instead, just be in need of a good moan.

Frances took a sip of tea and reached for her phone, just as it rang.

It was Callie Anson, and Frances sensed a certain urgency in her friend's voice as she delicately enquired whether they might meet up for coffee and a chat.

'Of course,' she said immediately. 'Come round here, whenever you like. I'm off today, and Graham is away, so we'll have the house to ourselves.'

'Can I come ... now?'

'Just give me a quarter of an hour for a quick shower.'

Frances showered, dressed, and was just descending the stairs when the doorbell rang. She greeted Callie with a hug, then led her through to the kitchen. 'I'll put the kettle on. Tea or coffee?'

'Coffee, I think.'

'Coffee it is.' She filled the kettle while Callie sat down at the kitchen table.

'I'm sorry to bother you on your day off,' Callie said.

'You're never a bother,' Frances assured her, but she couldn't help wondering what urgent matter had brought Callie to her door on a Saturday morning, when she'd seen her just a couple of days earlier. She made the coffee, then settled down across the table from Callie while the cafetière brewed. 'Okay, what's up?' she asked gently. 'Marco?'

Callie grimaced. 'Yes. Partly. Indirectly, I suppose. But he's really ... collateral damage.'

'Then what on earth?' It wasn't, thought Frances, like Callie to be so oblique.

'I've ... made a promise.' Callie looked down at the table and traced the pattern of the cloth with her finger. 'But I've thought about this carefully ... prayerfully ... and I don't think I'm breaking that promise by telling you about it. Getting your advice.'

Promises. Frances thought of the many times she'd made promises which she'd had cause to regret; it was one of the burdens of being a priest. 'Tell me,' she invited.

'I'm harbouring a fugitive,' Callie said baldly. Then she told Frances the long story: the girl lighting candles, the death in the hotel, the unexpected arrival of Tariq, the young man's tragic life, the promise she'd made.

Frances listened attentively. When Callie finally ran out of words and looked down again at the table, she took a sip of her cooling coffee and chose her next words with care. 'So you promised not to tell the police. Including Marco. And that's a problem for you?'

'Of course it's a problem!' Callie raised her head and gave Frances an anguished look. 'Marco and I don't have secrets from each other. I should never have agreed not to tell him.'

'So this *is* about Marco.'

'He came last night,' Callie confessed. 'He wanted to cook me a meal. But I had to send him away.' She gulped as the tears welled in her eyes. 'I feel ... awful about it. Tariq hid, and I lied. I said I had a migraine. He looked ... so hurt. And I don't know what I can do to make it right with him. Not now. Not when I'm still bound by the promise I made.'

THEY WERE on their way back to Devizes. Inevitably.

Fortunately the Saturday traffic wasn't as bad as it had been on Friday night, and Neville now knew the way. Miles and miles of the M4.

And Cowley hadn't put up any sort of a fight about the trip this time. In fact, he'd been positively insistent on it. Neville had suggested a short-cut, to free them up for other enquiries: asking Alan Chapman to come up to London for an additional interview. But Sid wasn't having it. 'We need to talk to that taxi driver ourselves,' he'd pointed out.

Neville acknowledged the sense in that. They really *would* need to interview the taxi driver, and perhaps it would be helpful to catch Alan Chapman off guard. He might be a bit more forthcoming if they didn't provide him a reason to be defensive and suspicious by demanding that he travel to London.

'So what's your take on the son?' Neville asked Cowley, once they'd hit the motorway.

'Poncey bastard. More money than he knows what to do wif. And up himself, wif it. But no reason to kill his mum, that I can see,' he admitted.

'And his missus? Or should I say *partner?*'

'Bitch,' Sid pronounced with feeling. 'Gold-plated. God, I wish we could figure out a way to put her in the frame for it.'

'That would be sweet, wouldn't it?' Neville smiled involuntarily and indulged himself in a moment of fantasy: Danielle being marched through the police station in handcuffs, then the cell door slamming behind her.

'Dead sweet.' Cowley contemplated the glowing tip of his cigarette.

Neville had once again given up trying to keep his sergeant from smoking in the car; that wasn't going to happen, especially on a long trip like this. It was either put up with the smoke or stop for fag breaks every twenty minutes or so, and that just wasn't practical. Not when they had work to do.

'So how are we going to handle Alan Chapman?' Neville wasn't sure what approach would be most effective, and genuinely wanted Cowley's input. 'He won't be expecting us to show up again. What's the best way to do it, when we've presumably caught him off guard?'

'Hit him hard,' Sid said instantly. 'Tell him we know he's lying.'

FRANCES, fully cognisant of the dangers inherent in giving advice about matters of the heart – such as the problems Callie now found herself embroiled in with her fiancé – decided to tackle instead the more practical matters at issue.

'Tariq needs to talk to a solicitor,' she said. 'He really ought to get some proper advice about his position. I mean, he could apply for asylum. I'm not a legal expert, but it seems to me that it ought to be granted, under the circumstances.'

Callie shook her head. 'I suggested that. But he's terrified to take any chances that could possibly separate him from Zuzanna. He's afraid that they would deport him, or send him to some hell-hole like Yarl's Wood.'

'Well, yes. They might well do that,' Frances admitted. 'A detention centre would be likely, at least in the short term. But if the police are looking for him ...'

'He doesn't know for sure that they are. They might not even be aware that he exists.' Callie took a sip of her coffee. 'It was his boss, Mr Wicker, who told him to clear off – it sounds to me like that Mr Wicker has something to hide, and doesn't want the police to talk to his employees.'

Frances nodded shrewdly. 'Something to hide, like the fact that he's employing at least one illegal immigrant. Maybe more – who knows?'

'Well, yes. I don't suppose the police would look very kindly on that.'

'Nor would the Home Office. Wicker would be in at least as much trouble as Tariq.'

'So you think ...'

'I think,' Frances said, shaking her head, 'that this is a real can of worms you've managed to get yourself in the middle of.'

'But didn't Jesus tell us to take in the stranger?' Callie's eyes were shining with unshed tears. 'Isn't that part of our calling?'

Frances thought back on her ministry, recalling the times she'd been faced with difficult issues of confidentiality. Usually the right thing to do was the opposite of the easy thing to do, and that indeed was one of the burdens of priesthood. She reached out and patted Callie's hand, choosing her words carefully. 'It is,' she acknowledged. 'But he never promised that it was going to be easy, Or that it would come without a cost.'

10

Neville pulled the car to the kerb in front of Kennet House. 'Show time,' he said.

Cowley, signalling his eagerness to get on with it, opened the car door and dropped what was left of his fag into the road.

They strode up the long drive to the house, then Neville rang the bell. Three times.

'He's here,' Cowley observed while they waited. 'His car's in the drive.' It was a black BMW, Neville noted – just the sort of car that a bloke like Chapman would drive. Expensive, conservative. Nothing flashy, but no expense spared.

A minute later he thumbed the bell again, impatiently, and a short while after that the door opened a crack. A spectacle-less Alan Chapman peered through the crack, blinking at them short-sightedly.

Neville spoke first. 'Mr Chapman, could we come in?'

'But ... do you have some news, then?' Chapman opened the door a bit wider. Neville could see that he was wearing a dressing gown – woolen, tartan plaid, tied with a cord round the waist – and probably nothing else; his legs and feet were bare.

'Sorry if we've disturbed you,' Neville said, 'but it's rather important that we speak with you.'

Chapman ran a hand over his ruffled-up hair. 'All right, then,' he said with seeming reluctance, moving aside and opening the door wide enough for them to get through. 'Have you found the person who killed my wife?'

'Not yet.' They stepped into the spacious entry hall, Neville blinking to readjust his eyes after the brightness of the sunshine.

'Allie?' A querulous female voice wafted down the staircase, followed by a descending figure. Bare feet – with pink toenails – were visible first, then bare legs, then a torso covered only by an unbuttoned men's shirt, and finally a head: the head of a young woman.

She was, Neville apprehended in that first glance, not quite what he would have expected in a home-wrecker. No *femme fatale* she – the bare legs were stocky, the torso on the chunky side, the face pudgy and without makeup. Her hair was bleached blond, but prominent dark roots were visible.

He turned his head quickly to observe Alan Chapman's reaction of abject horror – and caught Sid Cowley's expression as well. Triumph, vindication – and not a glimmer of lust. Well, that was something. There was enough to contend with here without Sid's libido added to the mix.

'What's going on?' said the woman, addressing herself to no one in particular.

Chapman seemed to be struck dumb. He closed his eyes, as if that could obliterate what was happening.

Neville gave her an exaggerated smile. 'I don't believe we've had the pleasure of your acquaintance. I'm Detective Inspector Stewart, this is Detective Sergeant Cowley. And you are ... ?'

LILITH HAD SPENT the morning familiarising herself with the neighbourhood in the vicinity of the Regent Hotel. Though Sussex Gardens was a fairly quiet street, it was just round the corner from the bustle that was Praed Street: Paddington Station, St Mary's Hospital, fast-food restaurants, ethnic grocery shops, red buses and tourists galore. She walked the short distance from the railway station to Sussex Gardens, dodging the rolling suitcases which rumbled along every pavement, dragged by people of various hues who spoke to each other in languages she didn't comprehend. Then she strolled down the length of Sussex Gardens, with its dozens of tacky tourist hotels inhabiting what had once been posh town-houses, and turned into the Edgware Road. There the predominant flavour was Middle Eastern, many of the restaurants and shops adorned with signs in Arabic script. If someone were dropped down here in the Edgware Road, Lilith reflected sourly, there would be nothing to tell them that they were in London rather than Beirut or Damascus. Apart from the red buses, of course.

She ventured tentatively into one of the grocery shops. It was redolent with unfamiliar smells, its shelves crammed with products she didn't recognise and wouldn't have had a clue what to do with. 'Can I help you?' asked a man with a fierce black moustache, heading in her direction.

'No, thank you.' Beating a hasty retreat, she returned to Sussex Gardens and stood in front of the Regent Hotel for a few minutes. This was the time of day – late morning – when people tended to be checking out or checking in to hotels, but she observed no activity at the Regent. Lilith hadn't quite decided on her strategy, and decided to play it by ear, mounting the steps to the entrance and pushing open the glass door.

The man at the desk looked up at her approach. 'Can I help you?' he asked, his thin lips stretched into a smile.

She made a guess that this was Ronald Wicker. 'Mr Wicker?' she said, matching his professional smile with one of her own.

His face altered, brows drawing together as the smile disappeared. 'Who wants to know?'

'I wonder if I might ask you a few questions with regards to—'

He didn't even let her finish. 'If you're Press, I'm asking you to leave the premises. Immediately.' He stabbed his finger in the direction of the door through which she'd so recently arrived.

'But ...'

'Go.'

Just then, though, the door swung open and a young woman entered, dragging a large suitcase behind her. Suddenly the man behind the counter resumed his perfunctory smile as he re-focused his attention. 'Can I help you?'

Lilith made a tactical withdrawal and hovered near the door while the manager went through the procedure of checking the woman in and handing her a key. 'It's on the third floor,' he told her with an apologetic shrug. 'No lift, I'm afraid.'

The woman flexed her shoulders and sighed. 'Can someone help me with my case?'

'Yes, of course.' He sounded reluctant, but nevertheless he came round the counter and grabbed the handle of her suitcase, dragging it towards the stairs.

As soon as he was out of sight around the bend of the stairs, Lilith made a quick decision. The stairs went both ways; he'd gone up, so she would go down.

The narrow steps took her to a semi-subterranean level which didn't seem to be part of the public space of the hotel. Cursing her bad luck, Lilith turned to go back up when she spotted a door. Nothing to lose, she said to herself, and pushed the door open.

It was a small room, meanly furnished and lit by a fluorescent strip light. A prominent 'No Smoking' sign was tacked to the wall, but beneath it, at a beat-up table, lounged a young man puffing away on a cigarette.

'I'M PAIGE,' said the semi-clad young woman. 'Paige Mason. I'm Allie's ...' She hesitated, as if searching for the acceptable word. 'We're together,' she said at last, moving to Chapman's side and linking her arm through his in a visual demonstration of the relationship.

Chapman spoke to her through clenched teeth as he quickly disengaged himself. 'Go upstairs, Paige.'

She tossed her bleached mane. 'No. It's time they know the truth.'

'Then at least ... cover yourself.'

'Just a mo', then.' Paige scampered up the stairs and returned a couple of minutes later, wrapped in a dressing gown. It was extravagantly flowered, expensive-looking, silky; it also didn't quite span her generous frame, gaping in the front, and Neville guessed instantly that it had belonged to the late Felicity Chapman.

If anything, Alan Chapman looked more pained than ever, but he refrained from comment. 'Shall we go in here, then?' he said, gesturing them into the drawing room where they'd interviewed him the previous day.

Paige went in first and selected a wing chair, where she established herself defiantly – every inch the lady of the house. 'Like I said,' she addressed Neville when they'd all taken seats, 'it's time you know the truth about Allie and me.'

'And what *is* the truth, then?'

'We're together,' she repeated.

Neville framed his next question carefully. 'You're telling us that you and Mr Chapman are having an affair?'

She gave him an imperious glare. 'Affair is a horrid word. It's not like that. We're ... soulmates, like.'

Neville took a quick look at Alan Chapman, who was grey-faced and silent. 'And that involves a ... physical relationship, I assume?'

Paige nodded. 'Yeah, 'course. I mean, men do have ... needs. And that Felicity was a selfish, frigid cow. She didn't treat Allie right, and she didn't deserve him.'

'That's not really fair,' Chapman protested weakly.

She ignored him. 'And we love each other,' Paige stated, as though that were the definitive last word. Having had her say, she rose from her chair. 'Would you gentlemen like a coffee?'

'Yes, please,' Neville said, and Cowley nodded.

Paige made a grand exit, swishing out in her silky dressing gown. Alan Chapman put his head in his hands.

'Well,' said Neville pleasantly, 'that's made it quite a bit easier for us, hasn't it?'

'Saved us some time,' Cowley added. 'Now we don't have to ask you lots of questions.'

'At least not the questions we were going to ask you. We can cut to the chase, Mr Chapman. Did you by any chance kill your wife?'

Chapman raised his head and stared at him. 'Are you mad?'

'It's a perfectly reasonable question,' Neville said.

'You've seen what she's like. Paige. My secretary. She ... she pursued me. Every single day. She wouldn't leave me alone until ... until I'd slept with her. I was weak, I admit it, but it was never my idea. She made all the running.'

'That doesn't mean that you didn't kill your wife,' Cowley pointed out. 'During a row, maybe, even if you and your mistress didn't plan it in advance.'

'But don't you see?' Chapman spread his hands in a pleading gesture. 'I'm the last person who would kill Felicity, and not just because I loved her. Because I did – love her, that is. I may not have been the world's best husband, but I did love her.' He shuddered. 'And now – don't you see? Now that Felicity's dead, I'm doomed. Now that I'm free, as she puts it, Paige isn't going to leave me alone until I've married her!'

THE YOUNG MAN looked up as Lilith edged her way into the room. 'Hiya,' he said, with neither interest nor alarm.

He was, she noted, a particularly unprepossessing teenager, his sallow face – revealed in the unforgiving glare of the fluorescent light – disfigured with angry eruptions of acne. In front of him on the table were two open cider cans. He took a swig from one, then tapped the ash from his cigarette into the pop top of the – presumably empty – other.

'Hello,' said Lilith. She tried out a smile; it had no visible effect on him. 'Do you work here, by any chance?'

'Yeah, I do.'

Lilith pulled out one of the beat-up chairs and looked at it closely to make sure there was nothing unpleasant on the seat before sitting down across from him. 'Would you mind if I asked you a few questions?'

He narrowed his eyes. 'What about?'

She didn't want to tip her hand too soon, but decided that some degree of honesty was called for. Obliquely she said, 'There's been a death in the hotel, I understand.'

'Yeah.' For the first time his face showed some emotion. His eyes lit up; he licked his lips in an almost lascivious way. 'Yeah, some woman croaked. In room nine, second floor. Da cops have been here, ya know. Dey took my fingerprints and all.' He studied his hands with what seemed to be awed interest. 'I guess somebody did her in, innit?'

'So it would seem.' Lilith put her handbag on the table, opened it and extracted her notebook. 'So you don't mind answering a few questions?'

'Well ...' He took a drag on his cigarette and blew some smoke in her direction. 'I don't know, like.'

Was his reluctance because he really didn't know anything, Lilith wondered, or was there another reason? Loyalty to his employer, perhaps, or maybe greed?

She opened her handbag again and took out a roll of fifty-pound notes, peeled off five of them and put them on the table, just beyond his reach.

The boy stared at the notes, then raised his eyes to hers and licked his lips again. 'Well, I guess maybe.'

'That's excellent, Mr ... what is your name, then?'

'Les,' he said. 'Les Fielding. And who are you? You're not a cop, are ya?' he added as she wrote his name in her notebook.

That was rich, but she didn't have time to enjoy the irony of it. 'No, I'm not a cop. I'm a representative of the press.'

It took him a moment to process that. 'Oh. Like a reporter?'

'Exactly. Is it all right if I call you Les?'

'Yeah. Dat's me name, innit?'

'Okay, Les. Would you mind telling me what your job is here at the hotel?' Lilith scribbled down his inarticulate reply, which amounted to the fact that he was employed in the kitchen, mainly to prepare and serve breakfast to the hotel guests. 'And what about the other people who work here?' she went on. 'Zuzanna, is it? The chambermaid who found ... the body?'

'Yeah, Susie. Susie's Polish, like.' He took a slurp from the can of cider. 'And there's Angel. She's de ovver cleaner, like.'

'Where is Angel from, do you know?'

Les shrugged. 'She's foreign. Brown skin, like. Her English ain't so good, like, so I'm not sure where she's from.'

'Anyone else?'

'Terry. Terry what works wid me in da kitchen, like.' He looked thoughtful for a few seconds. 'If he ever like comes back, dat is.'

For some reason, Lilith's skin prickled. 'Tell me about Terry,' she said.

'He's an okay bloke, like. Talks good, too, for a foreigner.' Les took a final puff on his cigarette and drowned the end in the makeshift ashtray.

'But he's not here now?'

'Nah.' The boy shook his head. 'And dat's what's weird. Cuz he lives here, like. In da back room, behind da kitchen. But he skived off yesterday, after breakfast. And he ain't been back since den.'

Lilith took a deep breath. 'Where do you think he's gone?'

'Dunno.' The inevitable shrug. 'He didn't say nuffink to me. He just cleared off, like. And he took his sleeping bag wiv him.'

Sleeping bag? Something about that didn't sound right. 'Doesn't he have a proper room with a bed, then?'

'Nah.' Les shot her an almost pitying look. 'Nuffink like dat. He just dosses down in one of da store-rooms. On account of him not being legal, like.' He explained it to her then, as though she were a simple-minded child. 'He don't have no papers, see? Couldn't rent a room, not even round here in one of da doss houses.'

Her heart was beating faster; she tried not to betray her excitement, keeping her voice steady as visions of Sunday's front page danced in her head. 'So Mr Wicker – the manager – has allowed him to stay on the premises? And presumably pays him in cash, under the table?'

'Yeah, dat sort of fing.'

'So Wicker knows that Terry's an illegal immigrant?'

Les snorted and rolled his eyes. 'Course he does.'

'And I don't suppose Terry is the first? There have been others?'

He nodded. 'Yeah. A couple, like, since I been working here. One was some African bloke. Black as coal. Didn't speak no English at all. Didn't last more dan a couple of weeks. Den dere was a bloke from Syria, like. He stayed a while longer. And Terry – he's been here da longest. Almost a year, maybe.'

'Where is Terry from, then? Did he say?'

'He's from Syria, too, like. Nuffink left dere to go back to, he told me.' Les shrugged again.

Lilith made a quick note. 'Do you think that Terry's ... disappearance ... had anything to do with the woman's death?' she asked casually.

The boy stared at her, his eyebrows raised. 'I never fought of dat. Do you fink Terry might of done her in, like, den done a runner?'

'There might be some connection,' she suggested.

'Cor.' He sat still for a minute, taking it on board. 'And are yer gonna write dat in da newspaper, den?'

'I'm not sure,' she said primly. 'I'm still asking questions, aren't I? Trying to get an idea of what's been going on.'

Suddenly his eyes went squinty; he seemed to be working through something in his mind. 'Are yer gonna use my name?' he demanded.

'That's up to you, Les. I'd prefer to quote you by name, but I can refer to you as an anonymous source, if that's what you want.'

He allowed his gaze to move along the table to the pile of fifty-pound notes. 'Cause I wouldn't want me Uncle Ronnie to fink dat I'd grassed him up, like.'

It was Lilith's turn to stare. 'Uncle Ronnie? Ronald Wicker is your *uncle*?'

Les Fielding shrugged. 'Yeah. Din't I say?'

Callie found herself alone on Saturday afternoon: Tariq had gone out to meet Zuzanna at some unspecified location, which theoretically left Callie free to get on with her sermon – now a matter of some urgency.

But hard as she tried to concentrate on the miracle of Pentecost, all she could think about was Marco.

She should ring him, she knew. But she didn't know what she was going to say to him. In spite of her secret hope that Frances would somehow absolve her from her promise, that hadn't happened. Her friend's advice, ultimately, had been to tell Marco that she was involved in a matter involving the church which she was unable to share with him, and he would just have to trust her. Would that be good enough?

She should ring him. Instead she grabbed the phone and rang the vicarage, telling herself that she needed to know whether Brian was back home from his son's wedding.

Usually, on a Saturday – Brian's day off – Jane would run interference, answering phone calls and fending off visitors at the vicarage. Callie was prepared for that; she would be pleasant to Jane, ascertain that they were home, and ring off quickly. This time, though, Brian picked up the phone himself.

'Oh!' said Callie. 'Brian. I was just checking to make sure you were back. I was expecting Jane to answer.'

'Janey's lying down,' Brian told her. 'The wedding – I think it took it out of her a bit. You know. Quite a busy day, and all that.'

'It went well, though?' she asked politely.

'Oh, fine. It was a lovely wedding. They're young, but Ellie's a smashing girl, and Simon's mad about her. They'll make a go of it.'

Callie seized her opportunity. 'Speaking of weddings,' she said, 'I've been hoping that you'd have a look at the church diary and see if there's a date this summer for mine.'

'Yours?'

'My wedding,' she stated firmly, ignoring her own doubts on the subject. 'Like I told you, Marco and I would like to be married this summer. July or August.'

'But it's nearly June already!'

Callie took a deep breath, biting back the furious words of blame. 'Yes, I know,' she said with forced calm. 'That's why I want to set a date.'

'Tomorrow,' said Brian. 'After the morning service. We'll look at the diary then. I'm sure we can come up with something.'

She would believe that when she saw it, Callie reflected once the call had ended. She focused on the computer screen, added a sentence to her sermon, then promptly deleted it as unsatisfactory and picked up the phone again, punching the button for her brother's mobile number.

Peter answered after a couple of rings. 'Sis? What's up?'

'I could ask you the same thing. It's been ages since I've seen you. Since we talked, even. Is everything all right?'

There was a tiny pause before he replied. 'Yes, fine,' he said. 'I've been ... busy, is all. We'll have to get together soon.'

'Have you seen Mum?'

This time the answer came out quickly. 'No. Not for ... a while.'

Something else for Callie to feel guilty about, then. She hadn't talked to their mother in over a week, and neglect had never sat well with Laura Anson.

'How's Marco?' Peter asked.

'Fine,' Callie said.

'Good. Have you set a date yet?'

'No,' she admitted. 'I'm working on it.'

'Well, let me know when you do.' He gave a little laugh. 'Gotta go now, Sis. Take care of yourself.'

'You too.'

And then he was gone. Callie looked at the phone, puzzled. What on earth was up with her brother? If it was yet another love affair gone wrong, she surely would have been the first to hear about it, as she always was. So what could it be?

As if she didn't have enough to worry about.

NEVILLE CLIMBED BACK into the driver's seat of the car and looked across at Sid Cowley. 'Well. He certainly made that one easy for us, didn't he?'

'Or *she* did.' Cowley snorted. 'What a piece of work.'

'You've almost got to feel sorry for the bloke.'

'You believed him, then? That he didn't have any reason to kill his wife?'

Neville thought about it for a minute. 'He was pretty convincing. I mean, given the choice between his wife and that woman ...'

'A fate worse than deaf, if you ask me. Though he *did* shag her.'

'And,' Neville reflected, 'a couple of days after his wife died, he's been shagging her again. That's a bit off. Bad form for a bereaved man, if he really did love his wife like he said.'

'I imagine it was her idea,' Cowley pointed out. 'She would have said he needed comforting.'

Cold comfort, Neville said to himself, all too easily imagining Paige Mason climbing into his bed. He'd slept with a few women like that back in the day, and it wasn't something he was proud of – even though he hadn't been married at the time.

Cowley cracked the window and fumbled in his pocket for his fags. 'So now we go and interview the taxi driver?'

They'd discussed their strategy on the drive to Wiltshire: first talk to Chapman, then contact PC Grace Long and ask her to arrange an interview with the woman who had alerted her to the row which had taken place before Mrs Chapman's departure. 'Do we really need to?' Neville wondered. 'I mean, he's confessed to the affair. He's admitted they had an argy-bargy. We don't really need the driver's testimony about that.'

'But she was the last person to see Felicity Chapman – to talk to her – before she fetched up at that hotel in London,' Cowley pointed out. 'That makes her an important witness. We should talk to her now, while we're here. Save us another trip to bloody Devizes.'

Neville knew he was right, though he was uneasy about extending their absence from London any longer than was necessary. He pulled his mobile out. 'Let me ring Triona,' he said. 'Then I'll ring PC Long and see what she can do for us.'

But when he thumbed the button on his phone, the screen remained blank. 'Bloody hell,' he swore, adding a few other expletives for good measure. 'Battery's dead. I bleeding forgot to charge it last night.'

Cowley reached for his phone with ill-concealed eagerness. 'Never mind, Guv. I'll ring Grace Long.'

THE VOICE in Callie's head was insistent: ring him. Ring Marco.

By sheer force of will she'd managed to concentrate on her sermon, and brought it to some sort of conclusion. She wasn't totally happy with it, but at least it was done.

And she needed to ring Marco.

She still wasn't ready to do it. Instead she picked up the phone again and rang her mother.

Laura Anson answered after the first ring. As if she'd been sitting there staring at the phone for weeks. 'Caroline! I thought something terrible had happened to you!'

'I've been ... very busy,' she said lamely, aware that she was echoing her brother's weasel words.

'That's hardly an excuse for neglecting your mother.'

She accepted the rebuke with meekness. 'No. It's not. I'm sorry.'

'And as for that brother of yours – well! It's shocking. I haven't seen him for weeks.'

'Neither have I,' Callie said truthfully.

'Are you going to make time to see me any time soon?'

She sighed, reached for her diary, and flicked through the pages. Get it over with, she told herself. 'How about tomorrow afternoon? I could come to you after Evensong. For a cup of tea.'

Her mother's reply was typically ungracious. 'All right. Tea. But don't expect any cake – it's a little late today for me to get to the shops.'

Callie said her farewells and ended the call.

Well, that was done. At least, Callie reflected, since her mother had only been to her flat once, there was little danger that she would burst in on her unannounced. That was one small blessing.

But she needed to ring Marco.

The phone weighed heavy in her hand for a few minutes before she finally summoned up the courage to push the speed-dial button.

'Hello, this is Mark,' said Marco's pre-recorded voice. 'Please leave a message and I'll get back to you.'

GRAHAM HAD TOLD Frances to pamper herself while he was away for the day, but that wasn't really in her nature at the best of times. She found some left-overs in the fridge and ate them for lunch, thinking all the while about her disturbing conversation with Callie. Had she given her the right advice? Was there anything she could do to help her friend on a practical level with her refugee dilemma?

Only later did she remember what she'd been about to do when Callie's call interrupted her: she was going to ring Triona and see how she was doing.

Guiltily she found her phone and rang Triona's mobile.

'Hello?' The voice that answered was unrecognisable, faint, scarcely more than a whisper.

'Triona? Is that you? Are you all right?'

'No, not really.' There was a pained sigh.

'What's the matter?'

The other woman groaned; her words came in short, breathy bursts. 'I've been having Braxton Hicks. For days, off and on. Been to hospital, a couple of times. They keep sending me home. I'm sure they think I'm hysterical. A mad Irish cow. But I just feel ... like shit. Worse. Like I'm going to die.'

Frances had heard this a number of times, from other expectant mothers at the hospital. She always counselled them to believe the doctors and the midwives, who had seen it all before and knew what they were talking about. But Triona was her friend, and that made it different somehow. 'What does Neville say?'

An unamused bark of laughter. 'He's not here. Surprise surprise. Off on a case. I tried to ring him. His bloody phone's not switched on.' A gulp; a stifled sob. 'He probably wouldn't believe me anyway. The bastard.'

'*I* believe you,' Frances said. 'Hold on, Triona. I'm coming, okay?'

11

'No.'

'But it's dynamite,' said Lilith.

'It's also too late in the day,' her boss reminded her. 'I agree that it's dynamite. And that's why we need to wait and do it properly.'

Lilith resisted the impulse to terminate the call on the spot. Here she was with the hottest story in town, and Rob Gardiner-Smith was telling her that it wouldn't be going onto Sunday's front page. Not into Sunday's paper at all, in fact. 'But someone else might beat us to it if we wait,' she persevered.

'Did you see anyone else in the neighbourhood? Had anyone else been on to the gormless nephew?'

'No,' Lilith admitted.

'Waiting another day isn't going to hurt. If anything, it gives you time to talk to a few more people, strengthen the story. Beef it up a bit. Really nail that bastard Wicker.'

'I've got all I need to nail him. He's a real piece of work.'

'Yes, and I'll need to run it past the lawyers, as well. Especially since the nephew's involved, and doesn't want us to use his name. We've got to make sure it's water-tight from a legal point of view.'

Deflated, Lilith conceded defeat. 'Monday, then?'

'All being well. Monday.'

FRANCES RANG the bell of the flat. A minute later, the door swung open. 'Thanks for coming,' said Triona, hanging onto the door handle as if for strength and support.

The words flew out of Frances' mouth before she could stop them. 'You look terrible!'

'Thanks.' She produced a twisted smile. 'I feel even worse.'

Terrible was a mild word for the way Triona looked: pale as a ghost, her face sheeny with sweat, huge dark shadows under her sunken eyes. Her curly hair was untamed, and evidently hadn't seen a comb for days.

'Tell me exactly how you feel,' Frances invited.

Triona let go of the door handle and cradled her bulging abdomen with both arms. 'Like this little bugger is determined to get out. Right now. I know that Braxton Hicks feels like real labour. But ... God, it hurts. Like the devil.' She grimaced and gripped her stomach more tightly.

Frances made a quick decision. 'All right, then. I'm taking you to hospital.'

'But they'll just send me back home again. They keep telling me this is normal.'

It didn't look normal to Frances. 'I'm not a doctor. But I think you need ... medical attention.'

'I hate looking like a fool,' Triona protested, though she allowed herself to be led to Frances' car.

THIS WASN'T the way Neville would have planned it. Ordinarily, in circumstances like this, he would have arranged for them to talk to the taxi driver who had taken Felicity Chapman to Pewsey station at the local police headquarters building, in a proper interview room. But PC Grace Long had insisted that it wouldn't work: it would frighten the woman, she said. It needed to be informal, unthreatening. Neville suspected that it had more to do with the fact that Grace Long wanted her guv – Tom Burton – kept out of it. The taxi driver was *her* find.

And so they were going to meet in the stuffy residents' lounge of a very old-fashioned hotel in the centre of Devizes. Worn dralon sofas and wing-back chairs, dark oak tables, patterned carpet, faded prints on dingy murk-coloured walls. In dire need of a make-over.

They were definitely in the provinces, Neville realised. By the time they'd made all the contacts and the arrangements, it was past five and they were well into that deadly period of time: too late for tea, a bit too early for drinks, and way too early for dinner. Negotiating with the woman behind the reception desk, Neville thought longingly of London, where you could get anything you wanted to eat or drink at just about any time of the day or night.

'We could give you a pot of tea,' the woman said with obvious reluctance.

'Sandwiches?' he suggested hopefully. It had been a long time since he and Sid had eaten anything. 'Or cake?'

She shook her head. 'Oh, no. Nothing from the kitchen. The kitchen is closed.'

'Biscuits, then?'

'We'll see what we can do.'

It didn't sound promising, but he would have to live with it. 'Tea for four, then. In the lounge.' Turning away, he spotted an old-fashioned phone on the reception desk. 'Could I possibly make a call?' he asked impulsively. 'Just a quick one.'

She raised her eyebrows, but nodded in agreement. 'As long as it's quick.'

Neville punched in his home number.

It might take Triona a while to get to the phone, he reasoned, and turned his back on the receptionist's beady glare as it rang and rang, unanswered, until the answerphone kicked in.

FRANCES GLARED at the hospital receptionist with the fiercest stare she could summon up. The woman was unknown to her, unfortunately – a Saturday evening part-timer rather than one of the regular receptionists.

The woman tapped a few keys on her computer and concentrated on the screen, ignoring Frances. 'No,' she said at last. 'No, she can't be seen by a doctor. Nor a midwife. Not now. Not tonight.'

'But she needs to be seen. She's in a great deal of pain.'

The receptionist sighed. 'My guidelines are clear. She needs to go home now, and try to get some sleep. If she's still feeling poorly in the morning, she can ring us. Chances are, she'll be back to normal by then.' She glanced towards Triona, hunched over on one of the chairs in the reception area. 'Tell her to practice her breathing exercises. And drink plenty of water. Dehydration makes Braxton Hicks worse.'

Frances drummed her fingers on the counter. 'I'm telling you—'

'Aaayaiiiiii!' A shrill, unearthly scream cut Frances off in mid-sentence. She spun round.

Triona was now sitting bolt upright, struggling to get to her feet. 'Something's happening,' she gasped. 'Something's happening!'

CALLIE HAD BEEN STARING at her phone for so long, willing it to ring, that she snatched it up instantly, even as she registered the fact that it was Marco's ring-tone.

'Marco?'

'*Cara Mia*. You asked me to—'

'Yes. Yes.'

'Your headache is better?'

'Oh. Yes. Much better.' She took a deep breath. 'Marco, can we ... get together? Somewhere? Maybe go out for a meal?'

'You mean now? This evening?'

'Yes.'

'I could come to you,' he said. 'I can be there in, oh, say thirty minutes?'

'No. I mean, it would be better to meet somewhere else.' She thought quickly, but found herself drawing a blank.

'Well,' he said after a few seconds of silence, 'I suppose you could come here. To my flat. Geoff's gone out, so I'm on my own.'

As much time as Marco had spent at Callie's flat, she had never been to his place: he had always discouraged it, explaining that his flat-mate was usually in residence. And it wasn't very homely, he'd told her – just a place to lay his head. So she was curious, in spite of her nervousness at seeing him. 'All right, then. Shall I come a bit later? Seven, or half past?'

'Seven sounds good to me. I'll cook for you. I still have those porcini,' he reminded her.

'See you soon, then.'

It would be all right, she told herself. It *had* to be all right.

'THIS IS MAGGIE,' said PC Grace Long. 'Maggie Ruddle.'

Neville shook the woman's outstretched hand. 'Thanks for coming.'

Her handshake, he noted, was surprisingly firm for such a slight woman. She was short, slim, dressed in jeans and a donkey jacket. Mid-fifties, perhaps – possessing a strong-featured face etched with deep lines. 'If you think I can help, like,' she said in a voice thick with the sort of accent Neville had come to recognise as local to Devizes. 'I've already told Grace here everything I know.'

'We just need to tidy up some loose ends,' he said in what he hoped was a reassuring manner. 'Have a seat, Mrs Ruddle.'

'Just Maggie will do.' She shrugged out of the donkey jacket, draped it over the back of one of the dralon chairs, then lowered herself into its dusty depths.

At that moment the tea arrived, borne in on a tray by the reluctant receptionist. 'Tea for four,' she announced. 'And biscuits.'

'Thank you very much,' Neville told her. 'Much appreciated.'

'Ooh, I could murder a mug of tea,' Maggie said eagerly, then clapped her hand over her mouth. 'Begging your pardon. That wasn't the best thing to say, was it?'

Neville grinned, finding himself liking this blunt woman.

The receptionist held out the tray. 'Very welcome, I'm sure.'

'Sid, make yourself useful,' Neville ordered, realising that his sergeant was still standing like a lemon, staring at Grace Long.

Cowley, seemingly struck dumb, took the tray and deposited it on a table.

'I'll pour, shall I?' PC Long offered. She did it in a practiced way, asking each of them how they liked it before pouring them a cup.

The hiatus gave Neville the opportunity to look at the young PC properly. She was out of uniform this time, with her rich coppery hair loose round her shoulders rather than in a regulation bun. Skinny jeans showed off a more than acceptable figure; it was no wonder that the ever-susceptible Sid Cowley couldn't take his eyes off her. If he hadn't been an old married man, soon to be a father, he would have been ogling her himself.

'Sugar, Sergeant?' she asked when the other two had been served in order of protocol.

'Uh. Yes. Three.'

'Cat got your tongue, Sid?' Neville interposed wickedly.

Cowley tore his gaze away from the PC just long enough to give Neville a filthy look.

Once they'd drunk their tea and demolished the biscuits – a few custard creams in cellophane packets – Neville got down to the business for which they'd come: interviewing Maggie. He ran through his questions while Cowley took notes.

Everything she told them was consistent with the information that PC Long had already conveyed. Neville found her a credible witness – what reason would she have to lie? – and an admirably concise and insightful one as well. She had known the victim surprisingly well, given the difference in their stations in life, and had cared about her a great deal, without having the baggage which came with a familial relationship. That made her a rare and valuable witness.

'I was that worried about her, to be honest,' she said simply as she concluded her account of the morning in question. 'I'd never seen her in such a state. That's why I thought she might of ... you know. Done herself in.'

'But she didn't,' Neville assured her. 'She was definitely murdered.'

Maggie frowned thoughtfully, running a hand over her spiky hair. 'So he must of done it. That husband of hers. Somehow.'

Though Neville knew that he probably shouldn't offer his own opinion, he responded candidly to her honesty, feeling that she deserved the same in kind. 'I don't think he did, you know.'

Cowley spoke for the first time, with an expression of distaste. 'We met her. His mistress. Paige Mason.'

IF CALLIE HAD BEEN WORRIED that Marco wouldn't be happy to see her, she needn't have been concerned. He opened the door of his flat and kissed her warmly, then drew her inside.

'Risotto,' he said. 'Porcini risotto. I can't leave it too long. Come through to the kitchen.'

She had only a glimpse of the main living room of the flat as he led her through. Neutrally furnished, tidy – as she would have expected from Marco. He had grown up with a family in the restaurant trade, and was consequently the sort of cook who always cleaned up after himself in the kitchen. Tidiness was an ingrained part of his nature.

So, too – Callie had come to appreciate – was patience, a quality which very much came into play in the creation of risotto. Callie had never mastered risotto herself. She'd never really tried, knowing that during the time required for the slow stirring, she was likely to be interrupted by a phone call or some other demand on her attention.

Instead of a table, his small kitchen was furnished with a sort of breakfast bar with two high stools side by side. Callie settled herself on one of them and observed him at work: stirring, adding a ladleful of stock, stirring some more, tasting, stirring. It was soothing to watch him, almost hypnotic, knowing that conversation was neither required nor even desirable. Her mouth began to water when he heated up another pan, sizzled some olive oil and threw in a handful of fresh mushrooms. 'Oh, that smells amazing,' she couldn't resist saying. 'Do you want me to stir that pan?'

Marco smiled at her. 'No, but you could chop the porcini. They're soaking in that water over there. Save the water, of course. That will go in towards the end. To add flavour.'

In spite of everything, she felt ridiculously happy at that moment. Here in the kitchen with Marco, working together towards a common goal – even if that goal was nothing more profound than filling her empty stomach with something delicious that he had made for her.

'I love you, Marco,' she said impulsively.

'And I love you, *Cara Mia*.' He smiled again and blew her a kiss. 'But let's not get distracted, okay?'

'PAIGE MASON?!' Grace turned and stared at the Londoner – the lanky one who had been ogling her since she arrived, and whom she'd been trying to ignore. 'Paige Mason? I was at school with her!'

'She was wif him. At his house. This afternoon, This morning. Last night, I suppose.'

Unable to grasp the implications of what he was saying, she shook her head. 'But she's ... my age! That's just ... well, it's *wrong*. And she's ...'

'A piece of work,' he supplied.

'What was he *thinking*?' Grace remembered Paige Mason, all too well. Not the prettiest girl in their year – by a long chalk – nor the cleverest. But for some reason she'd decided that she was better than the rest of them: better than the farmers' daughters, and the girls whose fathers worked at the brewery.

Paige Mason didn't have a father – at least not one that she knew. Her mum had never been married, which would have been a source of shame for just about any other girl. But it didn't stop Paige from putting on airs and graces.

Grace hadn't seen Paige since they'd left school; even though they'd both still remained in Devizes, they evidently travelled in different circles. She hadn't actually thought about her in ages. But now she remembered, vividly, a conversation she'd had with her mother. Years ago, it had been: before Mum got sick. She'd probably been about fourteen, but she recalled it as if it were yesterday.

She'd come home from school, smarting at some nasty comment Paige Mason had made to her about her father having dirt under his fingernails. She wouldn't have told her dad, not in a million years, but she blurted it out to Mum. 'Why does she have to be so horrid?' she demanded.

Mum gave her a cuddle and sat her down at the kitchen table. 'She's insecure because she doesn't know who her own father is,' Mum said.

'But why doesn't she know?'

Her mother regarded her for a moment before answering. 'You're old enough now to understand this. And I know about it because your nan – my mum – was great friends with Paige's nan. Mrs Mason.

'Paige's mum – Sal, she was called – was the Masons' youngest child. Younger than me, so I didn't really know her very well. She was spoiled rotten, my mum always said. When she was about sixteen, she ran away from home. Went up to London, apparently. And while she was there, she had lots of ... boyfriends. Do you understand what I mean?'

Grace didn't, fully, but she nodded sagely anyway.

Mum went on to explain that when Sal Mason came back home, nearly a year later, she was in the family way. 'And Mrs Mason told my mum that Sal didn't exactly know who the baby's dad was. All she would say was that he was either a duke, or a famous rock star. One or the other, no names mentioned.'

Callie put down her fork. 'Marco, that was wonderful. I've never had better risotto. Not ever.'

'Mama's recipe,' he said modestly. 'I think the secret is the flavour from the soaking water. And that extra knob of butter at the end. Oh, and maybe the fried mushrooms on top. But I'll never make it as well as Mama does.'

She wanted to pick up the plate and lick it. Instead she sighed happily. 'I don't believe that. I think you're a fantastic cook.'

'Tell that to my sister. She won't even let me in the kitchen, unless there's the direst emergency.' Marco grimaced. 'On the other hand, let's not talk about my sister right now. Shall we take the rest of the wine through to the other room?'

'Good idea. These stools aren't the most comfortable place to spend an evening.' And, she thought, not the most conducive for more than desultory conversation – sitting side-by-side rather than face-to-face.

Marco slid off his stool, cleared the plates and cutlery, and gave them a quick rinse before stacking them in the sink. 'I'll deal with these a bit later,' he stated, then refilled their wine glasses, tipping the last drops into Callie's glass.

She followed him back into the living room and sat where he indicated, on an oatmeal-coloured sofa. He sat down next to her and clinked glasses.

'Thanks for a lovely meal,' she said.

'Thank you for coming.'

Up till now, Callie had felt no sense of awkwardness. But she wondered whether that was a freighted comment, requiring some sort of apology from her. She knew it was going to have to happen sooner or later, so she might as well get it over with. After a fortifying sip of wine, she began. 'About last night, Marco ...'

'You don't have to explain.'

'But I do.' She stared for a moment into her wine glass, seeking for inspiration. 'It's ... complicated.'

'Did you really have a migraine?' he blurted.

'No,' she admitted.

'You lied to me, then?' The hurt in his voice was so palpable that she winced.

'I didn't tell you the truth. But I couldn't tell you, and I still can't.'

'I don't understand.'

Callie took a deep breath. 'It ... has to do with ... my job. With promises,' she added. 'Promises I made to God, at my ordination, and promises I've made to ... someone else.'

'Someone else,' he repeated. 'Anyone I know?'

'No. Like I said, it's ... job-related. And it has nothing to do with you. With *us*. It's just ...' Callie paused, turning her head to look at Marco. His face was averted. 'I wish more than anything that I could tell you, but I can't,' she said at last.

He raised his head and met her eyes. 'This probably won't be the last time this happens, will it?'

An honest answer was called for, painful – and risky – as it was to say the words. 'Probably not.' She watched his face, trying to read his reaction and gauge his emotions, but couldn't tell what he was thinking. Would she show her to the door, tell her to get out of his life?

After a long moment, Marco nodded. 'All right, then.' He put down his wine glass and reached for her hand.

She couldn't believe what she was hearing. 'All right?'

'It's one of the things I love about you, *Cara Mia* – your integrity. Being true to yourself, even when it's not easy. Even when it affects ... me. Us.' He wrapped his arm round her shoulders and drew her closer. 'My job can be like that, too. There will probably be things I can't tell you, at some point in the future. That's something I suppose we'll both have to accept.'

'So we have a future, then?'

His answer didn't take the form of words.

BY THE TIME Neville got back to his flat, he was absolutely exhausted. He couldn't believe how late it was, either: the interview had gone on longer than he'd expected, and Cowley – obviously smitten by PC Grace Long – had been in no rush to get away. Then, finally on the way back to London, they'd got caught up in a massive tailback caused by an accident on the motorway. With traffic at a standstill, they'd been overtaken by numerous emergency vehicles careering along the hard shoulder, while Cowley rabbited on endlessly about Grace Long, about his sister, about Grace Long. Eventually he'd just told Sid to shut up; the rest of the journey – involving a long and complex diversion onto minor roads – had taken place in injured silence. Vastly preferable, on the whole.

But now he was home, at last. Putting his key in the lock of the door into the building. Hungry, he realised as he noticed that the takeaway on the corner was still open and doing a thriving business, but he was also too bone tired to be bothered.

He dragged himself up the steps and unlocked the flat door, trying to decide how to handle the situation with Triona. Would she be asleep? That would be the easiest: he could creep into bed, or maybe just crash on the sofa, and deal with the apologies in the morning. If she was awake, waiting up for him, that would be a different story altogether.

There were no lights on in the lounge. Good sign, he decided, though it seemed odd that the curtains weren't drawn. The room was dimly lit by the streetlights, the headlamps of passing traffic, and the fluorescent glare from the takeaway. In the corner of the room, the answerphone was blinking green.

Neville crept towards the bedroom and paused at the open door. Again, the curtains were undrawn. In the ambient light from the street he could see that the bed was unoccupied but also unmade, the duvet in a tangle at the foot of the bed.

'Triona?' He headed for the bathroom, abandoning the need for stealth. 'Are you okay?'

No reply. And no Triona, either in the bathroom or in the kitchen.

'Triona?' he called out, unable to believe that she wasn't here.

Neville stood still for a moment, trying to think over the pounding of his heart. If she wasn't here ...

Get a grip, he told himself. *You're a detective, for God's sake.*

Returning to the lounge, he punched the flashing button on the answerphone.

The first message, unsurprisingly, was the one he'd left hours earlier. 'Triona, I've been held up. I'll be back as soon as I can.'

The second was a voice he didn't immediately recognise. 'Mr Stewart?' a female voice said, then identified itself. 'This is Frances Cherry. Triona's friend. When you get this message, you need to come to the hospital. As quickly as you can. Ask for me.'

Neville went, his exhaustion forgotten. He took the car; it was a familiar route – the same one he used nearly every day to get to the police station – through Holland Park, Notting Hill and Bayswater to Paddington. Autopilot – no need to think about it. Traffic this late on Saturday night was less hectic than on a weekday morning, so he made reasonable time, and pulled into the hospital car park at just past midnight.

He went to the general enquiries desk and asked for Frances Cherry.

A phone call was made; a few minutes later she was standing before him. 'Mr Stewart,' she said.

That didn't sound right. 'Call me Neville,' he said automatically, though there was something that didn't feel quite right about that either.

'Neville. Would you come with me, please?'

'What the ... what's going on?' he blurted. 'Where's Triona?'

Not speaking, she led him down a corridor and into a small private room. The sort of room, he realised at the back of his mind, where doctors took people to give them bad news.

'What's going on?' he repeated.

She turned and looked at him; he couldn't read her expression. 'You have a daughter,' she said with a smile that didn't reach her eyes. 'She was born several weeks early, so she's very small, but perfect. They say she's going to be fine.'

The words caught him completely by surprise; he repeated them stupidly. 'A daughter.'

'She's to be called Annie, Triona said. After her mother.'

'Annie.'

Frances Cherry swallowed; he could see her throat moving, and he noticed then that there were tears in her eyes.

'Triona?' he said. 'Where is she?'

She blinked rapidly; a tear ran down her cheek. 'Triona haemmoraged. Very badly. They couldn't stop the bleeding.' She reached out a hand and touched his arm. 'I'm so sorry, Neville. She's ... gone.'

12

Callie slept soundly that night. Things were all right between her and Marco, and that made all the difference. Their canoodling on his sofa had been cut short by the untimely arrival of his flatmate, but that didn't matter. Neither did the fact that she still had a young man sleeping on the floor of her sitting room, nor her dread of the impending visit to her mother. As long as she and Marco were okay ...

Her alarm went off at the usual hour, affording her sufficient time to shower and prepare herself for the morning service.

Or at least it would have given her sufficient time, if Tariq hadn't been in the bathroom.

When she'd got back from Marco's last night, Tariq had already been asleep, and she'd managed not to wake him. But that meant she hadn't had a chance to communicate with him about her schedule for the morning. She recalculated, made herself a cup of tea, and was just consuming the last few sips when he emerged from the bathroom, damp and apologetic.

'I am sorry, Miss Callie. I thought I would use the bathroom before you were up. I hope it is not a problem for you.'

'No problem,' she assured him. 'I still have time for a quick shower and a quick trip out with Bella.'

'I can take Bella out,' he offered.

She thought about it: tempting, but there would be quite a few more people coming and going from the church this morning than there had been during the week. What if someone – some self-righteous nosy parker – were to see a young man coming out of her flat with her dog? She couldn't take that risk, for all sorts of reasons. 'I don't think that would be a good idea,' she said reluctantly.

'Ah.' He nodded, quick on the uptake.

What she didn't have time for was another read-through of her sermon. She printed it off while she dressed in her clericals, then took Bella out for the briefest of walks round the precincts before entrusting her to Tariq's care and rushing over to the church to robe.

Brian was in the vestry, putting on his chasuble – red, for Pentecost.

'Sorry I'm a bit late,' she said, addressing his somewhat disapproving expression. 'A few ... complications ... this morning.'

'Never mind. You're all right for the sermon?'

She flapped the bits of paper she had in her hand. 'Yes. All set. "Come Holy Ghost, our souls inspire".'

'GRAHAM, it was ... awful. Terrible. The worst night of my life. And that includes the night I was arrested.'

She'd come home late – very late. Or early, depending on your definition. Not wanting to disturb her husband, Frances had gone to bed in their daughter's vacant room. Unsurprisingly, even exhausted as she was, it had taken her ages to fall asleep and then she'd slept badly. Graham had let her sleep; when he returned from his morning service he checked on her, found her awake, and sat on the bed beside her to talk.

Sometime during those nightmarish hours at the hospital, she'd sent him a text to let him know where she was, and warned him not to expect her home any time soon. Now she needed to tell him, face to face, what had happened.

'Start at the beginning,' he invited, reaching for her hand. She grasped it gratefully.

'I rang her. Just to see how she was doing.' Swiftly Frances recounted the opening scenes of the long drama: her arrival at Triona's flat and realisation that something was badly wrong, the struggle with the receptionist, the breaking of Triona's waters in the waiting room. And then the blood. So much blood.

'It was like a nightmare,' she told him, closing her eyes at the memory. 'They rushed her off to theatre. They did everything they could to save her. But she'd just lost too much blood.'

'And the baby?'

Frances nodded. 'The baby is going to be fine. A girl. She's very small, of course. But they say there's nothing wrong with her that a few weeks in the neonatal unit won't sort out.'

'Was Triona conscious?'

'Barely, at that point. But she saw the baby, even if she wasn't able to hold her. And she told me that she wanted her named for her mother.'

'So you were able to be with her? I'm surprised.'

'They let me stay with her. Not as her friend, but as the chaplain. When they realised she probably ... wasn't ... going to make it,' she added.

'Oh, poor Fran.' He squeezed her hand. 'So you were with her till ... the end?'

Frances suddenly felt as if she was going to cry, but she gulped back the tears. 'Yes. It's one of the privileges of priesthood, as you know, but somehow it's different when it's a friend.' She took a deep breath. 'It was ... very peaceful at the end. She wasn't conscious. She just ... slipped away.'

'And where was her husband while all of this was going on?' Graham asked pointedly.

'Working, evidently. With his phone switched off.'

'Typical.'

'But, Graham.' She struggled to sit up in bed. 'Later, when he came. And I had to tell him. He was ... devastated. Heartbroken.' Frances knew she would never forget the look on his face. 'You know I've never really ... got on ... with Neville Stewart.'

Her husband grimaced. 'To say the least.'

'Apart from anything else, anything personal, I've never been convinced of his commitment to Triona, and to their marriage. But last night – this morning – I was convinced. He really loved her, Graham. In all my years as a chaplain, giving bad news – the worst news – to people, I've never seen anyone so completely gutted. It was like he was ... hollowed out.'

Graham put his arm round her shoulders. 'Like I'd be, if I lost you.'

'But then I took him to see the baby,' she went on. 'In the neonatal unit. They let him hold her. And the look on his face then—' She stopped, remembering, trying to capture it in words. 'He was ... transfixed. With love, Graham. Total love. I was afraid that he might somehow blame the baby for Triona's death. Resent her, even. But he held her, and he talked to her.' Frances smiled, even as the tears began trickling down her cheeks. 'I found myself actually liking Neville Stewart. For the first time. And in spite of everything, as awful as all this is, I think it's going to be the making of him. He'll never get over it, of course, but I think it's going to be okay. For him and Annie.' Then she gave up the effort to hold back her tears, and sobbed in her husband's arms.

'GOOD SERMON,' Brian said after the service, at the back of the church, as soon as he'd finished the dismissal prayer for the servers.

It sounded a little grudging to Callie, but she was nonetheless grateful for any positive feedback. 'Thanks.'

He pulled the red chasuble over his head and handed it to the waiting MC. 'Good congregation today, for Whitsun. I suppose we need to mingle at coffee. Seek out the unfamiliar faces.'

'And then can we talk? In the vestry? With the diary?'

Brian sighed. 'All right.'

Twenty minutes later, having chatted with several parishioners, Callie spotted Brian making his escape. Apologising, she graciously disengaged from the woman she was talking to and followed him to the vestry.

Brian opened the large red church diary, then reached for his own personal diary as well. 'The summer is very busy,' he said. 'Quite a few weddings. Are you sure you wouldn't rather wait till autumn? Give you a bit more time to make plans. A wedding is a complicated thing, from what I've seen.'

'The sooner, the better,' she said firmly. 'It will be a small wedding. Mostly family. And the congregation will be invited, of course.'

'Well.' He tapped the book with his pen. 'There's a Saturday free in mid-August. I suppose we could squeeze you in then.'

Impulsively she gave him a hug. 'Thanks, Brian. That's perfect. I could kiss you!'

'I don't think that would be a very good idea,' he said wryly, disengaging himself.

SINCE MARK WAS NOT on speaking terms with his sister Serena, his Sundays no longer conformed to the old familiar pattern of Mass at the Italian church, followed by lunch with *la famiglia* at his sister's house. For his mother's sake, though, he had tried to establish a new pattern: Mass with his parents, then coffee at their house before they continued on to Serena's and he went home – to a solitary lunch at his flat.

His mother was in no way reconciled to these new arrangements. It just wasn't right, she insisted. Families should be together on Sundays. 'It breaks my heart,' she said as she oversaw the brewing of the coffee. 'You and Serena. Always you have been so close. Such good friends. *Migliori amici, veramente*. Talk to her, Marco. Talk to *la tua sorella*.'

'Not until she stops trying to run my life.' Mark crossed his arms across his chest. 'I mean it, Mamma. What she did – trying to set me up with Giulia – that was going too far. She might not like Callie, for whatever stupid reason, but it's time for her to respect my choice. My right to make my *own* choice.' He uncrossed his arms to accept a tiny cup from her. 'I'm going to marry Callie, whether Serena likes it or not. It's up to her to come to terms with that. Or not,' he added.

'But you are cutting yourself off from *la tua famiglia*!'

'Not from you, Mamma. Or Pappa.' They were sensible enough to keep their reservations to themselves, Mark reflected as he took a sip of his mother's fiercely strong and utterly delicious coffee. He knew that they liked Callie; he also knew that they would have been infinitely happier if Callie had been born to an Italian family. He respected them for being able to hold the two conflicting impulses at the same time, and to refrain from airing any doubts they might harbour.

'But to eat by yourself, *da solo*, *di domenica* ... *è sbagliato*. Wrong, Marco. *Lo sai*.'

'Soon I'll have my own wife to eat with,' he pointed out, then instantly regretted it as he saw the pain on his mother's face. 'Sorry, Mamma. But it's true.'

That reminded him that Callie was supposed to ring him, once she'd talked to Brian. He'd turned off his phone before Mass; now he took it out of his pocket and switched it back on.

There were two new voicemails waiting for him. '*Scusa*, Mamma,' he said, putting the phone to his ear. 'This could be important.'

'Mark, mate,' said a voice which was definitely not Callie's. 'It's Neville. This isn't ideal, but I wanted to tell you myself before you heard it from anyone else.' There was a pause, then the clearing of a throat – or it might even have been a sob – before the next, quieter, words. 'There's no easy way to say this. Triona's dead.'

TEA WITH HER MOTHER: not Callie's idea of the perfect Sunday afternoon. But needs must.

On impulse, and without much hope, she rang her brother's mobile to see whether he might be able to join her.

'All right,' Peter said, to her surprise. 'I'll meet you there. And maybe we'll have time for a chat. Afterwards.'

That sounded a bit ominous, but on the whole it was a move in the right direction, given her brother's recent silence.

He was waiting for her in front of Laura Anson's building, holding a cellophane-wrapped bunch of tulips. 'For Mum,' he said. 'From Tesco, which she won't like. But at least they're not lilies.'

'Marco brought her lilies.'

Peter grinned. 'I know. She told me. "Literally streaming" she was. She had to give them away.'

Callie thought back to that day: to her mother's watery eyes and sniffles. 'I didn't know she was allergic to lilies! I thought she had a cold!'

'Ever the martyr.'

You just couldn't win with Laura Anson. Callie reckoned she should have known that by now. She sighed, summoning up her courage. 'Ready?'

'Let's do it,' said Peter.

MARK COULDN'T GET his head round it: Triona dead.

Neville, now a widower. And a father.

Their conversation, when he'd rung Neville back, had been brief. Neville was obviously struggling to keep himself together.

What was he going to do? How was he going to cope?

Evans would probably take Neville off the Chapman case, Mark reckoned. Assign another CIO, put him on compassionate leave.

But there were so many things to think about when a family member died. Mark had recent personal experience of that, with his brother-in-law's death. And in his job as a family liaison officer he saw it every day. Most people just had no idea how many details – painful, routine or otherwise – they would have to deal with. Part of his job, inevitably, was to help them through the red tape, the minefield of bureaucracy surrounding a sudden death.

Neville was his friend. He could do no less for him.

He looked at his phone for a moment, pulling his thoughts and his words together, then rang Neville's number.

'Listen, Nev,' he said when Neville answered. 'I know you don't want to think about all this at the moment. But the funeral. And all that. It's what I do. I can help you. Whenever you're ready.'

'Thanks,' said Neville. 'Thanks, mate.'

CALLIE LOOKED across at her brother and sighed wordlessly. Their mother had just gone to the kitchen to top up the hot water in the teapot ('If I'd known you were both coming, I would have got out the bigger pot.').

Peter rolled his eyes at her. 'Well,' he said in a theatrical stage whisper, 'the one thing you can say about our mother is that she's consistent.'

'I really thought she'd be happy to hear that we'd set a date,' Callie whispered back. 'I mean, she's been on at me for years about getting married.'

'You should know her better than that. The only thing that makes her happy is finding fault.'

Far from being happy to get her daughter's wedding date into her diary, Laura Anson had immediately produced a long list of her friends who would be expecting an invitation. 'Though it's scarcely enough notice for most of them,' she'd said. 'They lead busy lives, you know. And quite a few of them will be away in August.'

She'd not taken it well when Callie had told her that her friends would not be on the invitation list. 'It's going to be a very small wedding. Just immediate family and close friends.'

'But these people *are* my close friends.'

'*My* friends,' Callie had summoned the courage to say. 'I'm inviting *my* friends, not yours.'

Laura Anson swept back into the room with the replenished teapot and a frown. 'About this wedding,' she said. 'What are you planning to wear, Caroline?'

'Oh, I'll find a dress. Frances said she'll take me shopping this week.'

There was no offer forthcoming from her mother to accompany her. Instead Laura Anson frowned thoughtfully. 'I shall need to buy something suitable, of course. You *will* let me know when you've decided on a colour scheme, won't you?'

'Yes, Mother.' Callie knew better than to look in the direction of her brother. Eye contact with him could be fatal.

FRANCES, still exhausted, went to her own bed and slept a little more in the afternoon, waking when Graham brought her a cup of tea after his return from Evensong.

'I'm going back to the hospital,' she told him. 'To see Annie, and make sure she's okay.'

'You could ring,' he suggested. 'You're the chaplain. They'll talk to you – tell it to you straight.'

She knew he was right, but she also knew it wouldn't be good enough. She needed to see the baby for herself; she owed that much to Triona.

The neonatal unit was state-of-the-art: one of the best in London, which made it one of the best in the world. That was reassuring. Frances was acquainted with many of the people who worked there; she knew how committed they were to providing the best possible care for the fragile, tiny lives entrusted to them.

When she arrived, she was pleased to see that the unit manager on duty was a capable nursing sister with whom she'd often shared a cup of coffee in the canteen. 'Kamala?' she said. 'I've come to see Annie Stewart. Born last night. Her mother ...' Frances' voice caught on the rest of the sentence.

The other woman nodded. 'Yes. Sad, that. Poor little scrap. But her dad is with her.'

'Neville Stewart? He's here?'

'Hasn't left her side all day.' She shook her head. 'I've been trying to convince him to go home. But he's not having it.'

'And how is Annie doing?'

The nurse beamed. 'The doctors say she's fine. Just small, is all. A few weeks in Special Care and she can go home.'

Home. But what sort of home would that be, with no mother and a workaholic father with nonexistent experience of children, let alone newborns? No other family, no support network.

Frances resolved there and then that no matter how she felt about Neville Stewart, she would do what she could for him and for Annie.

'WELL,' said Callie, once she and Peter were outside. 'I'm glad that's over with.'

'Until the next time.'

That was the problem: there would always be a next time. Their mother was never going to change.

'Thanks for coming,' Callie added. 'I appreciate the moral support.'

'Sis ...'

With that one word, spoken tentatively, Callie had a premonition of something bad to come. It didn't take long in coming, even without any encouragement on her part.

'Can we talk?'

She made a show of looking at her watch, though she knew she wouldn't be able to say no in the end.

'It's important,' he added, with a bit more urgency. 'Can I come back to yours?'

That, of all things, would not be a good idea. She thought quickly. 'Somewhere closer, maybe?'

'There's a Starbucks round the corner, then,' Peter suggested. 'I'll buy you a coffee.'

It wasn't too busy late on a Sunday afternoon; they found a private table towards the back and ordered their drinks.

Callie had a premonition what this might be about: when Peter sought her out to talk, it was usually about his latest relationship. His recent unaccustomed silence filled her with half curiosity, half dread. 'You wanted to talk?' she asked.

No further prompting was required. Peter leaned forward across the table. 'I just wanted you to know, Sis. I'm in love.'

This was far from the first time she'd heard those words from him. Peter was a serial romantic, and his older sister had been his chief confidant for a good ten years.

'Yes?' she said, trying not to sound as sceptical as she felt.

She must not have succeeded, as he assumed an injured expression. 'Oh, I know you think you've heard this all before.'

'That's because I *have* heard it all before.' She began ticking them off on her fingers. 'Jason, Nick, that boy at school, was he called Piers—'

'Oh, but this is different.'

'You always say that, as well,' she pointed out.

'But this time ...' Peter's clasped hands flew apart in a sweeping gesture. 'This is the real thing. I never imagined ... never could have imagined ... feeling like this. Like I could fly. Like my heart is going to burst with happiness.' His hands returned to his chest and pressed on his heart. 'Now I know what the poets and the song-writers have been going on about for all these years.'

This did sound different to Callie, in degree if not in essence. 'And it's ... reciprocated?' she asked cautiously.

'Yes. Oh, yes!' He grinned at her – a sappy, besotted grin. 'Yes, he loves me too. We're so happy together that it's ridiculous.'

'Well, I'm happy for you, then.'

And she *was* happy for him – happy that he'd seemingly found the person he'd been looking for at last. He was twenty-six: young, but a good age to settle down a bit. This relationship might tame some of his excesses, Callie reflected. No bad thing at all.

'He's the one,' Peter said solemnly. 'For always.'

'Does that mean ... are you planning to get married?'

Her brother grimaced. 'We want to. We'd ... we'd love to. But there's just one teensy-weensie little problem.'

'He's not already married?'

'No, not that.' He sighed and closed his eyes. 'No, the problem is, Sis – he's a priest.'

FRANCES TOOK a deep breath before she pushed the door open and went into the neonatal unit. She knew where Annie's incubator was located, so she headed in that direction.

The unit was as always humming with sound: the buzzes, clicks and beeps of the machines that kept the tiny babies alive and monitored their vital signs. Frances was used to the noise, but beneath it she identified the unaccustomed sound of song.

She saw Neville before he saw her. He was standing beside Annie's incubator, bending over it, singing a lullaby. His voice was rusty, croaky, and out of tune, but it was unmistakably singing a lullaby.

Unwilling to disturb him, she stood quietly for a moment. Then he raised his head, saw her and stopped singing.

'Sorry – I didn't mean ...,' Frances apologised.

'No worries.'

'How is she?'

'She's ... okay. Fine. She's perfect,' he said. 'She's a miracle. A bloody miracle.'

'And how are *you?*'

Neville shook his head and shrugged. 'I'm ... I don't know.'

He looked terrible, she realised: unshaven, bloodshot eyes, sagging skin. He looked like he needed a shower, a shave, and a good night's sleep. 'You should go home,' she said. 'I can stay with Annie for a while.'

He shook his head again, emphatically this time. 'I'm not leaving her.'

'But you need to look after yourself, or you won't be much use to her.'

'I'm not going ... home. I can't go back there. Not yet.'

Of course. His wife was dead. How could he face going home to that empty flat?

Neville's honesty disarmed Frances, transforming her instinctive wariness into empathetic warmth. 'Then I'll have a word with Kamala,' she said. 'Kamala Gupta, the unit manager. She might not have mentioned it to you, but there are rooms here. For parents. There are showers, a kitchen, and a couple of bedrooms. I'm sure she can arrange a room for you for a night or two.'

'Thanks,' said Neville. 'That would be brilliant.'

13

Mark Lombardi's first thoughts, on awakening to his alarm on Monday morning, were happy ones: at long last, he and Callie had a wedding date. She had rung him yesterday evening with the news that they would be getting married in mid-August. In less than three months, he would be starting a new life with the woman he adored. With or without his sister's approval and blessing.

Then, almost immediately, he remembered Neville, and thought with a pang of empathetic pain how he must be feeling. Surely Neville wouldn't be at this morning's briefing on the Chapman murder; he would have to ring him later and repeat his offer of concrete assistance.

But first he needed to get to work. It was a Bank Holiday, but he was a police officer and the Chapman murder took precedence over personal considerations.

He showered, dressed, ate a quick breakfast, then headed for the Holborn tube station as usual.

Mark didn't usually stop to look at the news stand offerings, but something compelled him to do so this morning. And it was the *Daily Globe* to which his eye was drawn, with its screaming headline: 'Illegal Immigrant - Did He Commit Murder?'

He fumbled in his pocket for a pound coin, bought a copy, and read it during his journey.

> ILLEGAL IMMIGRANT - DID HE COMMIT MURDER?
> By Lilith Noone
>
> Mrs Felicity Chapman, aged 56, of Devizes in Wiltshire, was murdered in her room at the Regent Hotel in Paddington last week. An inquest has not yet been held, and no arrests have been made in connection with her death. But this reporter has learned that the Regent Hotel has a history of employing illegal immigrants with NO PAPERS.
>
> One such illegal immigrant, a man from Syria who goes by the name 'Terry', has been employed in the kitchen of the Regent Hotel for over a year, according to informed sources. He went missing from work on the morning after the murder, and his whereabouts are currently unknown.
>
> The manager of the Regent Hotel was unavailable for comment.
>
> Are the police actively searching for this man 'Terry' in connection with the murder? Official police sources declined comment, but if this man is not being investigated, the public will want to know WHY.

It was short, if not very sweet.

There was a sidebar featuring some sketchy information about Felicity Chapman; Mark wondered how that had been obtained.

He soon found out; as soon as he was out of the Underground, his mobile phone rang.

'Sergeant Lombardi?' demanded an aggressive voice.

'Yes.'

'This is Ben Chapman. How the hell did that reporter get my number? Did you give it to her?'

'Of course not.'

Unmollified, the other man went on in the same tone of voice. 'Then how did she get it? Can't everyone just leave us in peace? My mother is dead, for God's sake.'

'Lilith Noone is known for her ... aggressive techniques.'

'And is she right about this immigrant? Did he kill my mother? And are you looking for him?'

Mark sighed. 'I'll have to get back to you, Mr Chapman. I'm on my way right now to a briefing about the case. And it's probably better for everyone concerned if you don't speak any further to Lilith Noone, or any other members of the press,' he added.

Ben Chapman uttered an obscenity – which Mark chose not to take personally – and disconnected.

PETER – in love with a priest.

That was all she needed, Callie reflected.

Peter was in love with a priest, and was seeking not just her acceptance but her approval and wholehearted support.

He wanted her to perform a service of blessing. Not a wedding, but a blessing.

The Church of England's position on the matter was completely muddled yet unswerving: no matter what the law of the land allowed, priests were not permitted to enter into same-sex marriages. If they did so, they would be subject to all sorts of unpleasant consequences up to and including losing their jobs. And while the Church didn't seek to prevent lay people from taking advantage of their legal right to marry a person of the same gender in a civil – not religious – ceremony, it underscored its disapproval by forbidding services of blessing following same-sex marriages or civil partnerships for anyone, clergy or lay.

Peter, who had no great love for the Church of England, didn't care. And evidently Peter's new love was prepared to risk episcopal wrath: not going as far as marriage, but with a civil partnership, followed by a blessing. According to Peter, the blessing was Michael's idea, and Peter had told his lover that if it was going to happen, he wanted Callie to do it.

What a can of worms.

In vain she had tried to explain the Church's official stance to her brother. 'It's not allowed,' she'd said. 'There are no sanctioned forms of service.'

Peter had shrugged that off. 'Michael says he knows for a fact that it happens anyway. He has several friends who have had services of blessing. There are priests who are willing to do it, whether it's allowed or not.'

'Then why don't you just go to one of them? If Michael knows who they are?'

'You're my sister,' he'd said stubbornly. 'Family. It would mean a lot to me, Sis. I mean, I'm going to walk you down the aisle for your wedding, aren't I? It's the least you can do in return.'

She hadn't said yes, but she hadn't managed to say no either. Not in any way that Peter would accept.

Once again, her thoughts turned to Frances – sensible, grounded, experienced Frances.

Frances would know what to do, how to handle it.

On impulse she rang Frances' mobile number and caught her at home.

'Bank Holiday,' Frances said. 'I have the day off, amazingly.'

'I don't,' Callie confessed. 'But I really need to talk to you. Again. This time it's about Peter.'

'Can it wait till this afternoon?'

'Yes, of course. That's better for me – I have my weekly meeting with Brian this morning, Bank Holiday or not.'

'Well, then.' There was a slight pause on Frances' end. 'How about killing two birds with one stone, and hitting the bridal shops? We can find you a wedding dress and talk while we're doing it!'

MARK WAS on his way to the briefing room when he rounded a corner and almost literally ran into Detective Chief Superintendent Evans, coming the other way. 'Oh! Sorry, Sir.'

'Lombardi. Have you seen Stewart?' Evans demanded. 'He's not at his desk. He's not answering his phone.'

Was it possible that DCS Evans didn't know what had happened? 'Uh, Sir, his wife,' Mark stammered.

Evans narrowed his piggy eyes. 'She's had the sprog, I suppose.'

'Well, yes. But ... Triona died, Sir. I thought you would have known.'

'Good God.' The DCS, well known as an uxorious family man, seemed momentarily taken aback. 'That's a damned shame. Bad luck. And the sprog?'

'She seems to be doing okay, Sir, from what I've heard.'

Evans nodded thoughtfully and stroked his enormous chin. 'Well, it's a damned shame,' he repeated. 'But I need Stewart here. See if you can raise him, will you? Tell him to get here as soon as possible.'

IT TOOK a number of seconds for the vibration of the phone in Neville's pocket to percolate through to his sleeping brain and wake him up.

He was, he realised as he struggled to consciousness, sitting in a chair beside Annie's incubator. He must have fallen asleep at some point, overcome by the weariness he'd been ignoring for ... how long? What time was it now? What day was it, even?

The first thing he did, before reaching for his phone, was to check on Annie. She was asleep; she seemed to be fine. With a sigh of relief, he fished for his phone.

Mark Lombardi, he saw on the screen. That was okay.

'Hi, mate,' he said.

'Neville. Where are you?'

'At the hospital. With Annie. Where else would I be?'

There was a slight pause at the other end. 'Well, actually,' Mark said, sounding apologetic, 'Evans is expecting you to be here. At the station. For the briefing. He ... was looking for you. He didn't seem to know about ... what's happened.'

'Bloody hell!' As soon as the words were out of his mouth, he felt guilty, and looked round to make sure that no one had heard him. And he hadn't waked Annie – that was the main thing. 'Sorry. Sorry, mate. I guess I should have rung him. But I just ... didn't think about it.'

'That's completely understandable. But ... can you come? Soon?'

'I need to be here. With Annie,' Neville stated. He put his hand on the incubator.

'The thing is ...' Mark paused. 'The thing is, there are ... developments. The *Daily Globe* is stirring things up. Apparently there's been an illegal immigrant employed at the hotel, and he's gone missing.'

This time Neville kept his voice down, but his words were even more heart-felt. 'Bloody Lilith Noone!'

'I'm afraid so. It's on the front page. Evans is having a coronary.'

Neville closed his eyes and tried to apply some logical thought to the situation. The station was only a few minutes away; he was much nearer to it than he would have been if he'd been at home. With every fibre of his being he felt the necessity of being there with his daughter, but he knew that Annie didn't really need him every second of the day. She was being looked after by competent, caring professionals, and she was in stable condition. And as soon as the briefing was finished he could be back here quickly. He would tell Evans to replace him as SIO, and come straight back to Annie.

'All right,' he said grudgingly. 'Tell Evans I'll be there in a quarter of an hour.'

ALL WEEKEND, ever since they'd returned from Oxford, Brian Stanford had been getting calls from Mildred Channing, demanding to know when he was going to visit her in hospital. He'd managed to put her off till Monday morning, when Jane urged him to go and get it over with.

'You're sure, Janey?' he'd said. 'I can go later if you'd prefer. If you need me here.'

Her morning sickness was relatively mild that morning – and there wasn't anything he could do about that in any case, apart from offer slightly irritating moral support. 'Go,' she said. 'Before your staff meeting.'

But it was time for the staff meeting, and he wasn't back yet.

As luck would have it, Callie was on time. Jane answered the door, as she usually did, and explained the problem to her. 'Brian isn't here,' she said, furrowing her brow, as she admitted Callie to the vicarage. 'He went off on an early hospital visit this morning – Mildred Channing. She was ringing him all day yesterday, wanting to know when he was coming to see her. And he's not back yet.'

Callie nodded, with an understanding smile. 'I went to see her on Friday. She's ... difficult.'

Jane wasn't in the mood for discussing her husband's parishioners with the curate. 'Come in and wait for him,' she invited. 'Would you like something to drink? Tea or coffee?'

'No, thanks.'

She led the way into the sitting room and gestured for Callie to sit down on the sofa. 'How was Simon's wedding?' Callie asked. 'Brian said that it went well.'

Jane smiled involuntarily. 'Oh, it was lovely. Just lovely. It was at the Randolph Hotel, you know. No expense spared. The food was amazing. All vegetarian.' For the next few minutes she carried on in that vein, describing the dishes they'd been served, then moving on to the bride's dress.

'Where did she get it?' Callie enquired. 'Was it in London, do you know?'

'I have no idea,' Jane admitted. 'Oh, that's right. You're getting married, aren't you? Brian said.'

'Yes. In August. Everyone is telling me that I need to get busy planning everything. It's less than three months away. But it will be a small wedding,' she added.

'Simon and Ellie's wedding was small. And her parents planned it ... very quickly. In a matter of days, it seems. We didn't even find out about it until the day before.'

'I don't have anyone to plan my wedding for me.'

'Your mother?'

'She's not that ... interested. I'll be lucky if she turns up on the day.' Callie's voice was light, yet Jane couldn't help but feel that it wasn't really a joke.

'Well, if there's anything I can do ...' Jane offered. It was a typical vicar's wife thing to say, but she regretted the words as soon as they were out of her mouth. What if Callie actually took her up on it?

'Thanks. That's very kind.'

At that moment Brian arrived home, calling as he let himself in the front door. 'Sorry I'm late. I was delayed.' He came into the sitting room, rubbing his hands together. 'Have you heard, Janey? There's been a murder in the parish.'

'A murder?' she echoed, startled. 'Anyone we know?'

'No. It was in one of the hotels in Sussex Gardens. One of the guests, apparently, done in by someone on the staff. Some illegal immigrant who worked in the kitchen, and has gone missing. Anyway, everyone on the wards was talking about it – it was on the front page of today's *Daily Globe*. You can imagine what Mildred Channing had to say. "We shall all be murdered in our beds by foreigners." That sort of thing.'

'Oh!'

Jane turned at the sound from Callie. The other woman had gone very pale, she noted, and she was slumped back against the cushions of the sofa as if suddenly boneless. 'Are you all right?' Jane said.

Callie swallowed visibly; after a few seconds she spoke in a shaky voice. 'Do you think I could have a glass of water?'

NEVILLE HAD SUCCUMBED to a few hours of sleep over the past day or so, and he'd had a shower at some point in the family rooms at the neonatal unit, but he had no change of clothing, and he hadn't shaved since Saturday. So he knew that he wasn't looking like an oil painting, but he wasn't prepared for the level of distaste on the face of the guard at the entrance to the police station – a man who obviously knew him by sight. 'Sleeping rough, are you, mate?'

'Something like that.'

DCS Evans was waiting for him just inside the door. That was a first. His boss looked him up and down, frowned, then seemed to choose his words carefully. 'Well, Stewart, you made it. About time, too.'

Neville grunted noncommittally.

'I'm sorry to hear about ... your wife.'

He wasn't ready to talk about Triona. Not now. He wasn't even ready to think about her, to process the reality of what had happened to her. To him. So he grunted again.

The awkward preliminaries out of the way, Evans turned and headed for the stairs, speaking over his shoulder as Neville trailed behind. 'Lombardi told you about the *Daily Globe*?'

'Yes, sir. Bloody Lilith Noone. As usual.'

'As usual. And there's something else you need to know about, Stewart. Before the briefing.' Evans stopped on the empty landing, where there was no one who might overhear their conversation. 'The SOCO chap was looking for you earlier. He came to me instead, when he couldn't find you. They've run the fingerprints from the hotel room. There were quite a lot of them.'

'Yes?'

'The victim, obviously. And the cleaner – chambermaid, housekeeping, whatever she's called. The Polish girl.'

'She's turned up, then?' Neville realised, to his surprise, that he was actually interested.

'No. But they were able to match her prints to the ones on her cleaning trolley. Pretty straightforward, that.'

Neville nodded, guessing there was more to be revealed.

'Then there were others,' Evans stated. 'A few from the manager.'

He snorted in disgust. 'Wicker. He went in and messed with the crime scene after the cleaner found the body. Bloody idiot.'

'So that's no surprise, either. But there were some very clear prints from someone else, in unexpected places. Mainly on the headboard.'

'Of the bed?' Now he really was interested.

Evans nodded. 'Remind me what the postmortem said about sexual activity?'

He thought back to his conversation with the pathologist. 'None. At least not recent. She wasn't raped or interfered with before or after the murder.'

'That's what I thought. But someone had their mitts on the headboard.'

'And they don't have any idea who it was?'

'I didn't say that, boyo.' Evans narrowed his piggy eyes at Neville. 'They're pretty clever, our SOCOs.'

'Yes?'

'They found the same prints all over the hotel's kitchen.'

'The nephew?' Neville pictured the gormless lad and reached in his memory for the name. 'Les Fielding, is it?'

'No. They took his prints and eliminated him straight away.' Evans waited for Neville to reach the next logical step himself.

The missing man. Terry, Neville dredged up from his memory. That's what the nephew had called him. 'The other bloke, then. Terry.'

Evans grinned. 'Got it in one, boyo. Bloody Lilith Noone's illegal immigrant. She was right, damn her. But find him, and I think we'll have found our murderer.'

PLEADING A HEADACHE, her second imaginary one in just a few days, Callie didn't demur when Brian cancelled their meeting and sent her home.

Part of her, though, didn't want to go back to her flat. What on earth was she going to say to Tariq? She needed time to gather her wits and think through the implications of what Brian had revealed.

She didn't for one second believe that Tariq was a murderer. But she could understand why people would jump to that conclusion, with or without the help of the *Daily Globe*. And that would possibly – probably – include the police. Now, melodramatics aside, she really was harbouring a fugitive from justice.

These things passed through her mind before she reached her flat. Before she did anything else – before she talked to Tariq – she needed to see exactly what the *Daily Globe* had said. Who were their sources? What was their evidence? How did they know about Tariq in the first place?

Putting her key in the lock, she said a quick prayer that she wouldn't have to talk to him right now. And her prayer was answered; he wasn't in the sitting room, so she passed quietly through it and shut herself in her study.

The first thing she did was navigate to the *Daily Globe*'s web site, where the article was displayed front and centre, as the lead story. It was just a short piece, with no named sources and no evidence. Nothing, really, but the *Daily Globe*'s usual xenophobic cocktail of speculation and innuendo. But nonetheless it was worse than she'd imagined: he was mentioned by name, even if they'd got the name wrong. Surely it wouldn't be long before the police discovered his real name, and then ...

She needed to talk to him, and urgently.

Callie found him sitting at the kitchen table, nursing a mug of coffee, his phone on the table in front of him. 'I am so sorry about this, Miss Callie,' he said miserably, before she opened her mouth.

Of course he would know about it: he had a smart phone, and was presumably very adept at using it.

'You must believe me,' Tariq went on. 'I did not do this terrible thing.'

'Of course I believe you,' she assured him. 'But the police will be looking for you now, even if they weren't before. If you just tell them the truth—'

'I cannot!' He raised his head to look at her; Callie observed, with a twist of her heart, that his dark eyes were swimming with tears. 'Don't you see? They know now that I am ... illegal. That I have no papers. That I was breaking the law by working at the hotel. Just by being in this country, I am breaking the law. They will take me away and lock me up. They will send me back to Syria. And I'll never see Zuzanna again. You cannot ask me to do this, Miss Callie!'

THERE WAS NOTHING FOR IT, Neville realised. He was going to have to continue as the SIO. Evans had been sympathetic – uncharacteristically so – about his situation, but he had no inclination to replace him on the case, when they were so close to solving it. 'I want you to find this foreign bastard,' he'd said. 'Wrap this case up. We're nearly there.'

Easy for Evans to say. But how was he going to find him? This was needle-in-a-haystack stuff. London was a vast metropolis, with innumerable places for someone to hide if they didn't want to be found. Hell, the bloke wasn't even necessarily in London. Five days on from the murder, he could be absolutely anywhere. The fact that he'd made it from Syria to London without getting caught meant that he was adept at evading the authorities. And they didn't even know his real name.

After the briefing, Neville sent Sid Cowley back to the Regent Hotel to lean on Wicker and the weasel of a nephew to produce a name other than 'Terry'. But he didn't have much hope of success: Wicker was unlikely to have kept any written records which implicated him in illegal employment activities, and the nephew was clueless as well as gormless.

'I fink it's about time to haul Wicker in,' Sid suggested. 'Frow the bloody book at him, like. Now that we know what the bastard was hiding.'

Sid was right: Lilith Noone's revelations about Wicker's history of employing illegals vindicated Neville's own instincts that the man was hiding something. No wonder he'd been so evasive and slimy. It was tempting to go for an easy, satisfying arrest – but that wasn't addressing their main problem. 'All in good time, Sid,' he said reluctantly. 'Let's find Terry first. Then we'll deal with Wicker.'

So what was the next step?

Because of the Bank Holiday, the inquest would be opened tomorrow, Tuesday. Ordinarily he would have considered calling a news conference following the inquest, hoping that something would come out of that normally perfunctory proceeding which might be of interest to the press and the news media. But it now appeared to Neville that an immediate appeal to the public might yield a result. He had nothing to lose and potentially all to gain – including the approval of the *Daily Globe* – in asking for help to identify the elusive 'Terry'. Yes, he would be admitting that the police didn't know who Terry was; that, he felt, was a price worth paying if it produced any sort of result.

Neville made his decision: he rang the press office and asked them to set up a news conference for that afternoon.

And then, as if drawn by a force over which he had but little control, he headed back to the hospital, the neonatal unit, and Annie.

14

It was a Bank Holiday, but that didn't mean that the Lombardi family restaurant, La Venezia, would be closed: quite the contrary, as it was likely to be a busy day, especially at lunch time. So Mark felt safe in ringing his niece Chiara on her mobile, confident that her mother would be otherwise occupied while Chiara herself was out of school.

'Uncle Marco!' she said, clearly delighted. 'I miss you! We haven't seen you in ever so long.'

'You know why,' he reminded her.

'Mum. And Callie. And the wedding.'

'Has she said anything?'

'No,' Chiara admitted. 'When I mention your name, she changes the subject.'

So Serena hadn't had second thoughts, or reassessed her position. Mamma's intervention had had no effect.

'I don't suppose she'd like me talking to you,' he mused.

'I don't care! Mum is just being horrid.'

At least his sister hadn't been able to turn Chiara against him – he should be grateful for small favours.

'I wanted to let you know that we've set a date for the wedding. It's in the middle of August, during the school holidays.'

'Brilliant! I get to be a bridesmaid, don't I?'

'That's what Callie wants. And what I want, for sure, *Nipotina*,' he added warmly. Of course Serena could – as she'd threatened – forbid it. But that would risk endangering her future relationship with her younger daughter, which he knew was complicated enough at the moment.

'And Angelina?'

'Of course.'

'What about our dresses? Do we get to help pick them out? Can they be pink, maybe? Pink is my favourite colour.'

Mark laughed as her eager questions tumbled out one after another. 'We'll see, *Nipotina*. We'll see.'

BY MID-AFTERNOON, Neville had managed to get a couple more hours of sleep at the hospital. He'd showered, shaved, and made an effort to tidy up his clothing as much as he possibly could. Later, he told himself, maybe he could summon enough courage to go back to his flat and collect some clean clothing. Either that, or go out and buy some new ones.

And he'd drafted a statement for the news conference, sitting beside the incubator with one eye on his tiny daughter.

Most of the time Annie was sleeping. But when she was awake, the nurses allowed him to hold her for a few minutes.

She was so small; she seemed so frail. Her skin was transparent – he could see the blue veins beneath it. But the nurses assured him that she was well, more than holding her own, in no immediate danger.

And she was perfect. Ten grasping fingers, ten flexing toes, each with their minute nails. A pink rosebud of a mouth. Eyes that looked at him without focusing, deep blue as the sea. It was the hair that had surprised him the most: she had lots of it, dark as her mother's. Neville felt that he could gaze at her forever, lost in the wonder of his love for this miraculous, beautiful, vulnerable creature.

'She's a lovely girl,' said Kamala, the unit manager. 'And a fighter. You see? She's already bigger, stronger than she was yesterday. Tomorrow she will be even bigger. Tomorrow maybe I will show you how to change her nappy.'

Tomorrow. Neville wouldn't allow himself to think any further into the future than that. Annie would be stronger tomorrow. That was enough for now.

CALLIE AND FRANCES MET UP, as they'd arranged, at Notting Hill Gate.

'Okay,' said Frances. 'I've googled it. And there are good bridal boutiques all over London. What sort of dress do you fancy?'

'A ... wedding dress?' Callie ventured, baffled.

'But what's your style? Are you looking for "Boho Parisian Chic", "Romantic Decadence", or maybe "Italian Elegance"?'

'Oh. I see what you mean. But ... I don't know. Boho and Decadent don't sound much like me, do they?' She struggled to imagine what either might look like.

'Italian elegance might be appropriate.' Frances smiled.

'Would it make Marco's sister like me any better? I doubt it.' Callie shook her head. 'Is "traditional" one of my choices at all? As in long and white?'

'Oh, we can definitely find traditional. But first,' said Frances, 'let's grab a bite of lunch. You haven't eaten, have you?'

'No,' Callie admitted. She hadn't even thought about food.

'Then we can decide which direction to head. And we can talk. Peter, did you say? I wait with bated breath to hear about your brother's latest ... exploits.' She stopped in front of an upmarket sandwich shop. 'Is this okay?'

'Oh, fine. Whatever.'

They went in and examined the contents of the chiller unit. 'It's a bit picked over,' Frances observed. 'I think I'll go for the chicken and avocado.'

Callie reached for a mediterranean tuna wrap and a bottle of fizzy water. 'My treat,' she offered, heading for the till.

There were plenty of empty tables. They chose one in a corner and unwrapped their sandwiches.

Frances leaned towards Callie across the table. 'Okay. What's all this about Peter?'

'Peter.' She shook her head, finding she didn't have the energy at the moment to go into her brother's woes. Not when there were more pressing matters on her mind. 'That will keep till later. But have you seen this morning's *Globe*?'

'That rag.' Frances frowned. 'It's not a publication I seek out. And I wouldn't have thought that you would, either.'

'I don't, normally. But ... oh, Frances! They know about Tariq!'

JUST BEFORE THE news conference was scheduled to begin, Sid Cowley caught up with Neville and updated him on his visit to the Regent Hotel.

'No joy with the bloke's name, Guv,' he said, pulling a regretful face. 'Though to be honest, we didn't expect anyfing. Wicker's a slimy bastard, and his nephew's fick as shit.'

'Well, thanks for trying, Sid.' Neville patted him on the arm. 'Were you able to find out anything else?'

Cowley reached in his pocket and produced a folded sheet of paper. 'I asked to see the guest register. Wicker didn't want to show it me, but in the end he gave in – he knows that we know he's in deep shit for hiring illegals, so he decided to play ball. He even let me photocopy the page. So we've got the details of everyone who was supposed to be in the hotel that night. I fought we might follow up on them and see if any of them saw anyfing, or anyone—'

'Good job, Sid!' Neville grinned. 'I'm not even going to ask you how you ... persuaded ... him.' He took the paper and stuffed it in his own jacket pocket. 'We'll talk about this after I've finished the news conference.'

The briefing room, he saw, was full to bursting – thanks, of course, to the bloody *Daily Globe* and bloody Lilith Noone. Lilith herself was sitting in the middle of the front row, smirking at him like the cat that got the cream. Neville allowed himself a scowl in her direction as he stepped to the podium and flattened out the crumpled bit of paper on which he'd written his statement.

His head felt like it was going to explode.

'Thanks for coming today,' he began. 'I'm Detective Inspector Neville Stewart, SIO regarding the murder of Felicity Chapman.'

Best to stick to the words he'd prepared; he squinted at the paper and read aloud. 'Mrs Chapman was unlawfully killed on Wednesday night last week, at the Regent Hotel in Sussex Gardens, Paddington. The Metropolitan Police are seeking a man to question in connection with this murder. His full name is not known to us, but he goes by the name of "Terry" and is believed to be of Syrian origin. If anyone has any information regarding this man or his whereabouts, we would urge you to contact us. We would also like to speak to a Zuzanna Dabrowska, an employee of the Regent Hotel, whose whereabouts are also unknown.' He read out the phone number. 'Are there any questions?'

A man towards the back of the room stood up. 'DI Stewart, can you tell us how Mrs Chapman was killed?'

It wasn't a secret. As far as Neville knew, it was on the Met website as a matter of record. 'She was suffocated,' he said.

Another man, identifying himself as a representative of the *Guardian*, stood. 'Mr Stewart, do you have any actual evidence linking this "Terry" to the murder? Or is this just a fishing expedition? Or maybe a witch hunt?'

This was a bit trickier for Neville: he and Evans had decided that the existence of the fingerprint evidence shouldn't be released yet. He realised that this question couched a bit of political point-scoring against the xenophobic *Daily Globe*, and wished he could help in putting Lilith Noone in her place. But he had to shake his head, albeit reluctantly. 'I'm afraid I can't comment on that,' he said.

At that moment Lilith Noone herself rose to her feet, smiling. 'Perhaps I can help, Detective Inspector.'

Neville narrowed his eyes at her. 'Miss Noone?'

'All of us at the *Daily Globe* are deeply concerned that such a dangerous individual remains at large, threatening the innocent population of London,' she said.

'Yes. That's what this news conference is about,' Neville reminded her testily.

'But the police have not yet made any progress in arresting him, or you wouldn't be having this news conference. So we at the *Daily Globe* are prepared to help.' She paused, looked directly at Neville and then turned to face the television cameras at the rear. 'On behalf of the publishers of the *Daily Globe*,' she announced, 'I would like to offer a reward for any information leading to the arrest of the person responsible for the death of Mrs Felicity Chapman. One hundred thousand pounds.'

FRANCES SIPPED coffee from a paper cup – compliments of the house – while Callie was in the changing room, being assisted into the first wedding dress. The coffee wasn't bad, she reflected. Certainly not the worst she'd ever had.

She'd been looking forward to this expedition with Callie, as a distraction from the grim realities of life and death in which she'd lately been embroiled. It was probably also, she recognised, a sort of compensation for the fact that she'd been deprived of shopping for wedding dresses with her own daughter. Heather, in addition to choosing what Frances regarded as a totally unsuitable husband, had married him in America and hadn't even informed her parents until it was a *fait accompli*.

Admittedly, Callie's revelations about her fugitive from justice were hardly conducive to a relaxing afternoon. Frances's thoughts kept returning to that unfortunate young man, terrified and pursued. She had no good advice to offer Callie on the subject, and tried to think what she would do in Callie's place. It would have been difficult enough for Frances to be trapped between her pastoral inclinations and her duties as a citizen under law, but for Callie there was the added complication of Marco. She really was caught in the middle.

The bridal shop assistant – a young girl with a heavily made-up Instagram face – appeared in the waiting room to announce 'So here she comes!'

Callie appeared behind her, wearing a white gown and a doubtful expression.

'So isn't it magnificent?' enthused the girl.

'I'm not sure,' said Callie, looking into the full-length mirror which covered an entire wall of the shop.

'Twirl,' Frances instructed.

Callie twirled. 'It's not quite right,' she said. 'I don't really like the way the sleeves fit.'

'So that can be fixed,' the girl stated. 'Anything can be fixed.'

Frances realised that Callie was now looking at her, awaiting her verdict. 'I think you can do better,' she offered candidly. 'That neckline doesn't really do you any favours.'

'It emphasises my bony collarbone, you mean?'

She shook her head. 'You have a nice long neck. Maybe something with a sweetheart neckline would show it off better. As long as there's not too much cleavage involved,' she added, envisioning the horrified expressions of Jane, Brian and the congregation if Callie were to appear at the altar with quantities of bare flesh on display.

'So maybe we need to keep looking,' said the girl, sighing. She stepped over to the long rack of dresses and pulled one out. 'So how about this one, then?'

NEVILLE LEFT the podium and walked out of the briefing room, virtually into the arms of a waiting DCS Evans.

'We need to talk,' Evans stated. 'In my office.' He gestured with his thumb at Neville, then at Sid Cowley, who was also hovering near the door. 'You too, Cowley.'

'I need to get back to my daughter,' Neville protested.

Evans glowered at him. 'We need to talk,' he repeated. 'Now.'

Bowing to the inevitable, Neville followed his boss up the stairs to his office, but he declined a chair. 'Sir,' he said. 'Could I request – again – to be replaced as SIO on this case? Sid can handle it. He's been in on it from the beginning. And I'd really—'

'Request denied,' Evans cut over the top of him. I want you to see this one through, Stewart.'

'But—'

'No buts.' Evans drew his heavy brows together over his piggy eyes and tried to stare Neville down.

Bastard, Neville said to himself, maintaining eye contact.

After a long moment, Evans was the one who looked away, and he went on in a very different tone of voice. 'Don't think I'm not sympathetic, Stewart. Damn bad luck, what's happened. But the fact is that nothing's going to bring your wife back. She doesn't need you now. And the sprog is in good hands, so she doesn't need you either. I, on the other hand, *do* need you.' He drummed his fingers on his desk. 'We're in the middle of what has suddenly become a high profile murder investigation, and we have to nail it.'

'Lilith Noone,' Sid Cowley put in. 'Maybe the reward ...'

Evans glowered at him. 'Bloody Lilith Noone. We have to do this without any help from the *Daily Globe*, thank you very much.'

Neville tended to agree with him. Lilith Noone's grandstanding had raised the stakes and made it all the more urgent to apprehend the killer. 'Sid has managed to get this,' he told Evans, pulling the folded paper from his pocket. 'A photocopy of the hotel register for the day in question. So we know who else was staying there that night.' He unfolded the paper and looked at it for the first time. Names, addresses, nationalities – as required by law. Even phone numbers, in most cases. It could be very useful, he realised. Assuming that the other guests had been more truthful in providing their details than 'Mary Smith', of no fixed address.

'Good work, Cowley,' Evans said approvingly. 'You should have got it a lot sooner, of course, but better late than never. Now you'd better get busy tracking all of those people down.'

'But Sir,' said Neville. 'We're going to need some help. There are more than a couple of dozen names here. Some of them might not be very easy to find. If you want it done quickly ...'

Evans waved his hand. 'I'm not averse to bringing in a few more people. The trouble is, we're overstretched at the moment and there just aren't that many officers available.'

'Sir,' said Sid Cowley. 'I have a suggestion.'

But before he could voice it, Neville's phone rang. 'Do you want me to answer it, Sir?' he asked.

Evans nodded. 'You'd better.'

He pulled it out of his pocket and saw that the call was from Danny Duffy, the young tech boffin. Pressing the green button, he put the phone to his ear. 'Hello? Danny?'

'Oh, hi, mate. Full marks for switching your phone on. This time, anyway.'

Ouch, thought Neville. 'Ha bloody ha.'

'Anyway, that phone that Sid Cowley gave me to look at?'

'You said you'd get it to it by Tuesday,' he recalled. 'Bank Holiday, and all that.'

'Well, today I got a bit bored. My girlfriend – she and her sister decided to go shopping. Blokes not welcome, assuming I'd want to go anyway. Which I definitely didn't. So I got a bit bored of watching daytime telly, and thought I'd take a look at that phone, just to pass the time.'

'And?' Neville prompted.

'Long story short,' said Danny, 'just like I thought, it wasn't hard to get into.'

'Did you find anything? Anything interesting?' he added.

'Yeah, I think so. That's why I'm ringing, mate. To let you know.'

In spite of himself, Neville felt his pulse quickening. 'Well, spit it out, then.'

'Long story short, I think we've hit paydirt.' Danny chuckled. 'In your investigation, have you by any chance come across a bloke called Julian St Clair?'

'IT'S PERFECT.' Callie twisted around in front of the full-length mirror so she could view the train. 'I love it. What do you think?'

She glanced at Frances, who was nodding her approval. 'It looks wonderful. Really suits your figure.'

Callie had tried on nearly a dozen dresses, none of them quite right. This one hadn't looked like anything special on the hanger, but the moment she'd slipped it on, she knew it was the one for her.

'Are you sure those sleeves won't be too hot in the middle of August?' Frances added. 'They're all right in May, but by August ...'

'They're lacy. I'm sure they'll be fine.' If there was one thing Callie abhorred, it was the fashion for strapless wedding dresses, exposing acres of flesh: arms and shoulders which in many cases should never see the light of day, not to mention cleavage in quantities more suitable to a boudoir – or a bordello. They seemed to her utterly inappropriate for a church wedding, and she was determined to cover herself comprehensively, even in the middle of August.

'Well, if you're sure ... it does look lovely. Marco will be knocked out when you walk down the aisle in that.'

Walking down the aisle. That reminded her of Peter, and the reason she'd asked Frances to meet her in the first place.

She turned to the hovering shop assistant. 'Yes, I'll have this one,' she said decisively, then turned back to Frances. 'I'll get out of this now. And maybe after I've done the paperwork, we could go somewhere for a quick cup of tea. And I can talk to you about Peter.'

'Let's go back to mine,' said Frances. 'I'm all ears.'

BEFORE MARK LEFT work for the day, he rang Ben Chapman once again, and received the usual ungracious reception.

'This had better be important,' Chapman said.

Mark kept his voice pleasant. 'This is a courtesy call, Mr Chapman. I just wanted to bring you up to date on the latest developments.'

'You've found my mother's killer, then?'

'No, not yet. But there was a news conference this afternoon, and it's likely that there will be extensive press coverage over the next day or so. We're hopeful that something positive will come out of that.'

'Just as long as the bloody press leaves me alone. Now if that's all—'

'One more thing,' Mark said. 'The inquest is tomorrow afternoon at the Westminster Coroner's Court. It's a matter of protocol at this point – the inquest will be formally opened, but since we're still in the midst of the investigation, it will be adjourned until a future date.'

'Waste of time, then.'

'You might look at it like that,' Mark acknowledged. 'But if, by any chance, you wished to attend, I would be happy to accompany you, as your Family Liaison Officer.'

'Not a chance,' said Ben Chapman, disconnecting his phone.

THE TEAPOT WAS EMPTY, and Callie had just about run out of words to describe her frustration with her brother.

'Well,' said Frances, shaking her head. 'I would have said that nothing your brother does ever surprises me, but this time he's managed to outdo himself.'

'So what do I say to him? He's going to keep at me until I give in and agree to do a blessing.'

They were in Frances' kitchen, the site of so many heart-to-heart conversations.

'More tea,' said Frances, getting up to re-fill the kettle.

'What do I say to him?' Callie repeated.

Frances leaned back against the sink and faced her friend. 'Well, the Church of England does say that we can offer "prayers". No full-blown service of blessing, obviously – especially since you're not even priested yet – but maybe he'd be satisfied with a little get-together and some prayers. Family, friends. Unofficial, as far as the Church is concerned.'

For a moment Callie saw a hint of light at the end of the tunnel. 'You're brilliant!' she said. 'That might just work.' And then, as she began to envision it, another thought struck her.

'Oh, Frances,' she groaned. 'What on earth will my mother say?'

MARK WAS HALFWAY to to the Tube station when he realised that he didn't really want to go home. It was a Bank Holiday; Geoff would either be out with his mates, in which case the flat would be empty and lonely, or entertaining his mates in the flat – which would be considerably worse.

What he wanted was to be with Callie.

And why shouldn't he?

On impulse, he walked past the station and continued down the Edgware Road to Sussex Gardens. He passed the Regent Hotel, sparing a thought for the events that had transpired there – and for the unfortunate Felicity Chapman.

And then he was at All Saints' Church, which he skirted to get to the church hall behind. As he'd done so many times before, he climbed the stairs to Callie's flat.

As Callie wasn't expecting him, he decided to ring the bell rather than use his key. It seemed strange – in a good way – to think that this would soon be his home as well. In ten weeks or so they would be married. He would move in with her here: it would be so much more convenient for his work. A quarter of an hour on foot versus at least half an hour on the Tube. That was a no-brainer. He would have to remember to tell Geoff – soon – to start looking for a new flatmate.

The door opened. The smile on Mark's face froze for just a second as he looked into the brown eyes of a young man: a young man whose expression of surprise surely mirrored his own.

15

PC Grace Long had the Bank Holiday off, but she hadn't been able to settle to doing anything. Yes, she'd run a few loads of laundry, done the ironing, cooked and served up two meals for her father and her brother, and prepared a third one, which was simmering away in the slow cooker, ready for later. Now she was giving the kitchen floor a good mop. But her mind was elsewhere.

She couldn't stop thinking about that strange triangle: Felicity Chapman, whom she'd never met; Alan Chapman, whom she'd met just the once; and Paige Mason, whom she knew all too well. Felicity was the one who haunted her, though – the poor woman, her illusions of a happy marriage shattered, dead in a hotel room a long way from home.

Why had she needed to die? Who had hated her enough to kill her? Or had there been something else in her life – something Grace had no knowledge of – which had led to her death? Perhaps it had nothing to do with her personally: had she just been the wrong person in the wrong place at the wrong time?

Grace thought about the crime novels she'd read over the years – the motives, the circumstances, the relentless trail of evidence which led the sleuth – amateur or professional – to the correct killer. None of it seemed to apply. Nothing she knew about murder, full stop, seemed to apply to the woman who had died in that London hotel room.

Not that it was any of her business, she reminded herself. Tom Burton had told her that more than once. It was someone else's case, someone else's problem. Yet she *had* been involved, and she couldn't help taking a personal interest.

That sergeant who kept making calves' eyes at her – the smoker with the Cockney accent: he'd given her his number, when his guv wasn't looking, and told her to ring him any time. For just a second Grace contemplated doing just that. She didn't fancy him – not in the least, not in a million years – but maybe she could get him to talk about the investigation.

And then her phone, stuffed in the back pocket of her jeans, bleated out the ring tone which told Grace that her guv wanted her.

JULIAN ST CLAIR.

Neville had never been the most technologically-minded of people, so while Sid Cowley googled around on his phone, Neville dug a London telephone directory out of his desk drawer. He thumbed through the pages till he got to the 'S' section, then ran his finger down a few columns.

'Found him,' he announced with satisfaction. 'St Clair J. The jammy bastard lives in Holland Park Mews.'

'Posh?'

'Dead posh.'

Neville had never had occasion to visit Holland Park Mews, but he knew where it was. His customary drive to work, from his flat in Shepherd's Bush to Paddington Green, took him straight through Holland Park. The neighbourhood was composed of a number of large mansions, including several foreign embassies – out of reach of all but the astronomically wealthy. But between two tree-lined avenues of double-fronted cream-coloured Victorian mansions ran a cobbled road which had once provided accommodation for the horses and carriages of the big houses on either side. These former stables and coach houses had been converted into characterful small dwellings which epitomised the 'des res' of London's aspirational class, selling for well upwards of two million pounds apiece.

'Shall we ring him?' Sid asked, flourishing his phone.

Neville shook his head with a grim smile. 'No, let's take our chances. It's not far. Let's just surprise him.'

OVER THE PAST FEW DAYS, Callie had found herself unsure of the appropriate etiquette at the door of her flat: should she knock, ring the bell, or just let herself in as usual? She got her key out, hesitated for a second, then realised that there were voices inside. The television, perhaps?

She unlocked the door, pushed it open, and stepped into her sitting room.

Tariq was on the sofa, his arm round Zuzanna, pressing her against his side.

And sitting across from them, Bella at his feet, was Marco.

They all turned to look at her. Bella thumped her tail.

'Hello, *Cara Mia*,' said Marco.

GRACE PROPPED the mop against the fridge, pulled the phone out of her back pocket, and pushed the button. 'Tom?'

'Gracie, sweetheart,' her guv said. 'Sorry to bother you on your day off.'

'That's okay,' she said automatically. 'What's up?'

'The thing is ...' He cleared his throat and started again. 'The thing is, I've had a phone call. From London.'

Her pulse quickened. 'About Felicity Chapman?'

'Yeah, that's right. Have you seen the telly, then?'

'The telly? No. What's happened?'

Tom Burton sighed. 'There was a news conference, apparently. In connection with the murder. It's been all over the telly. Especially down here, like. Seeing as she was local.'

She would be able to find it on her phone, then. 'And?' she prompted, willing him to get on with it so she could start looking.

'Well, the thing is, they're short-staffed. Like all police departments,' he added with a snort. 'And they need someone to, like, help with interviews and such. Tracking down the people who were staying at the hotel that night and interviewing them. That's what they told me.'

'And?'

'And they've asked for you, sweetheart. On secondment.'

Grace's heart thudded; her pulse quickened. 'Me? They want *me*?'

'They said you've been very helpful.' The reluctance and scepticism in his voice were obvious. 'Very nice, I'm sure, but I told them you couldn't do it.'

'You told them *what*?'

'There's your dad, for starters. You wouldn't want to be leaving him to look after himself, would you, sweetheart? And you've got your job to do here – I mean, what am I supposed to do without you? Lots of quad bikes get stolen this time of year, and this warm weather brings out all sorts. I told them there was more than enough to keep you busy in Wiltshire, thank you very much. London is no place for the likes of you.'

'London,' she echoed, stunned. 'They want me to go to *London*?'

'Tonight. Isn't that barmy? It's out of the question, and I told them so,' he said, adding reluctantly, 'but I promised I'd ask you, like.'

Grace took a deep breath. 'Well, you can ring them back, whoever "they" are. And you can tell them that I'm packing my bag.'

After his last high-profile murder case, Neville had hoped he'd never have to encounter Facebook again. But Danny Duffy's discoveries on Felicity Chapman's phone had brought him straight back into the realms of social media.

'I hate Facebook,' he stated with some ferocity. They were in the car, on the way to Holland Park but crawling along in rush-hour traffic.

'But Guv,' said Cowley. 'Just fink. If it wasn't for jolly old Facebook, we wouldn't have known nuffing about this St Clair cove. I mean, he must be in the picture. Stands to reason.'

'We'll see.' Neville frowned, fearing Sid's optimism was premature. Yet he had to admit to himself that the contents of Mrs Chapman's phone had provided a significant – and completely unexpected – development in the case.

Julian St Clair's name had not come up in their investigation because, it was obvious, no one else they'd interviewed knew of his existence. Felicity Chapman's husband certainly didn't, nor her son, and if she had talked about him to her taxi-driver friend Maggie, Maggie hadn't attached sufficient importance to him to mention it.

'Didn't I say from the start that there must be another bloke in the picture?' Sid reminded him smugly. 'And now we've found him.'

What they'd learned from the phone – to be specific, from a series of messages on the Facebook Messenger app – was that Felicity Chapman had been in touch with Julian St Clair for several weeks. He had initiated the contact, and although she had accepted his request to be a Facebook 'friend', at the start she had rebuffed his invitation to meet him. Everything had changed, though, on that day last week when she left Devizes and travelled to London. The day she'd found out that her husband was sleeping with his secretary.

She had sent a message to St Clair, telling him that she was on her way to London. He had responded with a suggestion that they meet up that evening, and she had agreed. A further message from him proposed a meeting place: a wine bar between Notting Hill and Paddington. 'Lots to catch up on,' he'd said. With a winking emoji.

A few minutes after that, as recorded on her phone, Felicity Chapman had sent the text to her son cancelling her visit to stay with him in Chelsea. And that afternoon she had – they knew – arrived at the Regent Hotel and paid cash for one night's lodging.

The exchange of messages with St Clair suddenly made sense of all of that. It was the missing piece of the puzzle, explaining actions which Neville – as well as Alan Chapman – had found inexplicable.

Neville realised that he was, in a perverse way, looking forward to meeting Julian St Clair. 'You may be on to something this time, Sid,' he acknowledged. 'Mr St Clair certainly has some questions to answer.'

CALLIE SAGGED into the nearest empty chair, trying to get her head round what she was seeing. Tariq, Zuzanna, and ... Marco? In the same room?

'You've introduced yourselves?' she asked weakly.

'We have,' said Marco. 'Your ... friends ... have been telling me how they come to be here. In residence, as it were.'

He sounded more baffled than angry, Callie thought. But she realised, almost immediately, that she'd never seen Marco when he was truly angry. Just a couple of times she'd observed the aftermath of his anger – enough to know that she wouldn't want to be there when his normally placid temper was riled to the breaking point. Before she could think of what to say, Zuzanna spoke.

'Miss Callie – she is very kind.' She stroked Tariq's arm. 'Tariq have nowhere to go to. I ask Miss Callie for help. She say he can stay.'

'It's my job,' Callie said.

Marco turned to face her. 'Does Brian know that you're ... harbouring fugitives?'

'No,' she admitted. 'No one knows.' Apart from Frances, she said to herself. Now was not the moment to confess that exception.

'You do realise that the police are looking for these people? As a matter of some urgency?'

She couldn't lie to Marco. Not now. Callie gulped and nodded, maintaining eye contact with him. 'It's my job,' she repeated.

HOLLAND PARK MEWS was accessed through a rather grand arch at one end. Neville manoeuvred the police car through the narrow gap and into the cobbled road.

'Cor,' breathed Sid.

'Quite.'

The flat-fronted two-storey dwellings in the facing terraces were all different – some plain brick, some painted white or cream, with doors of varying colours – but the overall effect was of a pleasing unity. They all had large garage doors at ground level and external flights of steps leading sideways to first-floor entrances. Neville drove along slowly until he found the number he was looking for, then pulled up on the yellow line, in between two of the garage doors.

'Garages like that in Central London,' Cowley said, shaking his head wonderingly. 'I'd guess there are some tasty little motors behind those doors. I wouldn't half like to have a butcher's.'

'Beemers, Jags, the lot,' Neville agreed. 'Not for the likes of us.'

Cowley behind him, he mounted the steps leading up to the door, painted a glossy black to match the garage. The narrow rectangular landing at the top was fenced in with black wrought-iron railings and contained a few pots with exotic stripey tulips.

Neville rang the bell. After a moment the door swung open. 'Julian St Clair?' he said, quickly assessing the man before him. He was in well-preserved middle age, with fair hair shading to silver at the temples and a neatly-trimmed beard to match; he wore what looked to be expensive jeans, a fine cashmere jumper, and an expression that could only be described as smug.

'Detective Inspector Stewart.' His voice was just as posh as his appearance.

'How—'

The man gave him a self-satisfied smile. 'I've seen you on the telly, of course. The news conference.' He waved his arm in a sweeping gesture of welcome. 'Do come in. I've been expecting you.'

'It's my job,' Callie had said, and Mark understood where she was coming from – of course he did. It *was* part of her job to look after other people, especially those within her parish. Her pastoral heart was one of the things he loved about her. But at this moment her duty to her job was in direct opposition to *his* job – his duty – and he couldn't just ignore that. He wasn't sure, at this point, what he ought to do; he only knew that he couldn't turn a blind eye.

Callie continued to look at him; he didn't look away, choosing his words carefully. 'And now it's *my* job, too. I'm sorry, *Cara mia*. I understand why you've protected them, but I can't be a party to that.'

The blonde woman – Zuzanna Dabrowska – started to cry, noisily and extravagantly. 'Don't arrest us!' she sobbed. 'Oh, please! Don't take us away!'

Mark didn't want to arrest them. Nevertheless, he was part of the team trying to solve a murder case in which this couple were significant material witnesses. One of them could even be described as a chief suspect, based on the fingerprint evidence.

He knew that he *should* arrest them, take them into custody, and turn them over to Neville for questioning as soon as possible. Nevertheless, under Callie's imploring gaze, he hesitated.

Perhaps he could ask them some preliminary questions himself, find out to what extent they were willing to co-operate voluntarily before taking the step of arresting them. It was clear that they'd been deliberately hiding from the police for days, but maybe the threat of arrest would be enough to get them talking.

'Could I speak to you for a moment?' Callie suggested quietly, perhaps sensing his hesitation. 'In the kitchen?'

Mark nodded. Relieved to escape, even temporarily, from Zuzanna's wailing, he followed her and shut the door behind them.

'Zuzanna is very afraid,' Callie said. 'That's why they're here. That's why they've been hiding. She's afraid that Tariq will be deported, that she'll never see him again.'

'Yes, but—'

'He's illegal. I'm sure you know that. But she loves him, Marco. And he loves her.' Callie took a step closer to him, reached out a hand and stroked his cheek, sorely testing his professional resolve. 'They're deeply in love. Like us. I can't even imagine what it would feel like, knowing that the person you loved could be taken away from you forever.'

Mark wanted to hold Callie in his arms and assure her that it would be all right. He couldn't do that – nor could he tell her the classified information about Tariq's fingerprints, so he chose his next words carefully. 'He's a suspect, Callie. The strongest suspect we have at the moment. And there are good reasons for that.'

Callie recoiled. 'But he didn't do it, Marco! He's innocent! You must know that!'

She was right that what he had seen of Tariq didn't square with the picture of a man who would murder a woman in cold blood. Mark reminded himself about the fingerprints. 'There is ... evidence ... linking him with the crime scene. Trust me, *Cara mia*.'

Callie shook her head. 'No. That can't be right. There will be an explanation. Tariq told me he had nothing to do with that woman's death. And I believe him.'

JULIAN ST CLAIR's home proved to be as sleek and fashionable as the man himself. The front door opened straight into a modern open-plan living area, with a kitchen at the back; a half-open door to the side revealed a glimpse of an elegant bedroom, decorated in shades of grey. From his own recent experiences in the property market, Neville understood that this was the the height of chic, and came at an enormous price.

'Would you chaps like a drink?' St Clair offered, as he ushered them to the cosy seating area. 'Or is that not allowed when you're on duty?'

Neville would have loved a drink – the stronger, the better. 'Very kind, but no thanks,' he said reluctantly.

'Tea, then, or coffee?'

'No, thanks.' He glanced at Cowley, who was staring round him at the understated elegance, his mouth open. 'We're fine, aren't we, Sid?'

'Uh, yeah. Fine.' Cowley shut his mouth, sat down on one of the chairs indicated by their host, and pulled out his notebook.

'Well, welcome to my home, Detective Inspector. And your colleague is ... ?'

'Detective Sergeant Sid Cowley,' Neville supplied.

St Clair nodded as he sat down. 'I imagine you have a few questions you'd like to ask me.'

This was not, Neville reflected, the sort of welcome they were used to in their line of work. It unsettled him, made him profoundly uneasy. Which was presumably exactly what Julian St Clair intended. 'Yes, Mr St Clair. Regarding Mrs Felicity Chapman.'

'Ah, Fliss.' St Clair shook his head. 'Very sad business, that.'

'You did know her, then?'

'Many long years ago, Detective Inspector. At school. We were ... I suppose what you would call sweethearts.'

Not what *he* would call it, thought Neville. Or Sid, who would probably have an even cruder description.

'You were ... intimate? Lovers?'

'Oh, no, Detective Inspector.' St Clair's mouth twisted. 'Those were more innocent days. Not that I didn't want to be,' he added. 'But Fliss was very ... proper. She was saving herself for marriage. Girls did in those days, you know. Well brought up ones, anyway.'

'But you didn't want to marry her.'

'Oh, but I did want to.' St Clair tented his fingers together and contemplated them. 'Very much. And she would have married me. Fliss was very ... fond of me. It was her parents who didn't think I was up to the mark. They made that very clear. And they sent her away – supposedly to a better school. But I knew exactly what they were about.' He shrugged. 'She met someone else, of course. Someone more suitable. She married that solicitor chap. Years ago.'

'And you never saw her again?' interposed Cowley.

'Not until last week. But in the mean time ...' He swept his arm round. 'I did rather well for myself, as you see. In the beginning I wanted to show her parents how wrong they were about me. I got a good job. Spent years in the middle east – oil, you know. Eventually started up my own business. I married. Twice. Neither one of them lived up to Fliss, so two failed marriages. Last year I sold up my business, came back to London.'

'And you contacted Felicity Chapman?' Neville asked.

'A few weeks ago. On a whim. I was reminiscing about her, looked on Facebook, and there she was. So I sent her a friend request. And she accepted.' He smiled. 'But you'll know all of this, presumably. From her phone. That's why you're here.'

'You asked her to meet you.' It was a statement, not a question.

St Clair nodded. 'As you know. And she said no, as you will also know.' For just a second he seemed to hesitate, then went on. 'There is one thing you may not know, though. We spoke on the phone, just once. I tracked down her mobile number and rang her.'

Neville sat up straighter; this was indeed something they didn't know.

They had all of the Facebook messages, and all of her texts, but hadn't had the chance yet to check through the records of her phone calls. 'And what did you talk about?'

'I told her that I wanted to see her – that my marriage was over, I was back in London, and I couldn't stop thinking about her.'

'And she said ... ?'

St Clair's mouth twisted. 'She told me in no uncertain terms that she was happily married and not looking for anything on the side. But she did say that if things had been different ...' He sighed. 'I felt she'd left the door open, just a crack. I still had a tiny bit of hope.'

'You didn't contact her again?'

'I didn't need to, did I? It wasn't much more than a week later that she messaged me to say she was on her way to London. She agreed to meet me, and I suggested a wine bar. But you'll know all that, Detective Inspector.'

'So you met her there,' Neville stated.

'She got there first. She was waiting for me.' St Clair smiled smugly. 'And she looked ... delicious. She'd been to the hairdresser's, she'd had her nails done. She was wearing her pearls, a silk dress, heels. She was dressed up for *me*. It was like we'd never been apart, like all of those years in between hadn't happened. Like we were both sixteen again. And I wanted her desperately, all over again.'

'So you took her back to her hotel room and killed her?' Cowley interrupted. 'I suppose it could have been an accident. A sex game gone wrong? Is that what happened?'

St Clair shook his head, laughing mirthlessly. 'You must be joking, Sergeant. Didn't you hear what I was just saying?'

16

Mark made up his mind. 'Listen,' he said to Callie. 'I'll talk to them. But I want you to stay here in the kitchen. 'And,' he added, as her face lit up with hope, 'I'm not making any promises.'

Callie gave a reluctant nod.

'You'll have to trust me,' he repeated.

'I do.'

Mark took a deep breath, planted a quick kiss on Callie's forehead, then returned to the sitting room. He resumed his seat; Bella leaned against his leg. Zuzanna Dabrowska fell silent, staring at him with huge, imploring eyes.

'I need to ask you both some questions,' he said.

They nodded in unison; Tariq's arm tightened round Zuzanna's shoulders.

'And I expect you to tell me the truth,' Mark added. 'Zuzanna, you found Mrs Chapman's body?'

Her face crumpled, the welling tears threatening to erupt into another weeping session. 'Yes,' she gulped. 'Was terrible.'

'You knew she was dead?'

'Oh, yes.'

'Did you touch her?'

She shook her head. 'No! I scream. I scream more, until Mr Wicker, he come.'

'And Mr Wicker touched her?'

'Yes. He grab her arm, he touch her neck. Then he say she is dead for sure. I ... I run away then.' She looked down, as if ashamed of her flight. 'Mr Wicker, he follow me. He tell me, go home. Do not come back. Not tomorrow. Not next day. Not until he ring me, tell me come back.'

'And you haven't been back?'

'No!'

Mark had no reason to disbelieve her account; it fit in with what the hotel manager had told Neville – at least up to the point of Wicker sending her away. And that part of it was entirely consistent with Neville's assessment of Wicker: a 'slimy bastard', Neville had called him.

'What about you, Tariq? I know that you work in the hotel kitchen. Why did you run away?'

The young man's face darkened. 'I didn't run away. Like Zuzanna, he sent me away. Wicker. He told me to take all of my belongings and clear out, until he rings to tell me to come back.'

Mark listened, with growing sympathy, as Tariq described his living arrangements. It was obvious that he had been exploited by the hotel manager, who had taken advantage of his desperate situation and then done everything he could to cover his tracks. Hiring illegal immigrants was a serious matter; Wicker could face severe consequences.

And presumably would, in due course, now that it was all over the front page of the *Daily Globe*. Mark reflected, just for a second, that he wouldn't want to be in the shoes of the person who had been Lilith Noone's source.

NEVILLE GLARED AT COWLEY. 'Shut it, Sid,' he said, then turned back to Julian St Clair. 'So what happened?'

He tented his fingers again and studied them as he spoke. 'We talked. We flirted a bit. We shared a bottle of wine. Then she told me that her husband – her perfect, wonderful husband – was having an affair. With his secretary. His *young* secretary. She'd just found out that morning.

Which explained everything – why she'd changed her mind about seeing me. So at that point I figured ... well, you can guess.'

He guessed. 'You thought she'd go to bed with you.'

St Clair glanced at him with a wry smile, then looked back at his fingers. 'It was a reasonable expectation, in the circumstances. And I really wanted her,' he added. 'We ... kissed. It was good. Very good. It was obvious that she wanted me, too.'

'What happened?' Neville repeated.

'I suggested that we go back to her hotel room. She was staying quite nearby, she'd told me. But she didn't want to. She said it wasn't a very nice hotel. Too sordid, she said.'

Remembering the small, shabby room, Neville couldn't help nodding. It wasn't the sort of place Julian St Clair was accustomed to employing for a romantic rendezvous, he was certain.

St Clair ran his fingers through the silver hair at his temples. 'I'd told Fliss that I lived not far away. So she suggested coming here instead.'

That seemed an entirely logical scenario; Holland Park Mews was a mere stone's throw from Paddington. 'And?'

His mouth twisted. 'It wasn't an option, unfortunately.'

'Why not?'

'Because my wife was here.' St Clair put his hand up to forestall the next question. 'Yes, I know I said that my marriage was over. And it was. It *is*. But not legally. Not yet. I'm still married. And she was here. So I had to come clean with Fliss.'

'And she didn't like that?' Neville guessed.

'She went batshit crazy.' St Clair's mobile face sagged into a frown. 'She accused me of being dishonest with her, of leading her on, of exploiting her vulnerability. And ... she was right. I didn't tell her the whole truth, because I wanted her. And I tried to explain that. But she turned out to be the same old Fliss I used to know – too prim and proper by half. She started spouting all the usual stuff about the sanctity of marriage. Then she stormed out. And ... that was it.'

It was time for Mark to get down to brass tacks, but he knew he needed to do it very carefully; he had to avoid both avoid scaring Tariq off, and saying anything that would compromise the investigation.

'So, Tariq,' he said. 'Were you there on Thursday afternoon when Zuzanna found the body? Anywhere in the hotel?'

The young man shook his head. 'No. Not in the afternoon. My work ... it is just in the morning, you understand. For breakfast. I prepare the food, put everything out, clear it up at the end of breakfast, and make things ready for the next morning. So I am usually free in the afternoon.'

'And what do you do, every afternoon? Do you always leave the hotel?'

Tariq hesitated for just a second. 'I would not want to stay there,' he said. 'It is ... not a very nice place. There is the staff room downstairs, and there is the store room where I sleep. Neither is a good place. So I go out. I walk a lot. All over London. London is a very nice city for walking.' He flashed his teeth in a brief smile. 'And there are good galleries, museums, lectures. All around London. All for free. I have become a cultured man in London, even with no money.'

Mark smiled back, in spite of himself. 'Sounds like a good way to fill your days.'

'Later I go back to the hotel. When Zuzanna finishes her work. Then we can spend some time together, before she goes home.'

'Where? Where do you spend time together?'

Tariq glanced at Zuzanna, squeezed her hand, then turned back to Mark. 'Outside, in nice weather. We walk in the parks. In bad weather we sit in the staff room. But outside is better.'

It was time to slip in the crucial question. 'You don't go into the upstairs hotel rooms, then? Like the room where Mrs Chapman was staying?'

'No,' Tariq said quickly. 'Downstairs only.'

'Have you ever been in the room where Mrs Chapman was murdered?'

It was direct, and it was effective. There was a sharp, indrawn breath from Zuzanna, even as Tariq pressed his lips together, then said 'No.'

'Never?'

He shook his head. 'No. Never.'

SHE WAS on her way to London.

Grace could scarcely believe it.

Two hours ago she'd been mopping the kitchen floor. Now she was sitting on the Great Western mainline train, heading for the nation's capital.

Up till now, she had been to London exactly once in her life: a Year Six school trip. The coach had delivered them to the Tower of London, and after the tour of that thrillingly grim edifice they'd embarked on a boat which had taken them along the river to Westminster Bridge, where the coach had collected them again. Her abiding memories of that day were the ravens in the Tower, the Beefeaters in their colourful uniforms – she'd made the mistake of calling them costumes, and been sharply corrected – and hearing Big Ben strike the hour before re-boarding the coach. A few brief hours in London, then back in her own bed that night.

And now here she was, London-bound. Her brother, bless his heart, had driven her to Pewsey station to catch the train. He'd promised to look after their dad as best he could. 'You'll do a grand job, whatever it is,' he'd told her, as her nerve nearly failed her at the very last minute, stepping from the platform into the carriage. 'I'm proud of you, Gracie.'

That had spurred her on, past the doubts which suddenly assailed her. Should she leave her father? Was it right and fair to abandon him to her brother's well-meaning but not always top-notch care? Could she really do what was being asked of her, with her limited experience in criminal investigation?

She'd stowed her bag – which had once belonged to her mother – in the luggage rack and snagged herself a seat at a table. Opening her book, she tried to read but found her eyes travelling over the same paragraph again and again, uncomprehending. So she closed it and checked her phone. Nothing.

Across the table from her was a girl about her own age with extraordinary hair in graduated shades of pink, pale at the scalp and a deep fuchsia at the ends, as if it had been dip-dyed. The girl rummaged in her backpack, set up a mirror on the table, then plopped a large, glittery makeup bag beside it.

For the next half-hour, Grace watched in fascination as the girl pulled brushes, tubes and pots from the bag and constructed her face, one painstaking layer at a time, staring intently at her image and seemingly oblivious to anyone or anything else. She started as a rather plain specimen, neither uglier nor more beautiful than the average girl on the street. By the time she finished, her face was a mask of perfection, worthy of any catwalk. The process was unlike anything Grace had ever observed. Her own make-up routine was quick and utilitarian: a few strokes of eye shadow, a flick of mascara, a dab of lip gloss, and if she felt like it and had the time perhaps a dusting of powder to minimise her freckles.

'The next stop is Reading,' announced a disembodied, crackly voice. 'If you are leaving the train at Reading, please remember to take all of your belongings with you.'

The pink-haired girl efficiently swept all of her equipment back into the glittery bag, stuffed it in her backpack, and slid out into the aisle, never once making eye contact with Grace. A moment later the train slowed, stopped, and the tannoy crackled into life again. 'This is Reading. The next stop is London Paddington.'

TARIQ WAS LYING.

Mark knew it, and he thought it probable that Tariq knew that he knew it.

The SOCOs had been thorough; they had provided all the evidence the police needed to prove that Tariq had indeed been in Room Nine – the room where Felicity Chapman had died.

Yet Tariq was looking him in the eye, doubling down on his assertion that he had never been there.

Neville wouldn't thank him if he asked the wrong question now. Perhaps it was best to stop right here, formally arrest and caution the fugitives, and turn them over to Neville to deal with. Callie wouldn't be happy about it – to say the least – but he'd given Tariq the opportunity to tell the truth, and he had nonetheless lied.

Mark took a deep breath; Tariq finally looked away.

'I'm afraid I'm going to have to ask you to come with me to the police station now,' he said quietly. 'And I'm going to caution you that—'

'No!' Zuzanna shrieked. 'No!'

'I asked you to tell me the truth.'

'I will tell truth!' Zuzanna shrugged off Tariq's encircling arm, jumped to her feet, and took a step closer to Mark. 'Yes, Tariq was in room. But not for killing that lady. Not to kill anyone!'

'Zuzanna, you don't have to—' Tariq began.

'Yes! Yes, I must!' She held her hands out towards Mark. 'Mr Mark, you understand this. You love Miss Callie. Yes?'

'Yes, I do.'

'So you understand.'

All of a sudden, he did.

Mark knew why Tariq had been in Room Nine. And why he had been reluctant to tell the truth about it. 'You were there ... together,' he said.

She nodded. 'Together. For ... making of love.'

An empty hotel room, two people in love. Two people who had nowhere else to go to be together. It all made perfect sense. And fingerprints ... on the headboard of the bed. And a man lying about it, trying to protect the reputation of the woman he loved.

'We cannot go to my bedsit,' she said. 'My sister, she would be angry. Krysia would not understand. But you understand.'

'Was it that day? Wednesday?'

She considered the question, counting on her fingers. 'Today is Monday? Yes, was Wednesday. Room was not ... how you say? Occupied? And not Reserved. Lady not come till later. Till afternoon.'

So they'd thought the room was vacant. Safe.

'Was my idea,' she stated. 'Tariq, he finish work. Room was clean. And ... empty. I want to show Tariq I love him. I tell him to come to room.' She smiled shyly, radiantly, eyes downcast. 'Was first time.'

NEVILLE WAS DEAD TIRED, exhausted to the bone. Shattered, knackered. All he wanted to do was go ... home?

No, not home. Back to the hospital, to the neonatal unit. To hold his daughter, tell her he loved her, and then to sleep. Hopefully for a very long time.

First, though, he had to drive Sid Cowley back to the station, and drop off the car.

And Sid was buzzing.

'I fink he did it,' said Cowley. 'Julian bloody St Clair. Smooth bastard. He went back to the hotel wif her, and when she changed her mind and wouldn't let him shag her, he killed her.'

Neville sighed. 'What about fingerprints?'

'Maybe he wore gloves. Or ... listen, he's a law-abiding bloke. Up till now, anyway. His dabs wouldn't be on file. We can send someone over straightaway to take them. I fink we've got him, Guv. The SOCOs will have found something to tie him to the scene. If not dabs, then somefing else. Mark my words. He's our bloke. I always said it would be anovver man, didn't I?'

It was always about sex with Sid. Neville shook his head. 'I think you're jumping the gun a bit. I admit he's a slippery piece of work, and I'm not convinced he was telling us the whole truth. But we're a long way from having a case against him.'

'We can check with the wine bar, Guv. Find out if anyone saw him leave with her. And at the bloody hotel. Don't they have someone on duty at night? Or CCTV in the lobby?'

If there had been someone on duty at the Regent Hotel, monitoring the comings and goings, or indeed CCTV cameras, they probably would have solved this case by now. Neville was too tired to summon the words to point this out.

He pulled into the station car park. Five minutes – ten minutes, tops – and he would be holding Annie.

His phone buzzed in his pocket. He waited until the car was safely parked in its allotted slot, then – against his better judgement – reached for the phone.

The call, he saw, was from Mark Lombardi. It was probably to remind him about something he certainly didn't want to think about:

now that the Bank Holiday was over, he would need to register Triona's death, talk to a funeral director, and tackle all the distasteful red tape that Mark was so expert at dealing with.

He pushed the button to answer the call. 'Tomorrow, mate,' he said, before Mark could speak. 'I can't even think about it tonight.'

There was an intake of breath, then silence on the other end.

'The funeral,' he amplified. 'I know we need to get the ball rolling. And it's good of you to remind me. But we'll deal with it tomorrow.'

'Uh, no.' Mark spoke quietly. 'That's not why I'm ringing. Not at all. I don't know where you are, Nev, but you need to come to the station. I have someone here that you'll want to talk to.' He paused, then amended, 'No, that you *need* to talk to.'

'London Paddington,' the tannoy announced. 'This is our final destination. All change.'

Grace took a deep breath and remained in her seat for a moment as the train slowed to a stop. Everyone else was getting up, collecting possessions, stowing phones, retrieving luggage.

Someone would meet her, she'd been told. During the last part of the journey she'd received a text to clarify further: by the Paddington Bear statue, on Platform 1. Under the clock.

The train had come in on Platform 1; that would make it easier. Grace's anxiety levels were high enough without the prospect of wandering round the huge station in search of the meeting place – and the unknown person who would be waiting for her.

The carriage cleared out rapidly. Through the window she could see that Platform 1 was thronged with people in a hurry, dragging cases. Grace stood, then pulled her bag down from the overhead rack. She slung her handbag over her shoulder, pulled up the handle of the case, and negotiated the narrow aisle to the carriage door.

Paddington Station was vast – larger than she'd ever imagined. Overwhelming, for a girl from Devizes. So many people, all of whom seemed to know where they were going, and were in a rush to get there.

Grace spotted the clock, suspended above the platform. Beneath it was the bronze statue of Paddington Bear, wearing his distinctive hat, sitting on his case. The crowds who had disgorged from her train streamed round it on either side without a glance, a minor annoyance in the single-minded rush to the ticket barrier, the rest of the station. And London.

Just a bit off to the side, out of the way of the relentless procession of travellers, a woman was standing, scanning the crowd. She was far from inconspicuous, and hard to miss: she was tall, dark-skinned, and wore her hair in a multitude of tiny braids. Her jacket was a riot of colour: orange swirls and hot pink curlicues, interspersed with lime green leaves.

Grace stopped in front of her and the woman smiled, a grin which lit her eyes and transformed her face. 'You're PC Long?'

She nodded. 'Grace Long.'

'Welcome to London, Grace Long.' The woman enveloped her in a fragrant and enthusiastic hug, released her, then grabbed the handle of her case. 'I'm Yolanda Fish, lovie. I'm going to look after you. And I can tell already that we're going to get along just fine.'

17

Callie's first thought when she woke on Tuesday morning was about the utter deliciousness of waking up next to a warm body, and even more so when that body belonged to Marco rather than Bella. She snuggled close to him sleepily and breathed in the slightly spicy scent of his skin. Soon they would be married, and this would be commonplace rather than unusual, but she hoped she would never lose this delight in his nearness.

And then she remembered why he was there in her bed. Suddenly she was wide awake.

It had been a very long night. Or a very short one, depending on how you looked at it.

She'd been alone for much of it. Marco had explained to her that he had no choice but to take Tariq and Zuzanna to the station for formal questioning by Neville Stewart. They were important material witnesses; Tariq was linked by evidence to the crime scene and had not been truthful about it. Callie had wanted to go with them, but Marco had vetoed that. He'd promised to come back and tell her what happened and he'd kept that promise, though it was very late when he arrived, and he'd virtually fallen into her bed, exhausted.

All she'd managed to get out of him before he fell asleep was that

Tariq and Zuzanna were still at the station but had not been charged with any crimes. Yet.

She kissed Marco's shoulder; he stirred, turned over, and opened his eyes. 'Cara mia!'

'Good morning, Marco.'

'What time is it?' His voice sounded panicky.

'Still early.' She peered at the clock on the bedside table. 'Just past six.'

He sighed. 'Good. I was afraid I was going to be late.'

'You have plenty of time.' She smiled. 'And so do I.'

'Good,' he repeated, stroking her face, returning her smile, leaning towards her for a kiss.

Callie resisted temptation. 'First you have to tell me. All about last night. At the station.'

He sighed and flopped onto his back. 'Okay.'

'Tell me everything.' She pillowed her head on his chest, listening to the steady beat of his heart.

Marco put his arms round her. 'It was ... intense. Neville got there quite quickly. He'd been tracking down another lead. He questioned them separately – Zuzanna first, then Tariq. Once Tariq got over being noble, trying to protect Zuzanna's honour, their stories matched up. They were in that hotel room for one thing only, and it wasn't murder.'

Callie could only imagine how upset and terrified they must have been, and wished again that she'd been able to accompany them for moral support. 'So what happens now? Did Neville believe them? If he did, why didn't he release them?'

'I think he believed them. But they're still material witnesses, even if they're innocent of murder. Neville still has a lot of questions that need answering. And don't forget that Tariq is ... undocumented.'

Callie groaned. 'This is just what they were afraid of – that he'd be deported. Back to Syria.'

'They're a long way from that happening,' Marco said reassuringly. 'I do think Neville was planning to let Zuzanna go home to her sister last night, eventually. But Tariq doesn't actually have a permanent fixed address, apart from the Regent Hotel.'

'He could have come back here.'

Marco shook his head. 'No way Neville was going to allow that.' He stroked her cheek. '*Cara mia*, it's out of your hands now. I understand that you were trying to help, to do your best for Zuzanna and Tariq, but there's nothing more you can do at this point.'

LILITH HAD ALLOWED herself a bit of a celebration on Monday night – a private celebration, but a celebration nonetheless. Alone in her Earl's Court flat, she'd opened a bottle of vintage champagne and downed a glass, then poured another.

She'd scored a bit of a coup, she congratulated herself. The front-page story in yesterday's *Globe*, and then the news conference. The look on Neville bloody Stewart's face, when she'd announced the reward, had been priceless. She hoped that expression had been captured by one of the cameras in attendance; when she had a little time, she would search online. It might even be on YouTube in another day or so.

It would certainly be front-page news in Tuesday's *Globe*. This story had legs; it could run and run.

Another glass of champagne was in order to toast herself. It was good champagne, its bubbles bursting deliciously on her tongue, and it would have been a great shame to waste it.

Everyone knew that once champagne had lost its fizz, it was worse than undrinkable. So Lilith finished the bottle, one happy glass after another. And then she fell asleep on the sofa.

She was still there on Tuesday morning. Her awakening was less gradual than it should have been, brought on as it was by the insistent ringing of her mobile phone.

Lilith opened her eyes – trying to figure out where she was and why that noise wouldn't stop – and instantly wished she hadn't. The sunlight was like a knife stabbing through to her brain. Her head felt as if it were being attacked with a jackhammer. Every muscle in her body ached. She quickly closed her eyes again; imprinted on the inside of her eyelids was a negative image of the table with its empty glass, its empty bottle.

She groaned, pressing both hands to the sides of her head, trying in vain to stop the agony. Now it felt like two tiny people were behind her eyes, trying to push them out from the inside of her head, while at the same time an iron band round her skull was being tightened.

Still the phone bleeped out its importunate ring tone.

Lilith reached for it, and somehow managed to swipe the screen to answer. 'Hello?' she croaked in an unrecognisable voice.

There was a pause on the other end, then a one-word code name.

Her police contact.

'Yes,' she said, her brain taking over from her suffering body. She managed to struggle into a sitting position.

'There have been ... developments ... overnight.'

'An arrest?' she demanded. 'Have they found Terry, then? Has he been charged?' That was quick work, she acknowledged; the *Globe* might have to make good on her promise of a reward sooner than she'd anticipated.

'Not an arrest, no. But a man is in custody. His name is Tariq Sadek. He's an undocumented Syrian national. I thought you'd want to know.'

MARK DID UNDERSTAND why Callie had withheld information from him: it was indeed part of her job – her calling – to care for the underdogs of society, those who had no one else to advocate for them. Her compassion, her tender heart, was one of the things he loved about her. Nonetheless it had made his life that much more difficult, and he had no illusions that it would be the last time it happened. It was just something he was going to have to live with – as she would have to live with the uncertainties of being the wife of a police officer. It would require constant awareness and accommodation on both their parts, but he had no doubt that it would be worth the effort.

Now, though, he had a pressing matter on his mind. Neville.

He'd been shocked at Neville's appearance last night. Even given all he'd been through in the last couple of days, Neville looked rough. He'd managed to hold it all together and present a reasonable facade of normality during yesterday's briefing and news conference, but by last night the strain was showing.

Mark had taken him aside for a word, after the interviews. Neville had confessed to him that he had nothing to wear but the clothes on his back – the same ones he'd been wearing since Saturday. All of his other clothes were at home, and he wasn't ready to go there. Not now. Not yet. He had a place to stay at the hospital, in the neonatal unit's family suite, and that was where he was going to remain.

Under the circumstances, Mark reflected, that wasn't surprising. Going back to the flat he'd shared, for a few happy months, with Triona was not going to be easy – however long he put it off.

Mark had offered to go with him, for moral support. When Neville refused, he'd promised that he would go on his own. As a friend. He would do the best he could to collect a few changes of clothing and other items Neville might need for the coming days. Neville had given him the keys. Now all he had to do was take the Underground to Shepherd's Bush, accomplish his errand of mercy, and be back to the station in time for the morning briefing.

And then, no matter what else was going on, there were things to be done, visits to be made: the registrar, the funeral director. He couldn't do those things on Neville's behalf, and Neville knew it. But he could go with him and try to make it as painless as possible. That was what friends were for.

THIS TIME YESTERDAY, waking up – late – on her day off, in the bed she'd slept in almost every night of her life, Grace could never have imagined how much could change in the space of twenty-four hours.

And now here she was in London. At Paddington Green police station, a member of the team. It was what she'd dreamed of for as long as she could remember, as she'd read all of those crime novels and imagined herself in the leading roles. When she'd joined the police force, as an idealistic young girl, this was what she'd had in mind: not the humdrum of rural quad bike thievery, but the buzz of solving real murders.

Yolanda Fish had looked after her exceedingly well, cosseting her, feeding her and delivering her to the proper place for her new duties. Yolanda – who was clearly known and respected by all of her colleagues – even introduced her to her everyone as they gathered for the briefing.

The tall Cockney sergeant – DS Cowley – made a beeline for her as soon as he came into the room. 'This is PC Grace Long,' Yolanda Fish told him. 'She's been seconded from the Wiltshire Constabulary.'

'Yes, I know.' He smiled at Grace and she felt herself warming towards him, just a little bit. 'I'm the one that suggested it. She's done a cracking job for us in Wiltshire, tracking down an important witness off her own bat, and I fought she'd be an ace addition to the team.'

Well, that explained it, Grace told herself, with a twinge of disappointment: she'd rather hoped it was DI Stewart who had asked for her. Nevertheless, she was grateful to Sergeant Cowley, and she favoured him with a smile.

He took a seat next to her, Yolanda Fish slipped away, and a minute later DI Stewart himself entered the room. He acknowledged Grace with a nod, though he didn't come over to speak to her. Clearly in a hurry, he wasted no time before launching into the briefing.

'It's been a busy twenty-four hours,' he said. 'There have been quite a few developments since yesterday morning. First and foremost, as you've probably all heard by now, we've got Tariq Sadek in custody, thanks to DS Lombardi.' He inclined his head towards a nice-looking man with curly dark hair. 'That's the good news. The bad news is that, in spite of what the *Daily Globe* would have you believe, it doesn't appear that Mr Sadek is our killer.'

'So Mark doesn't get the hundred thousand quid, then?' another officer said with a smirk, followed by general laughter.

'Ha bloody ha,' snapped DI Stewart.

CALLIE HAD BEEN to Morning Prayer; she'd taken Bella for a quick walk. All the while she was thinking about Tariq, about Zuzanna, expecting to get a call from one of them, or from Marco.

So she wasn't surprised as she mounted the stairs to her flat and heard the phone ringing. Marco would ring her on her mobile, though, she told herself as she fumbled for her keys, let herself in quickly, and made a dash for the phone.

'Miss Anson?' said a clipped voice.

'Yes, speaking,' she gasped, out of breath.

'You *are* a hard one to track down.' The words were followed by a disapproving clucking sound, then, 'This is the bishop's secretary, Miss Anson. The bishop would like to see you. At the earliest opportunity. In fact, there's a space in the bishop's diary later this morning, so if you're free, there's no time like the present.'

THIS WASN'T QUITE what Grace had envisioned, when she'd imagined herself as part of a detective team investigating a murder.

Not that she'd thought it would be particularly glamorous, or even exciting.

But she certainly hadn't expected it to be a desk job.

A desk, a telephone, and a list. That's what she had to work with; that was what she'd been brought in to do.

DI Stewart had explained it, when he introduced her at the end of the briefing: the manager of the Regent Hotel had made available a photocopy of the register listing the hotel's guests on the day of Felicity Chapman's murder. PC Grace Long had been seconded from the Wiltshire Constabulary to follow up on it, contacting each of the guests and determining whether they had anything to contribute to the investigation.

She could just as easily have done this at her desk in Devizes, Grace said to herself, running her finger down the list of names.

There were evidently thirty-two guest rooms in the Regent Hotel. Twenty-seven of them had been occupied on the night in question, and their occupants came from all over the globe.

Grace decided to start at the beginning. Ignoring the old-fashioned desk phone, she picked up her mobile and double-thumbed a number in Australia.

'Frank and Betty can't take your call right now,' twanged an Australian voice message. 'We're on the trip of a lifetime. Leave a message and we'll get back to you, eventually.'

Of course they wouldn't be home, she realised. They were undoubtedly still on their 'trip of a lifetime' – in Edinburgh by now, or maybe Paris.

The next name in the register was a domestic one: a Mr and Mrs Curry from Nottingham. Grace thumbed the number, and after a couple of rings a woman's voice answered.

'Is this Mrs Curry?' Grace asked.

'Yes. But whatever you're selling, I don't want it.'

'Mrs Curry, this is PC Long, ringing from the Metropolitan Police,' she said quickly, before the woman could hang up on her.

'Yes?'

'We're investigating an ... incident ... at the Regent Hotel in London. You and your husband were guests at the hotel last week, I believe?'

'No. You're mistaken,' she said flatly. 'My husband was on a business trip, but he was on his own.'

'I have your names in the hotel register. Mr Edgar and Mrs Teresa Curry, from Nottingham.'

There was a sharp intake of breath. 'That bastard,' the woman hissed. 'I'm going to kill him. Just see if I don't.' And then the call was terminated.

PUTTING off the inevitable for just a few more minutes, Neville decided to ring the Coroner's office to check on the scheduling of the inquest.

Hereward Rice's secretary was on top of the matter, and admirably helpful. 'I was going to ring you a bit later,' she said. 'As you know, DI Stewart, yesterday's Bank Holiday put us back by a day already, and Dr Rice was planning to open the inquest this afternoon. But we've had a phone call this morning from the deceased's husband.'

'Alan Chapman?'

'That's right. Mr Chapman wishes to be present at the inquest. I explained to him that it would be a mere formality at this point, but he said he wanted to be there. And that, of course, is his right, as next of kin. He'll be travelling from Wiltshire today, so Dr Rice has agreed to postpone the proceedings until tomorrow morning. Eleven o'clock.'

So any vague hopes that Neville had entertained of an excuse to postpone his errands with Mark Lombardi were dashed. 'Tomorrow, then,' he said resignedly. 'Thanks.'

Thirty seconds later, Mark tapped on the door and came into his office with a sympathetic grimace. 'It's time,' he said. 'This isn't going to be pleasant, but it's got to be done.'

After an hour's work, Grace contemplated her list. She'd spoken to seven people who had been registered at the Regent Hotel on Wednesday night last: two giggly American college students, travelling together; a Swedish backpacker, whose English was embarrassingly good; a Chinese tourist, whose English – in contrast – verged on the nonexistent; and three young men from Basingstoke who had been in London for a stag party and had seemingly been so wasted that they barely remembered the existence of the Regent Hotel. None of them recalled seeing Felicity Chapman, or a woman fitting her description.None of them had seen or heard anything that they would consider to be of possible significance. Grace had, in each instance, given them her number and asked them to ring her if anything occurred to them that might be of assistance.

There were still a lot of names on the list. She'd tried a few, like the Australian couple, who hadn't answered the phone. Some of the guests hadn't provided a contact number; several of her quarry were going to require additional tracking down, one way and another.

It was frustrating, but Grace had to admit to herself that it was also satisfying. Although she hadn't yet struck pay dirt, she could tell herself that the next call could be the one that would crack the case wide open. Police work, she'd realised a long time ago, was nothing like it appeared on telly or in her beloved crime novels. No glamour – most of it was just hard graft. Yet she liked the methodical nature of going through the process, one step at a time, until the graft paid off.

Having abandoned her initial strategy of starting at the top and working to the bottom for a more nuanced approach, she was deciding which name to try next when a face peered round the side of her assigned cubicle: DS Cowley.

'How're you getting on?'

'All right,' she said. 'Nothing yet.'

'I wondered if you're ready for a coffee, or maybe a bite of lunch. I can take you down to the canteen, show you the ropes, like.'

Her immediate impulse was to refuse, but if she did then she'd be on her own – sticking out like a sore thumb. A country bumpkin at the Met.

'All right, then,' she said. 'That's very kind. Thanks, Sergeant Cowley.'

'Call me Sid.'

She wasn't ready to do that yet, so she merely smiled she she shoved her phone in her pocket.

Frances Cherry, who'd had a busy morning on the wards with several frightened and talkative patients awaiting their operations, was feeling guilty that she hadn't yet managed to visit Annie Stewart in the neonatal unit. Hearing the food trolleys beginning to trundle down the corridor, she looked at her watch and realised that it was getting close to lunch time. The patients would be distracted by the arrival of food, making it a perfect time for her to disappear from the wards.

She slipped upstairs, and was pleased to find that Kamala Gupta was on duty. The nurse greeted her with a warm smile. 'Annie is doing very well,' she reported. 'That little one is a real fighter.'

'So was her mother.' Frances blinked back sudden tears.

Kamala patted her arm. 'You said she was a friend of yours?'

'Yes. I've ... I'd ... known her a long time. We were friends.'

'Bad luck. You wouldn't think that women would still be dying in childbirth, would you? Not in this day and age, in this civilised country. But it still happens, more often than you'd think.' Kamala lowered her voice. 'The father – Mr Stewart. Is he a friend of yours as well?'

That was a loaded question; Frances took a moment to think about her answer, and decided to be honest, if oblique. 'Well, I wouldn't exactly call him a friend. We have some shared history, let's put it that way. Why do you ask?'

Kamala leaned closer and spoke quietly. 'I am a bit worried about him. He doesn't want to leave.'

Frances glanced towards the door into the unit. 'You mean he's here now?'

'Yes. He's been away this morning – I believe he went to work, but he came back a few minutes ago. He sits by Annie's incubator for hours and talks to her, and at night he's been sleeping in one of the beds in the family suite. I told him he needs to go home and get some proper rest. But he seems a stubborn man, if it doesn't offend you for me to say that.'

Frances shook her head. 'It doesn't offend me. He *is* a stubborn man.' That, in her experience, was putting it mildly.

'He says he won't go home until he can take Annie with him. That could be a few weeks. And this isn't a hotel.' Kamala fixed her with large, liquid brown eyes. 'Maybe you could have a word?'

GRACE WAS glad she hadn't refused DS Cowley's offer; she wasn't sure she would have found the canteen on her own. Down a corridor, round a corner, another corridor and then a flight of stairs. 'What have you been doing this morning?' she asked him as they walked along.

'I've been tracking down Mrs Julian St Clair,' he said. 'You know. The guv was talking about her husband at the briefing. Felicity Chapman's fancy man. Pretty much the last person to see her alive. We need to talk to the wife, to confirm the bastard's alibi. For my money, he's our man,' he added. 'Too slick by half, that bloke. I don't trust him.'

'So you haven't talked to her yet?'

'Nah, the guv will want to do that. Once he gets back.'

'Where's he gone?'

DS Cowley stopped, forcing her to stop as well. He turned and looked at her with a furrowed brow, shaking his head. 'You don't know, do you?'

'Don't know what?'

'About the guv. His wife – she was having a baby, you know?'

'No, I didn't know,' she admitted.

Cowley continued to shake his head. 'She died. The other night, innit? After we got back from Devizes?'

Grace stared at him, appalled. 'Saturday night, you mean?'

'Yeah. So today he's got to do the necessary. See the registrar, the undertaker, and all that malarkey.'

'Oh, my God. I had no idea. The poor man!'

'Yeah, well, he's getting on with fings. He wanted off the case, but DCS Evans, he said he had to stick with it. Probably better that way,' Cowley added. 'Keeps him busy, like.'

She was almost afraid to ask. 'What about the baby? Did the baby die as well?'

'Nah. Might of been better if it had done.'

'What on earth do you mean by that? Is something wrong with it?'

Cowley shrugged. 'It's little, is all. Born too early. The guv showed me a photo. Ugly little fing. He's potty about it, mind, but what's he gonna do wif it? That's my point. Who's gonna look after it once it comes out of hospital? The last fing the guv needs right now, all on his tod, is a baby.'

18

By Tuesday afternoon, Lilith had begun to pull herself together. With the help of a handful of painkillers, she'd banished the crippling headache to a dull throb at the temples. She'd showered, washed and dried her hair, and changed into clean, fresh clothes. She'd even managed to rehydrate a bit, and nibbled on some dry toast.

Feeling marginally human again, she made some notes on her laptop, then cobbled together a story based on the information she'd received from her informant, and building on the edifice of speculation and xenophobia she'd already begun to construct.

Tuesday's cover story – written and filed before her private celebration – had featured the news conference, trumpeting the *Globe*'s instrumental role in flagging up the illegal immigrant now sought by the police. Information about the reward money on offer was front and centre, in a big box, filling half the page. That was scheduled to be repeated in tomorrow's edition as well.

But now the police had him in custody: Terry, the kitchen helper. Now known to be Tariq Sadek, a Syrian national without papers.

It was time to talk to Rob Gardiner-Smith.

JANE HADN'T HAD A VERY good morning, but as in previous days the nausea had retreated by afternoon. She was tired – tired of feeling sick, tired of throwing up, tired of lying in bed, tired of being tired. Fresh air was what she needed, she told herself. It was a beautiful spring day, and she hated to waste it entirely indoors. Besides, the fridge, the pantry and even the deep freeze were starting to look decidedly empty. Brian was no good at shopping, and she hadn't felt like thinking about food – let alone buying or preparing it – for what seemed like weeks.

She would go to the shops. It didn't need to be a major excursion at this point, but she could buy a few things. Things that might tempt her: some fresh fruit, a nice bar of dark chocolate, maybe even some ice cream.

Grabbing her handbag and a carrier, she let herself out of the vicarage and headed through the churchyard in the direction of the shops.

But by the church hall, near the door which accessed the curate's flat on the top floor, her eye was caught by a furtive movement, as someone ducked round the corner.

One of the churchwardens had recently caught a couple of teenaged boys hanging out in the churchyard, smoking something that probably wasn't tobacco. So Jane was on alert, and decided she shouldn't just ignore it. She went round the corner to confront the potential trespasser – who turned out to be not a teenaged boy, but a slight, fair girl with huge, frightened eyes.

'Can I help you?' Jane said in her most confident, proprietary, vicar's wife voice.

The girl cringed. 'Miss Callie,' she said imploringly. 'I look for Miss Callie. Miss Callie not here.'

WALKING BACK to the station from the hospital, Neville simmered with fury.

That woman – Frances Cherry. She had had the temerity to try to tell him what to do. Go home, she'd said. Sort yourself out. Let the nurses take care of Annie. That's their job, that's what they're trained to do. Take care of *yourself* instead.

Not her exact words, but that's what he thought she'd meant.

How dare she? Who did she think she was, telling him how to live his life?

He hadn't been very nice to her. From what he recalled he'd said, in the heat of anger, he'd pretty much told her to mind her own business. He might even have called her an interfering female.

Now, though – already – he was beginning to regret his untempered reaction to what was obviously well meant on her part.

After all, he reminded himself, she had been Triona's friend. She had been a good friend to her, in all honesty. And the night Triona died – the night Annie was born – Frances was the one who was there for her. She had been there for all of it, up to the end and beyond, waiting for Neville and breaking the news to him. She cared about Annie, clearly, and continued to check up on her.

So why was he so angry?

Neville realised the truth just before he reached the station, and it stopped him in his tracks.

It was himself he was angry at. Frances Cherry was just a reminder – a painful reminder – that he *hadn't* been there for Triona. Not when she needed him the most, when he should have been there at her side through that most gruelling and horrible of nights.

Maybe if he had been there, had been proactive and advocated for her at the hospital as he should have done, she would still be alive.

Not in a drawer at the mortuary or in a box at the undertaker's, but alive, and sitting by Annie's incubator herself, holding their daughter. Smiling up at Neville. Looking forward to the day that they could take her home – together – and be a family.

Neville swallowed hard, choking back a sob. There was work to be done, he reminded himself. He could think about this later. Now he needed to find Sid Cowley, and get on with it.

After his painful but necessary errands with Neville, Mark made a quick trip home to his flat to shower and change his clothes before returning to the station.

He was in the shower when he heard his mobile ringing in the other room, where he'd dropped it on his bed.

Whatever it was, it could wait for five minutes, he decided. He finished his ablutions, stepped out and towelled himself dry.

Once he'd donned some clean underwear, he went to his bedroom and picked up the phone.

A message had been left. He tapped the button to retrieve it.

'Marco, it's Serena,' said a voice that sounded far from serene. 'It's Mamma. She's had ... an episode. The paramedics ... the ambulance ... they're taking her to hospital. Ring me when you get this.'

Grace returned to her desk after lunch, increasingly confident of her ability to find her way around this enormous police station. She'd had a surprisingly pleasant meal – well-cooked food, and Sergeant Cowley was beginning to grow on her a bit. There was probably a good policeman, and maybe even a decent human being, lurking under all that Cockney bluster, she decided. Even if he was a smoker.

She had another scan through her list of guests at the Regent Hotel, the names now beginning to imprint themselves on her brain as she sought for a logical order of attack. Some of the names were scrawled, almost unreadable. One, she noted, was printed very carefully: Dr Sein Lwin. The address, also meticulously clear, was in Myanmar.

Grace wasn't entirely sure where Myanmar was, but on impulse she punched in the mobile phone number. Why, she wondered as the phone rang, would a doctor be staying at a place as grim and grotty as the Regent Hotel? She obviously hadn't seen it for herself, but Sid Cowley's description of it, over lunch, had been vividly evocative of downmarket squalor.

She wasn't really expecting anyone to pick up, so was surprised when a precise male voice said 'Hello?'

'Is this Doctor Sein Lwin?' She made her best stab at pronouncing the name, certain that she'd got it wrong.

The accented voice corrected her pronunciation gently.

'This is PC Grace Long, from the London Metropolitan Police,' she said. 'Dr Lwin, I believe that you were staying at the Regent Hotel in Paddington last week?'

'Yes, that is correct.'

'If you don't mind me asking,' she said impulsively, 'why were you staying there? Instead of somewhere ... better?'

There was a soft chuckle. 'I was ... misinformed,' he said. 'I did not know it was ... shall we say, not up to standards? I stayed there for one night only. The next day I found more suitable accommodation. But I also did not know,' he added, 'that staying at the Regent Hotel was a matter of interest to the police. Have I perhaps committed a crime by doing so?'

She guessed that he was making a little joke, but plunged ahead. 'Are you aware that a woman was murdered in the hotel on Wednesday night? The night you were staying there? It's been in the news.'

A gasp, followed by a murmured word in a foreign language. Then, 'No, I did not know. I am no longer in London, you see. I am now in Amsterdam, visiting a colleague.'

'Dr Lwin,' – she pronounced his name with conscientious care – 'I'm just checking to see whether you might have seen or noticed anything that would help us with our investigation. The woman's name was Felicity Chapman. She was staying in Room Nine, on the second floor of the hotel. She was a middle-aged woman with blond hair. Very attractive, apparently, and ... like yourself ... perhaps not typical of the hotel's usual guests.'

Another deep intake of breath. 'Yes, I do believe I know who you mean,' he said after a considered pause. 'A very attractive woman, indeed. Well dressed, well groomed. And I noticed her especially because of her pearls.'

Pearls? 'I beg your pardon? Her pearls, did you say?'

'Burmese pearls, they were. I recognised them as such. Burma – Myanmar, my country is now called – is well known in the world for the quality of its pearls, and hers were particularly fine examples. Perfectly matched, and with such a beautiful golden lustre.'

Grace struggled to figure out what he was trying to say. 'She was wearing pearls?'

'Yes,' he said patiently. 'Beautiful Burmese pearls. I could not help speaking to her about them. Telling her how much I admired them.'

'Where was this, exactly?'

'In the lobby of the Regent Hotel. I'm sorry, I did not make that clear.' He paused for a second, as if gathering his thoughts, then went on. 'I will tell you about it as it happened. I had just arrived at the hotel, and was waiting to check in. The lady with the pearls was in front of me at the reception desk. She asked the manager if there was a safe in the hotel for her pearls. In her room, or in the reception area? I could not help hearing,' he added apologetically.

'And what did the manager say?'

'He told her that there was no safe. But that it was not necessary, because only trustworthy people were employed at the Regent Hotel, and she did not need to worry that her pearls would be stolen.'

Grace resisted the temptation to laugh out loud. 'Was that when you spoke to her?' she asked.

'Yes. I told her that her pearls were very beautiful, and did she know that they were Burmese pearls? She said that she did know. They had belonged to her grandmother, she said. Her grandfather had bought them in Burma. As a child she had always admired them, and her grandmother had left them to her when she died. I told her that they were very valuable, and she should be very careful with them.'

'Was that the only time you spoke to her, or saw her?'

'Yes. After that it was my turn to check in, and once I saw what my room was like, I had other things to think about,' he stated candidly. 'I did look for her at breakfast – if you can call it that – the next morning. But I did not see her.' He paused. 'I am very sorry to hear that she is dead.'

The first thing Neville did, back at the station, was to check with the custody officer to confirm that Tariq Sadek was still in the cells, and okay. Also, he admitted to himself, he wanted to make sure that Sadek wasn't demanding to see a lawyer, which was entirely within his rights but would complicate matters at the moment. Neville was aware that he would soon have to make a decision what to do with him: they would either have to charge him with a crime, release him, or pursue some other path like handing him over to the Home Office to be dealt with as an illegal immigrant. He was reluctant to default to the latter option, and he certainly didn't want to release him. So he would probably, before the clock ran out that evening, charge him with something vague like obstruction of justice – anything that would keep him there under lock and key until he was ready to deal with him.

Then he went looking for Sid Cowley, and found him – unsurprisingly – enjoying a cig at the smokers' corner, behind the station.

'I hope you've had a productive morning,' Neville said. 'Have you managed to track down Mrs St Clair?'

'Not a problem, Guv.' Cowley grinned, took a quick final puff, then threw the fag end on the ground. 'She's at an 'otel. And it's not the Regent, I can promise you that. It's only the bloody Ritz, innit?'

'Did you speak to her?'

'Nah, I figured you would want to do that yourself.'

'You were right,' Neville acknowledged. 'Well, Sid, I guess we're about to see how the other half lives. When they're staying at a hotel, that is.'

They headed for the car park. 'How did you find her?' Neville asked.

'Rang up old Jules himself and asked him where she was. Simple as.'

Admirably straightforward, Neville acknowledged. The only drawback was that if Julian St Clair knew they were looking for his wife, he could contact her before they got there and make sure she would confirm his alibi. Still, St Clair was an intelligent man, and would have figured out for himself that they would want to talk to her.

Mark checked his phone for the best way to get to the Royal London from his flat in Holborn, and decided that the quickest – if not the cheapest – would be to take the Tube to Liverpool Street, then grab a taxi to the hospital from there.

Still, the journey was slower than he would have liked. The Tube seemed exceptionally crowded, so it took forever at each station stop to disgorge disembarking passengers and cram in those who wanted to join the train. At Liverpool Street the taxi rank had a long queue of waiting hopefuls with suitcases; Mark decided to take his chances in the street instead. Eventually he managed to hail a passing empty taxi.

The driver evidently spoke no English, but he did understand 'Royal London Hospital'. He put the taxi into gear and crawled along in traffic. Mark was relieved that he didn't have to attempt to make conversation with him. Most taxi drivers, in his experience, were all too happy to enter into an opinionated discourse, if not a dialogue, on at least one of a triumvirate of topics: football, cricket, or politics. As he didn't follow even one of the three with any degree of enthusiasm, silence was preferable by far.

The taxi dropped him at the main entrance to the sprawling hospital. In the brief conversation he'd had with her, Serena had said that she would be waiting for him by the front doors, and she was as good as her word. He approached her with some trepidation, given the state of things between them, but she stretched out her arms towards him. 'Oh, Marco,' she said, her voice almost unrecognisable. 'Thank you for coming. I'm so worried about Mamma.'

'Is there a car park at the Ritz?' Cowley wanted to know.

Neville shrugged. 'We'll soon find out, won't we?'

There was, instead, a valet at the main entrance of the hotel; he approached the car as Neville pulled up and Cowley rolled down his window. 'Can I help you?' the uniformed man asked.

Cowley stuck his head out. 'Where do we put the car, mate?'

The man looked startled, but Neville added, 'Police business. We need to interview one of your guests.'

'Leave it with me, sir.' He reached for the keys, and within seconds Neville and Cowley were in the sumptuous lobby of one of London's poshest hotels. To call it a hotel, reflected Neville – to put it in the same category as the Regent Hotel or even the old-fashioned provincial hotel in Devizes – was to do it grave injustice. It was, simply, palatial – Buckingham Palace itself couldn't possibly be any posher than this.

'Cor blimey,' said Sid, but he didn't hesitate to march up to the carved oak registration desk. 'We're looking for Mrs Julian St Clair,' he stated.

The immaculately turned-out young woman behind the desk must have been very well trained indeed; she didn't even raise an eyebrow, but gave Sid a neutral, meaningless smile. 'I'll ring Mrs St Clair's suite,' she said, reaching for her phone. 'Whom shall I say is asking for her?'

Cowley looked at Neville, who stepped up close to the desk, lowered his voice, and said, 'Police.'

At that, the woman did betray by the merest blink that this was not everyday business-as-usual at the Ritz. But she didn't comment – she just made the call, spoke a few words quietly into the handset, then hung up and turned back to Neville. 'She will receive you in her suite,' she said, then gave concise directions for finding it.

'Thank you,' said Neville. They headed to the lift, ascended to the third floor, then went down a long corridor.

Mrs St Clair was waiting for them at the door to her suite. 'Come in, gentlemen,' she said. 'I believe you wish to ask me some questions?'

Neville pulled out his warrant card. 'Detective Inspector Stewart, Detective Sergeant Cowley. And you are Mrs St Clair?'

'Olivia St Clair,' she affirmed, stepping aside to let them in. 'For the moment, anyway. I'm not sure whether I'll keep the name or not.'

Just the money, then, thought Neville cynically as he entered the suite. It was beyond posh: with its glittering chandeliers, its antique furniture, and its extravagant swags of drapery, it made Julian St Clair's two-million-pound house in Holland Park Mews look like a shabby-chic dump by comparison.

Then, having taken in her surroundings, he looked more closely at Olivia St Clair.

She was, to put not too fine a point on it, a younger version of

Felicity Chapman: the same sleek blond hair, the same trim figure. Felicity Chapman would have looked exactly like this, twenty-five years ago.

He must have been staring. 'Yes, I know,' she said. 'I look like her, don't I? Like his bloody Fliss. It's why he married me, I know now. I wish I'd realised it sooner. I've wasted ten years of my life with Jules, trying to be someone else. Someone he could love.'

Her blasé cynicism – a match for his own – somehow shocked Neville into silence. Sid, too, seemed to be struck dumb by the magnificence of their surroundings, staring at the chandelier with his mouth hanging open.

Olivia St Clair gestured in the direction of a collection of spindly antique chairs. 'Would you like to sit down? Or shall we just cut to the chase, and save us all time?'

Neville found his tongue. 'You have something to tell us?'

She nodded. 'My husband may be a bastard, but he's no murderer. And even if he were, the last person he would murder is his precious Fliss. You can take my word for that.'

'So you're confirming his alibi, then?'

'I can confirm that he came back to the flat that evening, about half past eight. And he didn't go out again.'

Surely he wouldn't have told his wife that he'd been meeting up with an old flame, Neville reasoned. 'Did you know where he'd been?' he asked.

'Not at first. He'd just said he was going out, and didn't know what time he'd be back. So I was watching telly when he came in. The programme they run every evening during the Chelsea Flower Show. He was ... well, let's say he was feeling amorous. He wanted to go to bed, right there and then.'

'Randy bugger,' Cowley muttered.

Neville ignored him. 'And did you ... ?'

'Well, at that point I was still ready to do just about anything to save my marriage. So I went into the bedroom with him. I let him undress me. I started getting into the mood. And then ... then I smelled her scent. All over his neck.' She clasped her hands together; her knuckles were white. 'I asked him what the hell was going on. That was when he told me. He told me about bloody Fliss, and how he'd never stopped loving her, and how they'd met up again, but nothing had happened. "It's not too late for us", he said. And that's when I knew. That it *was* too late. That he'd never get over her, no matter what I said, or did, or was. I realised that he'd married me because I reminded him of her. And he was only settling for me now because she wouldn't have him. I knew it was over, from that minute. The next morning I packed my bags and came here. I haven't seen the bastard since.'

'And you know he didn't go back out that night because ...?'

'Because I didn't sleep a wink the entire night. We rowed and rowed. Went over and over the same ground. He finally turned his back on me and went to sleep. But I didn't sleep.' She raised her chin. 'I kept thinking about those wasted years. And I knew that I didn't want to spend another minute with the man who had stolen them from me, pretending to love me when he was in love with someone else the whole time.'

Before they left, Neville had one more question for her – just to satisfy his own curiosity. 'I wonder, Mrs St Clair – what about your husband's first wife? Was she like Felicity Chapman as well?'

Olivia St Clair laughed – a laugh of genuine amusement. 'That's the funny thing, Detective Inspector. If she had been, I might have twigged sooner. But she was just the opposite. She was small and dark-haired and very intense. I suppose after he lost Fliss, he went for the farthest thing he could find to her. When that didn't work, he found *me*.'

MARK and his sister sat together in a small, private room – the sort of room that hospitals provide for people who are waiting for bad – or occasionally good – news. The walls were pale blue; there were several framed prints on the walls, featuring chocolate-box cottages surrounded by spiky hollyhocks and fluffy pink roses. On one wall was a flat-screen television with the sound off, displaying an incomprehensible game show. The chairs were upholstered in a durable dark-blue fabric. An untidy stack of ancient magazines inhabited the low central table.

Serena explained that she hadn't yet managed to contact their father.

'Pappa doesn't have a mobile, you know. And he's not answering the phone at home. I'm not sure where he is, to be honest.'

'What about Chiara?'

'It's half-term week. She's gone to a friend's for a sleep-over. So I don't need to worry about her.'

The preliminaries out of the way, Mark got down to the essentials. 'Okay. Tell me about Mamma. Tell me what happened.'

Serena closed her eyes for a moment, then turned her head towards one of the chocolate-box cottages. 'It was after the lunch service. All the customers were gone, we were clearing up. Loading the dishwasher, refilling the salt shakers, changing the tablecloths for evening service. You know.'

Mark knew very well; having grown up in a family of restaurateurs, the routine was familiar to him. 'Yes.'

'Once the kitchen staff and the servers had gone, when it was just the two of us, Mamma started having a go at me. Again. She told me that you'd set a wedding date. Then she started in on me. "It breaks my heart that my children aren't talking to each other," blah blah blah. And then, all of a sudden, she stopped. She put both of her hands on her chest, and stopped talking. Her face went all queer, and she just ... went down. On the floor. It was lucky that she didn't crash into anything and hurt herself. I talked to her, tried to bring her round, but I could see that she couldn't hear me. She was breathing, but ... only just. And she was cold. Clammy. So I rang 999. They told me to cover her with a blanket. They – the paramedics – came really quickly. It seemed like ages to me, but it was probably less than five minutes. They got her stabilised, they put her in the ambulance. I tried to ring Pappa. Then I rang you. And now she's in theatre, and we're waiting ...' Serena gulped.

Mark was overwhelmed with emotion. Mamma – the matriarch – was the rock of the family, and always had been. 'I'm really sorry you had to deal with it on your own,' he said, knowing how inadequate that was to express how he felt. Serena had lost her husband to a heart attack, only a few months ago. Now it must seem to her that she was re-living that nightmare, that her world was crashing down on her yet again. If Mamma didn't make it ...

His sister finally turned towards him, and stretched out her hands, palms up. 'Marco,' she said, 'I am so sorry. Sorry for everything. Mamma was right. It's crazy for us to be like this. I've been thinking about it – about why I've been so dead set against you marrying Callie. And I realise that I've been ... jealous.' She spat the word out, like it was poison. 'Jealous because we've always been so close, the two of us, and now you have ... someone else. Jealous of both of you, I suppose. Jealous of her because she's the one you talk to now, and jealous of you because you have someone you love, to share your life with. And I don't.'

'Oh, Serena.' He stood up and gathered her in his arms, hugging her tight. 'You'll always be my special big sister. No matter what happens.'

A man in a white coat came into the room. 'Mrs di Stefano?'

She turned quickly to face him. 'Yes?'

'Your mother, Mrs Lombardi? She's had a heart attack. But we've managed to contain the damage, and her chances of survival are very good. She'll be in ICU shortly, and you'll be able to visit her. You and ...?' He looked enquiringly at Mark.

'My brother,' Serena gulped, squeezing Mark's hand. 'My brother Marco.'

Callie, exhausted after a long and eventful day, promised herself an early night. After her supper she took a bubble bath, put on her cosiest pyjamas, and snuggled on the sofa with Bella, watching a cookery competition programme on the telly. She was thinking about going to bed when her mobile rang.

It was Frances. 'Just checking to see how you're doing,' she said.

'Knackered,' admitted Callie. 'I've had quite a day.'

'Tell me about it,' Frances invited.

So Callie told her, starting with the developments of the night before – the events which had led to Tariq and Zuzanna being taken to the police station for questioning. 'I'm not really sure what's happening with Tariq,' she concluded. 'Marco says he's still in custody. Apparently he's going to be charged with a crime. But what he's most afraid of is being deported. And I think the police are trying to make sure that doesn't happen.'

'What about Zuzanna, then?'

'They released her. And this morning she came looking for me, but I wasn't about.' Callie paused. 'You won't believe this. Jane's the one who found her, and Jane has already taken her under her wing! For some reason, she's making Zuzanna her project. She's going to feed her up, she says – put some meat on her bones. Help her improve her English. And she'll do a brilliant job, I have no doubt.'

'Wow.'

'I mean, it could so easily have gone the other way,' she added candidly. 'Jane could have ratted me out to Brian, got me in trouble for harbouring a fugitive without telling him. But old Jane has really come up trumps this time.'

'Good for her. I always suspected there was a kind heart underneath all that vicar's wife armour.'

But Callie wasn't finished with her recitation. 'And then this afternoon, Marco's mum had a heart attack.'

'Oh, no!'

'She's going to be okay, apparently,' Callie assured her. 'Marco rang me from the Royal London, where they'd taken her. I went straightaway, and discovered that Marco and Serena had made up their differences. It took their mum's almost dying to do it, but all is now sweetness and light with Serena. She even gave me a big hug, and said she was so glad we'd set a wedding date.'

'Wow again. But you're home now?'

'I offered to hang about, but Marco and his sister had this huge Lombardi love-fest going on, and I felt like a gooseberry. I thought I'd just let them get on with it, so I came home.'

'Well, you *have* had quite a day,' Frances acknowledged.

'And I haven't even told you the biggest thing.' Callie stroked Bella's soft ears. 'I had a call from the bishop's office this morning. They wanted me to come in right away, so I went. That's why I wasn't here when Zuzanna turned up.' She went on, 'You know I told you, a while ago, that Brian wanted me to be priested at Petertide?'

'Yes?'

'Well, that's what it was about. The bishop wanted to talk to me, to satisfy herself that I was ready. We had a super meeting – she's brilliant, the bishop. I even 'fessed up to her about harbouring fugitives, and she said that Jesus would have approved.'

'Good for her.'

'Anyway, at the end of it, she said that as far as she was concerned, I was more than ready to be priested. So it's going to happen – next month!'

19

Grace woke in the middle of the night, in the cosy guest room at Yolanda Fish's house.

She'd had a memorable first day in London. She'd worked hard, doing what was asked of her. Making all of those phone calls, and meticulously making notes on the results. No breakthroughs, really. She'd talked to over twenty people; only one of them – the doctor from Myanmar – recalled having seen Felicity Chapman, and his recollection was specific to something as irrelevant as her jewellery. He hadn't observed anyone creeping along the corridor, opening the door of Room Nine, in the wee hours of Thursday morning. So what use was that?

And yet.

Yet there was something nagging her brain, continually recalling her from sleep. Something she couldn't quite grasp. She hoped she would remember it by the time she offered up her findings if called upon to do so at the morning briefing.

MARK KNEW that he couldn't spend the whole day – or even a significant part of it – at the hospital with his mother. So he set his alarm for an almost painfully early start, and went to the Royal Free before most of London was yet awake. Although it was still quite a long time until official visiting hours began, a sympathetic nurse allowed him to pop in and spend a few minutes at Mamma's bedside. He was reassured by what he found: she was breathing normally on her own, and though groggy and uncommunicative, she seemed to know that he was there.

He took her hand and told her, 'I wanted you to know that Serena and I are good. Just like you hoped. And you've got to get better soon, so you can come to my wedding.'

It might have been his imagination, but he was pretty sure that she gave his hand a faint squeeze. 'I'll be back as soon as I can, Mamma,' he promised, kissing her on the cheek before making his exit.

The news stand at the entrance to Liverpool Street Station was displaying the *Daily Globe*, front and centre. 'Police Nab Suspect in Hotel Murder' screamed the headline.

He wasn't even going to bother reading the story, Mark decided.

JANE WOKE ON WEDNESDAY MORNING – suddenly, as the rubbish collectors rumbled down the street, making their customary racket – with the sense that something was different.

She reached out her arm to the other side of the bed. Brian wasn't there: he was obviously letting her sleep while he went to Morning Prayer. Experimentally, she lifted her head from the pillow.

The movement didn't instantly make her feel nauseous. That in itself was different; it seemed to her that it had been weeks since she'd waked up and not immediately rushed to the loo to be sick.

Relishing the absence of the ongoing misery, she stretched out in bed. And then she remembered.

Zuzanna. The Polish girl was asleep in the spare room – the room that Callie had occupied a few months ago, while her roof was undergoing repairs.

Jane smiled to herself, already full of plans for Zuzanna. She would help her to improve her English – there were books that she could obtain to properly teach her the language. She would make sure that she had tasty and nutritious meals to fill out her waifish frame – the girl was practically skin and bones. They could provide her with a place to stay for as long as she needed it; the vicarage was spacious, with plenty of room for both Zuzanna and her sister. And even for Tariq, who could take over Simon's room. Brian would advocate for Zuzanna's fiancé, using all the power and authority provided by his dog collar – he would make sure Tariq went through all the proper channels to claim legal asylum, so there would be no danger of his being deported. As soon as possible, Brian would marry Zuzanna and Tariq. They were already residents of the parish, so there were no issues about residency.

Brian could employ Tariq as a caretaker at the church, Jane plotted. And when her baby came – Jane ran her hands over her still-flat belly – Zuzanna could help out. She could be a nanny, an au pair. Part of the family.

She looked at the clock. Brian would be home from Morning Prayer soon. It had been a long time – too long – since he'd had a cooked breakfast. That would be a nice treat for him. And for Zuzanna.

Jane threw back the duvet and got out of bed.

NEVILLE DRAFTED his testimony for the inquest – the bare bones of the facts about the discovery of the body and the ongoing investigation – in longhand on a scrap of paper, while sitting beside Annie's incubator. She was into her fourth day of life now, and already he could see that she was bigger, more robust, and rosier of complexion than she had been on that first traumatic day. He was beginning to believe what the nurses kept telling him: Annie was going to be all right. In a few weeks' time he would walk out of this place for good, carrying her in his arms.

This morning's briefing was going to have to be held early, on account of the inquest. So he finished his statement, tucked it in his pocket, then patted the incubator, and headed for the police station.

He needed to check with Mark Lombardi, he told himself – Mark would need to be available to the family, since Alan Chapman had travelled to London to attend the inquest.

Mark was just going into the briefing room. Neville caught up with him. 'Have you been in touch with the family at all?'

'They're all planning to be there,' Mark confirmed. 'Even Danielle. I spoke to Ben last night. He wasn't any more gracious than ever, but he said that his father had arrived, and wanted me to accompany them. I'm going to meet them there.'

'Good man.'

'Excuse me, Sir.'

Neville turned to see that PC Grace Long was waiting by the door, and was evidently speaking to him. 'Oh, hello, Constable. Everything okay?'

'Could I have a quick word, Sir?'

'Call me Guv. You're part of the team now,' he said, with a quick glance at his watch. 'You're getting on okay, I take it?'

'If I could just have a quick word,' she repeated. 'Guv. I wondered if you could tell me. Was Mrs Chapman wearing pearls when she was ... found?'

He stared at her. 'Pearls? No. She was in bed. People don't usually wear pearls to bed, as far as I'm aware.'

The girl's face went slightly pink, emphasising the freckles on her nose. But she persisted. 'Were there any pearls in the room? On the bedside table, or in a drawer, or maybe hidden in her case, or in her handbag?'

He didn't see the point of her questions, but he made an effort to recall. 'No,' he said. 'No pearls.'

She pressed her lips together and nodded her head, as if making up her mind. 'Then there's something I need to tell you ... Guv.'

THEY WERE WAITING for Mark at the entrance to the Coroner's Court: Ben and Danielle, whom he knew, and Alan Chapman, whom he'd not yet met. Chapman was a well-dressed middle-aged man with grey-tinged dark hair and spectacles, and he seemed possessed of better manners than his son had ever displayed. He extended his hand to Mark. 'Thank you for coming, Sergeant,' he said.

'This is a mere formality, as I said,' Mark warned them. 'You really needn't have come, though of course you're entitled to be here. The inquest will be opened by the coroner, the SIO will give a summary of the investigation to date, then the coroner will suggest a future date to continue the inquest – probably some time in the summer.'

Danielle shrugged and assumed a bored expression. 'Total waste of time, in other words,' she said.

'Dad insisted,' Ben Chapman put in. 'I told him not to bother, but he insisted.'

'I wanted to be here,' Alan Chapman said, with dignity. 'Felicity was my wife. I did love her, you know.'

Mark warmed to him, in spite of what he knew about the supposedly bereaved widower. At least he was making an effort.

'I hope it won't take long,' Danielle said, looking at her watch. 'We might even get back to work before lunch, if we're lucky.'

Out of the corner of his eye, Mark saw Lilith Noone sauntering towards the courtroom, looking exceedingly pleased with herself.

THE INQUEST WAS as cut-and-dried as expected, adjourned until July. Neville had taken Cowley with him; he didn't want to waste any time tracking him down before the next order of business.

They went straight to the Regent Hotel. 'Ready, Sid?' said Neville, pulling the car up on a double yellow line.

Cowley grinned. 'Let's nail the bastard, Guv.'

Ronald Wicker was behind the registration desk. The perfunctory smile he assumed as the door swung open immediately faded when he saw who it was.

'Good morning, Mr Wicker,' Neville said pleasantly.

The man blinked rapidly; beads of sweat appeared on his high forehead. 'Detective Inspector.'

'Do you have someone you can leave in charge here? Because we'd like you to come to the station with us now.'

Wicker gulped. 'I promise you, I didn't know he was illegal. You've got to believe me.'

'As a matter of fact, we don't have to believe you,' Neville said, still in a reasonable tone of voice. 'And we have no reason to think that you're telling us the truth. We'd like you to come to the station and answer a few questions.'

'But ... Les is on his lunch break. There's no one else to watch the desk. Maybe if you come back a little later ...'

Neville turned to Cowley. 'Do you have any cuffs, Sid?'

'There's some in the car, Guv.'

He turned back to Wicker. 'I'm going to ask you politely, Mr Wicker. Are you going to come with us voluntarily, or am I going to have to caution you? I'm quite happy to do it, if that's the way you want to play it.'

Now Wicker was sweating profusely; there were already damp patches under the arms of his shirt. 'No. I'll come. Let me get Les.' He edged his body round the reception desk.

Neville wasn't about to let him out of his sight at this stage. 'Sid can do that, can't you, Sid? You know where the staff lounge is, don't you? Pop down and ask Mr Fielding if he can interrupt his lunch and take over the desk for a while.'

Ten minutes later they were at the station.

'Sid,' said Neville as they got out of the car, 'can you arrange an interview room?'

Wicker climbed out of the back seat. 'I didn't know he was illegal,' he repeated, his voice just a bit more high-pitched than before.

'Yeah, yeah.' Neville took him by the arm and walked him into the station.

'My solicitor,' Wicker said suddenly. 'I want my solicitor.'

Neville had been hoping they could do an initial interview without a lawyer, but he realised with regret that Wicker was far too wily to allow that to happen. 'Yes, that is your right, of course,' he acknowledged. He led Wicker to a phone, while Cowley went off to see about an interview room.

'Half an hour,' Wicker said when he'd made the call. 'It will take him at least half an hour to get here.'

'We have all day, Mr Wicker,' Neville said breezily. 'I'm going to leave you with this nice custody officer for a few minutes. She'll get you a cup of coffee, if you want one.'

GRACE, in the absence of any other instructions, was still at her desk, and still working doggedly through the list of hotel guests. She'd managed to reach a few more of them, but was getting to the end of the phone numbers provided and thinking about how to best track down the ones who hadn't supplied a contact number.

She looked up as Detective Inspector Stewart came through the door, and gave him an involuntary smile. 'Hello, Sir. I mean Guv.'

'Good afternoon, Constable.'

'Call me Grace,' she blurted, before she could think about it and stop herself. She felt herself blushing. Now he really would think she was a gauche country bumpkin.

DI Stewart smiled, and the smile reached his eyes, crinkling them at the corners. 'Grace, I just wanted to commend you on your good work. It's early days yet, but I think you've given us the crucial information to crack this case. Good job, and thank you.'

'Have you made an arrest, then?' she asked, trying to cover her embarrassment.

'Let's just say that we're hoping to be in a position to do so very soon.'

She remembered, suddenly, what Sid Cowley had told her about DI Stewart's wife and baby. Surely she ought to say something, even if it was late in the day. 'Sir ... Guv,' she said, 'can I just tell you how sorry I was to hear about your wife?'

He shoved his hands in his pockets, hunched his shoulders, and looked down at the floor. 'That's very kind of you, Grace.'

'And your baby is ... well?'

He lifted his head; his face was utterly transformed by the smile that split it, ear to ear. 'She's called Annie. And she's absolutely beautiful. Would you like to see a photo?'

THE INTERVIEW ROOM – the state-of-the-art one, with video recording equipment – was ready. Wicker's solicitor eventually arrived, and he turned out to be exactly what Neville had expected: a slick character who had earned his bread for years by keeping members of the Garvey family out of spending any more time than necessary in prison, mostly on various technicalities. That meant, Neville realised, playing this one strictly by the book.

'Are the video cameras really necessary?' the solicitor demanded as they filed into the interview room. 'May I remind you that my client isn't actually under arrest.'

'And may I remind *you* that it is as much for his protection as anything else?' said Neville, consciously maintaining his attitude of scrupulous courtesy. 'We want an accurate and complete record of this interview.'

They sat down in their respective places: Neville and Cowley on one side of the table, Wicker and the solicitor on the other.

'My client tells me,' began the solicitor, clearly trying to grab the initiative, 'that this is a matter concerning employment. You are purporting that he knowingly hired an illegal immigrant at the hotel which he manages for his uncle.'

Neville raised his eyebrows, as if in mild surprise. 'Actually, we've said no such thing. Have we, Sid?'

'No, Guv.'

'We merely asked Mr Wicker if he would answer a few questions,' Neville went on. 'Your client has made the assumption that the immigration status of one of his employees is the subject of the questions.'

'And it's not?'

'No.'

The solicitor looked distinctly discomfited; he turned and glared at Wicker, who shrugged.

'We may get round to that eventually,' Neville said. 'But it's not what we want to ask him about.'

'Get on with it, then,' muttered the lawyer.

'Mr Wicker,' said Neville, 'I wanted to ask you about a pearl necklace. What I believe is referred to as a string of pearls.'

Wicker's adam's apple moved up and down convulsively; he licked his lips. 'Pearls?' he croaked. 'Are you having me on?'

'A string of pearls belonging to Mrs Felicity Chapman. She was wearing them when she stayed at your hotel.'

He shook his head. 'Nah. I don't remember any pearls.'

'You don't remember that she was wearing them?'

'Why would I even notice? What do I know about jewellery?'

'So you are claiming that Mrs Chapman was not wearing her pearls when she checked in to the Regent Hotel, or any time thereafter when you saw her?'

Wicker licked his lips again and glanced over at his lawyer, who was giving him no help at this point. 'Maybe she left her pearls at home,' he suggested.

Neville leaned back in his chair. 'What would you say, Mr Wicker, if I told you that I have a witness who can testify that he saw Mrs Chapman wearing her pearls in the lobby of your hotel, and heard Mrs Chapman asking you whether the hotel had a safe in which she could store them?'

Wicker's face drained of all remaining colour. 'Shit,' he muttered under his breath.

'And furthermore, Mr Wicker, my witness can testify that, in your hearing, he admired Mrs Chapman's pearls, and advised her to take good care of them because they were worth a great deal of money.'

The solicitor stood up abruptly. 'I am advising my client to answer no further questions until I have had a chance to confer with him privately,' he said.

IT WAS FRANCES' custom, on a Wednesday afternoon, to hold a communion service in the hospital chapel. She seldom had much of a congregation – a few devout staff members, if their schedules permitted it, along with whatever patients were mobile enough and motivated enough to find their way to the chapel.

On this Wednesday, there were a few more people than usual in the pews. She concentrated on the words of the service, and it was only as she stood behind the altar for the prayer of consecration that she spotted a figure standing at the back of the chapel. It was a very large black man with a very wide smile. 'Lift up your hearts,' she said, her own heart lifting to the ceiling and beyond.

He came forward at communion and took the wafer from her hands with a most unsolemn grin, then returned to the back of the chapel.

As soon as she'd said the dismissal, 'Go in peace to love and serve the Lord,' she rushed in his direction and met him halfway. He enfolded her in a huge bear hug, clasping her to his chest.

'Frannie, pet, you're a sight for sore eyes,' said Leo Jackson in his booming voice.

'Leo, you're back!'

'Like a bad penny.'

'I've missed you.' She smiled up at him through tears of joy. 'Oh, I've missed you. Why didn't you let me know you were coming back?'

'I wanted to surprise you.'

'You've done that, for sure. Are you back ... for good? Or just visiting?'

Leo chuckled. 'Well, the powers-that-be seem to think I've done my penance, working for six months in the West Indies. They're not going to put me back in a parish – not yet, if ever – but the bishop, bless her cotton socks, has found a diocesan job for me. It will keep me busy, but out of the public eye. And hopefully out of mischief,' he added. So I guess you could say that I'm back for good.'

GRACE WAS STILL PERSEVERING with her list when DS Cowley, closely followed by DI Stewart, virtually erupted into the office. 'Come on, Grace,' said the sergeant. 'We're going to the pub. We're going to celebrate!' He sounded half-drunk already.

'You want me to come with you? Now?'

DS Cowley winked at her. 'No time like the present, is there?'

Both of the men were grinning like fools. 'We'll tell you all about it,' DI Stewart promised.

One on either side of her, they marched her out the door, out of the station, and across the road to the nearest pub.

'I'll get the drinks,' said Cowley. 'What will you have, Grace?'

'A pint of whatever's going,' she said, and he looked at her approvingly before heading to the bar.

DI Stewart led her to a table in an unpopulated corner, as private as it was possible to be in a public house.

She was dying to know what was the cause of all the jubilation. 'What's going on, Guv?'

'We've got him, Grace! Wicker!'

'Got him? What do you mean?'

The guv smiled. 'I mean we've arrested him for the murder of Felicity Chapman. He's in the cells. He'll be charged before the end of the day.'

'But ... how?'

Cowley arrived with three foaming pints on a tray. He slid the dark one in front of the guv, one of the lighter ones in front of Grace, then took a big swig from his own glass before clinking it against hers. 'Cheers!' he said. 'Here's to us!'

They all clinked glasses, and Grace took a sip of her beer. 'Tell me,' she begged.

'It was all down to the pearls.' DI Stewart leaned closer and lowered his voice. 'Felicity Chapman wasn't wearing them when she was found, and they weren't in her room. Which means that someone pinched them, and we twigged pretty quickly – once we found out about the pearls, that is – that it had to be Wicker. Given what we knew about the man,' he added.

She felt like she was missing something. 'Why not someone else at the hotel?'

'Because someone else would have left something behind, something that would have been picked up by the SOCOs. Fingerprints, DNA, a hair, something.' He took a sip of the foam at the top of his Guinness. 'But Wicker made sure that he was the first one on the scene, when she was discovered by the cleaner. He told us himself, on the day – he checked for vital signs before he rang 999. I said to Sid at the time that he hadn't done us any favours by buggering up the crime scene. He did it deliberately. To cover his tracks.'

'The bastard,' said Sid.

'So we knew we had him,' DI Stewart explained 'He played all innocent at first, until we mentioned the pearls. He tried to deny that he knew anything about them – he even suggested that she wasn't wearing them.'

'But we had your witness,' Sid added triumphantly. 'Your Malaysian or whatever doctor. And as soon as we told him that ... he just caved. Totally caved.'

'His solicitor nearly had a coronary,' the DI said with a satisfied smile. 'He stopped the proceedings, took Wicker away to confer, and when they came back, it was clear they'd decided to cut their losses. A confession, hoping they can somehow bargain it down to a lesser charge than first degree murder.'

Grace's head swivelled between the two men. 'What did he say happened, then? In his confession?'

DI Stewart started. 'He admitted that he'd seen the pearls. That he knew they were really valuable. Then he told us that late that night, he used his pass key to get into her room, to suss things out. The curtains were quite thin, and the moon was bright that night, so he could see that she was asleep. And he spotted the pearls right away, on her bedside table. Easy pickings, for someone like Wicker,' he added. 'I'm guessing this wasn't the first time he's done it, on the rare occasion that anyone with something worth pinching stayed at that doss house. He must have thought he'd died and gone to heaven when he found out what those pearls were worth. So he spotted them, picked them up and was in the process of pocketing them when she woke up.'

Cowley continued the story. 'He said he was afraid she was going to scream, so he put his hand over her mouth to shut her up.'

'She must have struggled a bit, but she was probably only half awake, and he wanted to make sure that she didn't scream the place down ...'

'So he killed her,' Grace said flatly, feeling sick.

'He says it was an accident, of course.' Sid put in. 'That's his defence. He didn't mean to kill her. He didn't know she couldn't breathe. Didn't know she was dead until she went limp. That's what he says.'

'But I'm not at all sure that will hold water, once it gets to court,' the guv commented. 'I mean, what was he going to do? He'd been caught red-handed, as it were. Did he think she'd just roll over and go back to sleep and not mention it to anyone?'

Sid nodded. 'He was in deep shit, for sure. He might not have gone into her room intending to kill her, but he knew exactly what he was doing when he put his hand over her face.'

The picture was all too vivid in Grace's mind; she found it hard to share their jubilation as she imagined that poor woman's last terrified moments.

'And I'm not entirely sure he didn't make sure he'd finished the job by holding a pillow over her face for a few minutes,' DI Stewart added more seriously. 'We'll have to talk to the pathologist about that. Anyway,' he went on in an entirely different tone of voice, 'we've got him.' He raised his glass. 'Here's to a job well done.'

'Here's to us,' Sid added, lifting his as well.

The guv turned to Grace. 'We couldn't have done it without you, honestly. Have you ever thought about leaving Devizes and taking your chances with the Met? Because if you have ...'

'Well, said Grace, suddenly glowing, 'You never know.'

Before Evening Prayer, Callie rang Marco to see how his mother was getting on.

'I saw her this morning,' he said. 'I think she's improved a bit. And I talked to Serena this afternoon. She sounded very positive.'

'Oh, that's good news.'

Callie's doorbell rang.

'Oh, it's the door,' she said to Marco, wondering who it could be this time. Hopefully no fugitive from justice, carrying a sleeping bag.

'I'll ring you later, *Cara Mia,*' he said.

She opened the door to see her brother's smiling face.

'Hiya, Sis,' he said, breezing in. 'I thought it was about time for you to meet my other half. Though I think you already know him.'

Behind Peter was ... Father Michael Fairfax, vicar of St John's, Lancaster Gate. She'd been introduced to him at the last Deanery Clergy Chapter meeting.

'Oh,' said Callie, momentarily at a loss for words. Eventually she summoned a few. 'Peter didn't tell me it was ... you. He just said "Michael".'

'I hope I'm not an unpleasant surprise.' Father Michael favoured her with a high-wattage smile which demonstrated all too well to her why her brother – and no doubt all his female parishioners and not a few of the males – found him irresistible.

'Well, welcome,' she said, dazzled in spite of herself.

Father Michael took a step closer to her and fixed her with his laser-blue eyes. 'I just want you to know,' he said quietly, 'that your brother is the best thing that's ever happened to me. I'm going to look after him and love him for the rest of my life. Are you okay with that?'

Callie smiled, feeling a burden lift from her shoulders. 'I'm *very* okay with that.'

20

A faint heat haze hung over the lagoon as the flight from London Heathrow to Marco Polo came in for landing. In mid-August, that was to be expected, Callie realised. Her only previous trip to Venice, last October, had been quite different. In every possible way.

She and Marco held hands. Their hands – her right, his left – had been clasped together for most of the flight; now, as the plane decelerated and descended, he gave her hand an extra squeeze. 'Ready, Mrs Lombardi?' he said.

Mrs Lombardi. She wondered how long it would take to get used to it. The Reverend Mrs Callie Lombardi, priest.

Her priesting, a mere six weeks ago, had been a wonderful occasion, but it now seemed almost a distant memory, eclipsed by all of the preparations leading up to yesterday's wedding. Everyone had been right when they said that planning a wedding took time. Well, they'd managed it, hadn't they? And it had been wonderful. Glorious weather – which they couldn't have planned, no matter how much time they'd had – had been the crowning touch to a joyous gathering of loved ones and well-wishers from near and far.

She smiled at her husband. 'Ready.'

The wheels touched the runway with a faint bump, and most of the passengers jumped out of their seats immediately, before the seatbelt lights went out or the plane stopped moving.

Callie and Marco stayed in their seats. 'I don't know what the great rush is all about,' Marco murmured. 'Venice will still be there in an hour or two.'

They were the last ones off the plane. By the time they got through Passport Control to the baggage reclaim, their cases were circulating on the carousel in solitary splendour.

The plan was to take a private water taxi across the lagoon – booked in advance, a honeymoon splurge. Marco retrieved the cases and they passed through Customs and out to the dock. 'It's the only way to approach Venice,' Marco said. 'Across the lagoon. The only way to appreciate how magical this city is.'

A few minutes later they were skimming over the sparkling water of the lagoon, as Venice shimmered in the far distance like a mirage of almost unimaginable splendour.

'It was a good day, wasn't it?' said Callie.

'Better than good. It was a *perfect* day. And you were the most beautiful bride. Ever.'

'I think you're prejudiced,' she smiled.

'Even Serena said so. When I danced with her. She said that you looked amazing. And,' he added, 'she said she was very happy for me – for *us* – and wished us every happiness together.'

'She looked pretty amazing, too,' Callie said generously. 'Your sister is a beautiful woman. And the girls – they were a picture, in their pink bridesmaid dresses, with their dark hair all done up.'

'I can't wait for the photos.'

The contrast between the two slim, dark-haired di Stefano girls and the other bridesmaid, her friend Tamsin, had been marked: Tamsin was small and round, with a head full of bouncy blond curls. The photos were going to be interesting, to say the least.

Neville had served as Marco's best man, and he'd almost stolen the show. He'd arrived, in his hired wedding garb, wearing a sling round his front in which reposed a rosy-cheeked, black-haired 10-week-old Annie. Annie had been good as gold, and pretty much the centre of attention –

especially among the Italian contingent: the numerous friends of Marco's parents, and parishioners from the Italian church.

'It was good to see Neville,' Callie said. 'He seems to be doing okay.' Neville had taken an indefinite leave of absence from his job, and – funded by Triona's generous life insurance policy – was devoting himself to raising Annie, so no one, including Marco, had seen much of him lately.

'I never would have believed that he'd have taken to being a dad like he has.' Marco shook his head. 'But he just worships Annie. And she's thriving.'

'She's a precious little thing. One of those babies who looks like they've been here before, with very wise eyes.'

'It's not going to be easy for him,' Marco said candidly. 'As time goes on.'

'Do you think he'll marry again?' They'd discussed this question before, but Callie posed it yet again.

'Early days, *Cara Mia*. He loved Triona to distraction, but his life with her wasn't a fairy tale. He may find someone else one of these days. I hope he does.'

'Speaking of babies,' Callie said, 'hasn't Jane blossomed recently? One day you could hardly tell she was pregnant, and the next – well, you saw her yesterday. She certainly isn't trying to hide it any longer.'

'And she seems to have had a personality transplant, as well.' He raised his eyebrows. 'Laughing, smiling – pregnancy seems to suit her.'

'That, and having her "lodgers",' Callie reminded him. 'I realise now that she was a really lonely person after the boys went to uni, and before she took on Zuzanna, Krysia and Tariq. It makes me feel a bit guilty,' she confessed. 'I should have done more to be a friend her.'

'I don't think she was ready. They came along at just the right time.'

He was probably correct about that. And now, she reflected, Zuzanna and Tariq's wedding would be the next big celebration – probably before Jane's baby was born, if Brian was successful in sorting out Tariq's immigration status in the near future. Brian, surprisingly, had embraced that mission just as enthusiastically as Jane had taken on looking after the trio's material needs. Under Jane's relentless tutelage, Zuzanna's English had improved vastly in just a matter of weeks. And Krysia Dabrowska, far from being the strict, disapproving disciplinarian portrayed by her sister, had turned out to be a delight. The Stanford's son Charlie, home from Oxford in the long vac, seemed more than a little taken with her – and Jane was evidently doing nothing to discourage it.

'So who did you talk to at the reception?' Callie asked Marco. There had been so many people there – frustratingly, it hadn't been possible to speak to everyone she'd wanted to catch up with, in more than just a superficial way.

'Well, I had to spend some time with the police contingent,' he said. 'Neville, of course. And Sid. And DCS Evans – I was actually surprised that he came, and brought his wife. And did you see that Yolanda and Eli Fish were there?'

Callie laughed. 'Yolanda is hard to miss. They both are, for that matter. Mildred Channing must have had a fit.'

'Who is Mildred Channing, again? Sorry, should I know her?'

'She's just one of my parishioners, and there were a lot of them there. But she's one of my more *difficult* parishioners. The one who hates foreigners. She managed to get to the wedding, though, with her new knee.'

'Was she the one in the wheelchair?'

'Oh, no,' said Callie. 'That's Hilary Dalton. She's lovely. But unfortunately for her, the wheelchair means she can't escape so easily from Mildred Channing and her poisonous wingeing.'

'Well, if she hates foreigners, she had plenty of grist for her mill yesterday,' Mark pointed out. 'Not just the Fishes. The Dabrowska sisters, Tariq. Leo Jackson. And all my Italian lot, as well.'

'At least they're *white* foreigners, your lot.'

'Ha ha.'

'Did you see that Morag Hamilton was there? With Alex? They came all the way down from Scotland. Wasn't that sweet?' Callie smiled. 'I was able to talk with them a bit. Alex has grown like a weed. And she's so much happier. And Morag's cancer treatments have been effective, she told me. She's not totally out of the woods, but the prognosis is pretty hopeful.'

'It was great that so many of your theological college chums were able to make it – from Cambridge and wherever they are now,' Marco said.

Callie pulled a face. 'Well, Adam could have stayed away, and I wouldn't have minded. He and Pippa both. But of course he's so clueless that it wouldn't occur to him not to come.'

'Twat,' Marco stated with feeling.

'But yes – it was practically like Deacon's Week all over again, with Tamsin, and Nicky, and Val and Jeremy. And wasn't it nice that Margaret Phillips, the Principal, came? With Mad Phil, my tutor, no less! Apparently they're a couple now. That was a bit of a surprise, to say the least.'

Marco shook his head. 'I don't think I got to meet them.'

'They were having a great time, apparently. That's what Frances told me. Margaret knew Frances from way back, so they had a good old chin-wag. And Margaret was also old friends with the bishop, and spent most of the reception talking to her.'

'Did the bishop have anything to say about Peter and his boyfriend? Though I noticed that Michael wasn't wearing clericals.'

Callie shook her head. 'If she had any thoughts about that, she kept them to herself. They weren't making any secret of being a couple, though. I think they're amazingly brave.'

'They're in love,' said Marco, putting his arm round her and giving her a squeeze. 'Aren't you happy for your brother?'

'Totally delighted. Even if my mother's not.'

Marco sighed. 'I knew we'd get round to her sooner or later. The expression on her face – all day. She looked like she was attending a funeral, not a wedding. Like she had a bad smell under her nose.'

'Well, one thing you can say about my mother is that she's consistent.' Callie shook her head. 'I just can't let it bother me. I know I'll never be in the right where she's concerned, and that's the way it is. I'm not going to waste any more of my life worrying about it.'

'Glad to hear it. Anyway, now you have a new family,' Marco said. 'My parents adore you.'

'And I think they're pretty fantastic, too. Not least for producing and raising the most amazing man to be my husband.' She smiled, fingering the unfamiliar weight of her wedding band.

They were drawing nearer to Venice and its shimmering edges were hardening; the city was becoming more substantial, less ethereal, but no less magical for that.

'Your parents were on really good form,' Callie went on. 'Your mum has made an amazing recovery, hasn't she? But it was a shame that your grandmother couldn't make it.'

'Nonna just isn't up to travelling any more. That's why we're going to her instead.'

One of the benefits of travelling by private boat was avoiding being dumped off at the public dock, as Callie had been on her first trip. At the mouth of the Grand Canal, their taxi swerved off to the left and went down the Giudecca Canal, then turned into a small side canal. '*Ecco, grazie*,' said Marco to the captain, pointing to a little private dock. The boat pulled over and the captain unloaded their cases onto the dock.

Marco stood up and offered Callie his hand. 'Come on, *Cara Mia*. Mrs Lombardi. Let's go and meet my nonna.'

THE END

ALSO BY KATE CHARLES

Book of Psalms Series

A Drink of Deadly Wine

The Snares of Death

Appointed to Die

A Dead Man out of Mind

Evil Angels Among Them

Callie Anson Series

Evil Intent

Secret Sins

Deep Waters

False Tongues

Desolate Places

Other Novels

Unruly Passions

Strange Children

Cruel Habitations

ABOUT THE AUTHOR

Kate Charles was born in the US but has lived in England for many years. Her novels are set – mostly – against the colourful background of the Church of England. She is a former Chairman of the Crime Writers' Association and the Barbara Pym Society, and a member of the prestigious Detection Club.

https://www.katecharles.com/

www.ingramcontent.com/pod-product-compliance
Lightning Source LLC
Chambersburg PA
CBHW030534310726
48979CB00010B/1909/J
9781641971720